escapism. This series is just pure fun, and the humor is a treat. Fans of 'Storage Wars,' take note."
—***Somebody Dies***

"Here's something to brighten your day . . . very funny, with lots of great dialogue. There's even a Nero Wolfe homage, along with a cliffhanger ending . . . good news for us fans."
—***Bill Crider's Pop Culture Magazine***

"This humorous cozy is framed by life in small-town Iowa and teems with quirky characters. It will appeal to readers who enjoy Donna Andrews' Meg Langslow mysteries."
—***Booklist***

Antiques Knock-Off

"If you like laugh-out-loud funny mysteries, this next Trash 'n' Treasures installment will make your day."
—***Romantic Times Book Reviews***, 4.5 stars

"Stop shoveling snow, take time to chuckle: *Antiques Knock-Off* is a fitting antidote to any seasonal blues. Plan to shelve this one next to your Donald Westlake caper novels or just before Lawrence Block."
—***Kingdom Books***

"Scenes of Midwestern small-town life, informative tidbits about the antiques business,

and clever dialog make this essential for those who like unusual amateur sleuths."
—*Library Journal*

Antiques Bizarre

"Auction tips and a recipe for spicy beef stew enhance this satirical cozy."
—*Publishers Weekly*

"You'll laugh out loud at the screwball dynamics between Brandy and Vivian as they bumble their way through murder investigations."
—*Mystery Scene*

"Genuinely funny . . . another winner! The funnest mystery series going."
—*Somebody Dies*

"If you need a laugh and enjoy a neatly plotted mystery with a lot of engaging characters and lots of snappy patter, not to mention a little romance, read *Antiques Bizarre*."
—*Bill Crider's Pop Culture Magazine*

Antiques Flee Market

"Fast-paced . . . plenty of humor and tips on antiques collecting will keep readers engaged."
—*Library Journal*

Antiques Chop

A Trash 'n' Treasures Mystery

Barbara Allan

KENSINGTON BOOKS
http://www.kensingtonbooks.com

KENSINGTON BOOKS are published by

Kensington Publishing Corp.
119 West 40th Street
New York, NY 10018

All Kensington titles, imprints and distributed lines are
available at special quantity discounts for bulk purchases
for sales promotion, premiums, fund-raising, educational,
or institutional use. Special book excerpts or customized
printings can also be created to fit specific needs. For details, write or phone the office of the Kensington Special
Sales Manager. Attn: Special Sales Department. Kensington
Publishing Corp., 119 West 40th Street, New York, NY
10018. Phone: 1-800-221-2647.

Kensington and the K logo Reg. U.S. Pat. & TM Off.

ISBN-13: 978-0-7582-6363-6
ISBN-10: 0-7582-6363-5
First Kensington Hardcover Edition: May 2013
First Kensington Mass Market Edition: April 2014

eISBN-13: 978-1-61773-043-6
eISBN-10: 1-61773-043-2
Kensington Electronic Edition: April 2014

10 9 8 7 6 5 4 3 2 1

Printed in the United States of America

In memory of Martin H. Greenberg,
who gave Barbara her start

Brandy's quote:
*"No one ever keeps a secret
so well as a child."*
Jean de La Fontaine

Mother's quote:
*"Be who you are and say what you feel
because those who mind don't matter
and those who matter don't mind."*
Dr. Seuss

Cast Of Characters

Note from Brandy: *Mother has been begging me to open one of our books with a cast of characters—no doubt this reflects her theatrical background, but also she recalls reading Agatha Christie, Erle Stanley Gardner, and other Golden Age mystery writers, and relishing this "helpful aid" in keeping track of who's who. I am giving in to her, just this once, because (A) it will help catch new readers up, (B) refresh readers who've been following our exploits, and (C) shut Mother up (temporarily). This cast list pertains only to recurring characters—you'll have to keep track of the new ones on your own.*

Brandy Borne, thirty-one, bottle-blonde Prozac-popping divorcee who came running home to live with Mother in small-town Serenity, Iowa.

Vivian Borne (a.k.a. Mother), widow, seventy-ish, bipolar, part-time community theater actress and antiques hound, full-time sleuth.

Sushi, blind, diabetic shih tzu.

Jake, Brandy's thirteen-year-old son who lives with ex-husband Roger in Chicago.

Roger, ex-husband, forties, investment broker.

Peggy Sue, early fifties, recently widowed and Brandy's sister. Also Brandy's recently revealed biological mother.

Ashley, twenty, Peggy Sue's daughter attending college out east.

Senator Edward Clark, sixty, Brandy's recently revealed biological father.

Brian Lawson, early thirties, chief of police and Brandy's current flame.

Tony Cassato, late forties, former chief of police and Brandy's former flame. Currently in WITSEC (Witness Protection Program).

Rocky, Tony's black-and-white mixed breed dog with a K.O. circle around one eye; currently living with Brandy and Mother.

Back to Brandy: Got all that? Yeah, me neither. . . .

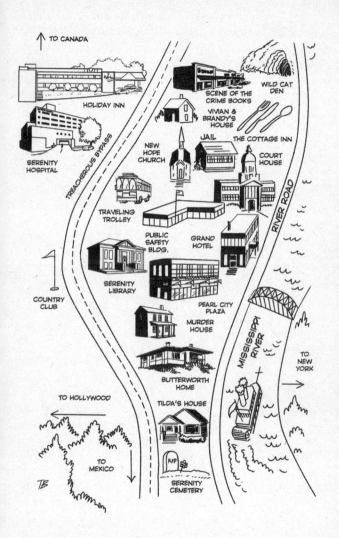

From *The Encyclopedia of Heartland Murders* (Kensington, 1995), Patrick Culhane. Used by permission.

Archibald Butterworth (1908–1950) was the victim in an ax murder that the *Des Moines Register* called "a modern-day Lizzie Borden mystery." Butterworth was a distinguished if little-liked member of the small river community, Serenity, Iowa. But there was nothing serene about the circumstances of his death on the hot, muggy afternoon of Sunday, August 27, 1950.

Butterworth was a failed Republican candidate for state senate, a longtime city council member, and a staunch member of the Amazing Grace Baptist Church. He was said to have prided himself on his piety, sobriety, and frugality. Others apparently considered him a hypocritical latter-day Scrooge. Left a small inheritance by his farmer father, Butterworth spent the Depression years shrewdly (or perhaps heartlessly) buying up foreclosed homes on the northwest edge of town. During the post–WW2 housing shortage, many veterans returning to Serenity became Butterworth's tenants. Pious or not, Butterworth was considered by many a notorious slumlord.

Apparently no more generous to himself than his North Side tenants, Butterworth lived modestly, his home—on the edge of Serenity's downtown, at the bottom of West Hill, which rose to the mansions of other wealthy residents—a small, two-story clapboard with insufficient heating in winter and no air-conditioning in summer. Butterworth was rumored to live lavishly while on his frequent travels, while maintaining an austerely frugal front at home.

Butterworth's wife, Amelia, died in 1936, giving birth to the couple's only son, Andrew; a sister, Sarah, had been born in 1935. Young Andy excelled in sports and the arts and achieved a local popularity denied his father. After church on the sweltering morning of Sunday, August 27, 1950, the fourteen-year-old was heard arguing with his father in the church parking lot over money—apparently a simple matter of the boy wanting either an allowance or permission to work after school.

That afternoon, with daughter Sarah away for the weekend, Archibald Butterworth napped on his couch in his study at home. Midafternoon, someone entered with an ax and delivered half a dozen savage blows that killed the town miser in his sleep.

While not matching the mythical "forty whacks" of the *Borden* case, those half-dozen blows were enough to put sleepy Serenity on the map. The sole suspect in a case drawing national attention was son Andrew, who claimed to have spent the afternoon fishing, by himself, at a local pond. He had been noticed by neighbors early that afternoon, however, chopping wood furiously in the Butterworth backyard. But after the murder, that ax, usually seen deposited in a tree stump by the family woodpile, was nowhere to be found.

In addition to the well-known animosity between father and son, a major clue was that missing wood-chopping implement. Whether this was indeed the murder weapon remains unknown.

The youth was held for questioning. A young attorney, Wayne Ekhardt, came forward to represent Andrew, producing a witness who could confirm the Butterworth boy had indeed been fishing. Thanks to the sworn statement of a lovely little twelve-year-old girl—who lived in the neighborhood—no charges were ever profferred against Andrew.

Or anyone else. Police looked into rumors of an affair between Archibald and a married woman, but got nowhere. The idea of the tall, bearded, foreboding Butterworth as a Lothario seemed far-fetched to locals, and as the years passed, the notion that Andrew may actually have killed his father took hold in the small town. After all, the young girl who had cleared him was an impressionable child, prone to theatrics, it was said. Had indeed little Vivian Jensen been an accomplice of sorts to the crime?

Interviewed in later years, Vivian Jensen Borne—now known locally as the town's resident theatrical diva—denied any such complicity. Andrew rehabilitated his own reputation (if not his father's) by selling the rental properties at a loss to any interested tenants, and remodeling the rest of the properties.

While to this day he maintains a residence in

Serenity—in one of the mansions on the hill his father could have lived in, but chose not to—Andrew Butterworth has for many years lived primarily overseas. He has never married, and travels frequently, the latter perhaps the only thing he had in common with his late, murdered father.

Attorney Wayne Ekhardt, whose first well-publicized victory was won without stepping inside a courtroom, went on to fame as Iowa's most celebrated criminal attorney (see separate entries, **Ekhardt, Wayne**, and **Woman Who Shot Her Husband in the Back in Self-Defense, The**).

Chapter One

Chop Meet

Previously, in *Antiques Knock-off*...

I don't remember walking from the backyard, where I'd been working, to the front porch, to sit in the old rocker... but I must have, because half an hour later I was still there, rocking listlessly, letting the cool fall breeze rustle my shoulder-length bleached-blond hair, when a huge silver Hummer pulled into the drive.

I wondered what kind of moron would own such a gas-guzzling monster *these* days, when my question was answered by the driver who jumped out.

My ex-husband, Roger.

What was he doing here, showing up unannounced, coming all the way from Chicago?

Wearing a navy jacket over a pale yellow shirt, and tan slacks, he hurried toward me, locks of his brown hair flying out of place, his normally placid features looking grim.

Immediately my adrenaline began to rush, and I flew down the porch steps to meet him, worried that something might have happened to our son.

"What is it?" I asked. "Jake?"

Out of breath, Roger asked, "Why haven't you answered your cell? I've called and called!"

Taken aback, I sputtered, "I . . . I've been in the yard all morning and didn't have it with me—what's going on?"

"Is Jake here?"

"No! Why?"

His words came in a quavering burst. "I was afraid of that."

"Roger! Stop scaring me."

A deep sigh rose from his toes. "I think he's run away."

As confused as I was concerned, I asked, "Why would he do that? He seemed fine yesterday when I talked to him." Then I frowned, recalling what our conversation had been about. "Only, uh . . ."

Roger gripped my arm. "Brandy, if you *know* something that might have motivated Jake taking off like this, you need to tell me *now*."

Removing his hand gently, I said, "Roger, you better come sit down. Of *course*, I'll tell you what I know. . . ."

And turning, I led him toward the porch.

As we sat in matching rockers—like the married couple we'd be if I hadn't ruined everything—I told Roger of my recent discovery of my true parentage: that thirty-one years ago, my older sister Peggy Sue had conceived me with then-state representative Edward Clark, while she had been a summer intern on his campaign. And that the grandmother I still called "Mother" had raised me as her own.

Roger's shock morphed into irritation, his eyebrows trying to climb to his hairline. "And you thought this information should be shared in a *phone call* with an impressionable thirteen-year-old boy?"

I spread my hands. "There was no other way—with the senator's reelection campaign all over the news, my soap-opera parentage was going to be everywhere. I'm surprised you didn't hear about it."

He frowned, but his irritation had faded. "I've been away on business, pretty much constantly in meetings. When I got back, Jake was gone."

"Have you notified the police?"

Roger shook his head. "Hasn't been twenty-four hours yet. What a damn dumb rule! Don't they say that the more time that goes by, the colder the trail gets?"

I stiffened. "You don't think Jake has been *kidnapped*? Is *that* what you're saying?"

Roger certainly had the kind of money to warrant our son being that kind of target.

My ex leaned forward, rubbing his forehead. "No . . . no . . . I don't think there's much chance it's anything like that. There's been no phone call or note or any such thing."

"Then . . . what *do* you think this is about?"

Roger took another deep breath. "Jake's been, well, a lot more of a handful than usual. Acting out at school and at home. All because lately he's been unhappy. He doesn't say so, but it's clear that's the problem. That's why I thought he might have come here. He's always been able to talk to you."

"What's he unhappy about, Roger?"

He shook his head. "Who knows what a boy of his age is thinking? School, friends, girls, he keeps it all inside. His grades are okay but his teachers complain about his attitude."

Suddenly I thought of someone who *might* know.

"I'm going to ask Mother when she last heard from Jake," I said, already on my feet. "You think he talks to me? He and his grandmother are thick as thieves, texting each other fast and furious."

Which she'd just mastered, after having a cell for five years.

He nodded his okay and I left my dejected ex on the porch while I headed inside.

Just under one minute later, I returned. "You should come in," I said, crooking a finger.

Roger followed me back in the house, and I led him into the dining room where Mother sat drinking a cup of coffee at the Duncan Phyfe table. She was wearing her favorite emerald-green pantsuit, her silver-gray hair neatly pinned in a bun, her magnified eyes behind the large glasses turned our way.

Next to her sat Jake.

He had on jeans and a gray sweatshirt with the Chicago Bears logo, and held a can of Coke in one hand, while the other draped down, scratching the head of Rocky, the mixed-breed mutt (complete with black circle around one eye) that we had recently taken in.

Sushi—my blind, diabetic, brown-and-white shih tzu, the "child" *I'd* retained custody of after the divorce—sat a few feet away, her little mouth in a pout, apparently due to the attention Jake was giving the new-dog-on-the-block.

"Oh, hi, Dad," Jake said, layering on a matter-of-fact attitude that didn't fully mask his sheepishness.

For a moment Roger's anger trumped his relief, but only for a moment. Father ran to son, throwing his arms around the boy's shoulders, hugging him.

Roger quite naturally scolded Jake for disappearing; Jake just as naturally apologized to his father for scaring him; Mother came to the defense of her grandson; Rocky—a former police dog—growled at my ex for his threatening tone of voice; and Sushi started yapping, not to be left out. For a while, I was glad just to be an interested spectator.

But finally, to stop the commotion, I raised my voice. "Jake, how did you get here, anyway? And if you hitchhiked, please lie to me and say you took a bus."

The boy looked my way. "I really did take the bus. Then walked from downtown."

Mother said to me, "You were out back, dear, when he arrived, about forty minutes ago. You seemed to have a lot on your mind, and I didn't want to disturb you."

Before I could decide whether to shake her till her bridgework rattled or just kick her in the keister, Roger exploded, "Forty minutes!"

"Well, of course, that's an approximation. . . ."

"And it didn't occur to you, Viv, to *call* me? You didn't think I'd be worried half to death?"

Mother lifted her eyebrows above the big glasses. "I *would* have gotten around to it, Roger dearest, but my immediate concern was that Jake was all right. Besides, talking to the boy, he indicates you've been away on business for several days, and called him only once."

"That isn't fair."

"Leaving him alone in that big house. Why, he might have had one of those wild rock 'n' roll parties you see in the movies! Dancing in his underpants and with nubile young things doing the boogaloo in bikinis around the back-yard pool!"

"I wish," Jake said.

Roger's mouth was open, but words weren't coming out.

Leaning against the doorjamb, arms folded, I said quietly, "Let's not make a federal case out of it, Roger. Mother was dealing with things in her own inimitable fashion. Our son has been found, and he's fine."

Or was he?

Suddenly impatient, Roger tapped Jake's shoulder. "Get your things, buddy boy."

Uh-oh—"buddy boy" was never a good sign. . . .

Roger was saying, "We're going home *right* now."

But Jake stuck his chin out. "I just got here," he said stubbornly. "Why can't I stay a few days?"

And before Roger could protest, Mother said, "I understand that the boy has all of this week off. A rare benefit of being in one of those year-round schools."

Roger trained hard eyes on her. "And *you* want *me* to *reward* him for what he did?"

"No, dear," Mother said patiently. "Jake staying here for a few days wouldn't be a reward exactly . . . more an opportunity for him to see that . . . despite this distressing news about our, well, family tree . . . nothing has *really* changed in our lives. Same-o same-o!"

"Even *I* can see that," Roger muttered, rolling his eyes. "Doesn't seem to really matter which branch of the family tree *you* swung in on, Vivian."

Did I mention that my ex never had gotten along with Mother?

Suddenly Jake's eyes became moist. "Does this mean I have t'call *Aunt Peg* 'Grandma'?"

"Certainly not, sweetheart," I interjected. "We're not at this late date changing the lineup on the team. Peggy Sue is still 'Sis' to me. . . . Just because she screwed up as a kid, that doesn't mean anything has changed."

Roger gave me an arched-eyebrow look that said: *Screwed up? Really?*

And I gave him a pained look that said: *Double entendre* not *intended.*

Mother leaned closer to Jake, peering into

his face. "And so *what* if I'm technically your great-grandmother? Can you imagine a greater grandmother than *moi?*"

That made Jake smile. "You *are* great, Grandma." He met his father's eyes. "Can't I stay, Dad? Please. I realize I was out of line, just taking off like that. Cut me a break, and I'll clean up my act back home. I promise."

Roger thought about it.

"Just for the week, Dad—I promise I'll behave."

Roger, with a half smirk, glancing Mother's way (and mine), said, "It's not *your* behavior that worries me, son."

"Oh, *we'll* behave," Mother responded, smiling a little too broadly. Sort of like the Cheshire Cat in Disney's *Alice in Wonderland* (cartoon version), right before he disappeared. "Won't we, Brandy, dear?"

"Sure. You're in luck, Roger. We're not involved in a murder investigation at the moment."

Roger shot me a reproachful glance. "I don't really find that funny, Brandy."

Wasn't meant to be. It was *Mother's* propensity for getting involved in such investigations that got us into trouble—not mine!

Jake jumped to his feet, threw his arms around his dad, gazed up with angelic innocence—it was over-the-top acting worthy of his grandmother. "Can I please stay?"

I already knew what my ex was going to say; I'd fallen prey to my offspring's baby blues many times.

"All right," Roger said, then waggled a finger. His next move on the parental/child chessboard was predictable and even kind of pitiful. "But when you get back, I want that room of yours cleaned."

Oh, so very little has changed in the negotiations between kid and parent. Well, some things have changed—you used to get sent to your room for punishment. Now every kid's room is a technological Briar Patch.

And before Mother could say something that would give Roger a change of heart, I offered to walk with him out to his Hummer, so we could finalize plans. Roger and I did get along, and we made a point of not using Jake to get back at each other.

As we descended the porch steps, I asked, "You'll be back on Sunday, then?"

Roger, digging in a pants pocket for keys, responded, "Late afternoon. That way we can be home in time for Jake to clean his room."

Did he *really* think that was going to happen?

"I could meet you halfway on the interstate," I offered.

Roger nodded toward the beast parked in front of his Hummer. "Not if you're still driving that broken-down Buick."

He had a point; last week a windshield wiper flew off while I was driving in pouring rain— luckily, on the passenger side.

We were by his Hummer now.

"Why don't you get a newer car?" he asked. "I'll buy it for you, if that's the problem. . . ."

I looked at him sideways. Yes, we were on increasingly better terms, as the divorce faded into history; but things hadn't gotten *that* much better.

Then my astonished ears heard myself saying, "No, thanks. The Buick keeps me from having to take Mother very far on her escapades."

Wait, what? I could *use* a new car!

He grunted. "Speaking of escapades—do you think you can manage to keep that woman out of trouble for an entire week?"

"I'm sure."

"You are?"

"Pretty sure."

"Nothing homicidal in the works?"

"Really, Roger. Get serious. It's incredibly unlikely that Mother manages to get herself involved in these, well, mysteries as often as she has. This is a small town. If there's one more homicide, the police will start looking at us as the real perpetrators behind all this carnage."

He laughed. "You're right. Statistically speaking, you're safe. Another murder in sleepy little Serenity? Not going to happen."

"Right."

His eyes narrowed at me. "And there's no other trouble she could get herself into?"

"I'm sure not."

Pretty sure. Almost sure. Not sure at all.

He read my expression and asked, "She *is* current on her meds, isn't she?"

I nodded; Mother was bipolar, which was why I was also current on my meds. Prozac.

"And you'll keep a *really* close eye on Jake?"

Roger was saying. "And call me if *anything* seems wrong?"

"Roger . . . what aren't you sharing with me?" Adding, without contention, "I *am* his mother."

He looked down at his feet for a moment. "I said earlier that Jake's been unhappy. But I wasn't, uh, as frank as I should have been."

"Then you *do* know why he's unhappy."

He nodded. "It's that private school. He hates it."

"Is he being bullied?" I couldn't imagine anyone picking on him, or him letting them do it. But bullying was so common these days. . . .

Roger shook his head. "Claims the other kids are snobs, and into drugs."

I didn't like the sound of either of those.

Shielding my eyes against the sun, I asked, "Why don't you just move him to a public school?"

Roger laughed once, humorlessly. "A public school might be fine in Serenity, but not in Chicago."

I touched his arm. "Look, Roger . . . don't worry about our son. Jake is one tough kid. We'll figure this out."

My ex cocked his head. "He misses you, you know."

"And I miss him."

"Brandy?"

"Hmm?"

"I . . . I shouldn't have punished you by taking sole custody of our son. I was angry after . . ."

"After what I did?" *Went to my ten-year class reunion without him, and slept with an old boyfriend?*

Oh, did I mention? I'm not perfect, but I am trying. Some of you have probably already found me "trying," at that.

Roger winced. "Yeah. After what you did, I was . . . you know how bent out of shape I was."

Actually, I didn't. He'd taken it stoically. I would have preferred screaming and kicking and crying and . . . and anything that would have indicated there was still something emotional going on between us.

"If it's any consolation," I said, "I hear my 'mistake' is on his third wife, totally broke, gained fifty pounds, and has a terrible case of adult acne."

"That's supposed to make me feel better?"

"Doesn't it?"

He smiled. "A little."

I smiled back.

Roger said, "Look, uh . . . getting back to Jake? I think maybe it would be better for us to have joint custody." He put both hands on my shoulders. "Better for us. Better for Jake. A boy needs his mother, too."

My Prozac-protective emotional wall was crumbling. I felt tears trying to make a break for it from my eyes.

Roger, suddenly a tad uncomfortable, said rigidly, "We'll talk about it when I come back on Sunday."

"Okay," I sniffed, dabbing away tears with my fingers.

I stepped back as he climbed into the Hummer with a sad little smile and a sad little wave.

Then I watched until the vehicle disappeared down the street.

Returning to the house, I found Mother and Jake still at the table, having what looked disturbingly like a conspiratorial confab, and suspiciously like shenanigans.

How was I going to keep my promise to Roger with those two in cahoots? And what kind of mind in the twenty-first century comes up with words like *confab, shenanigans,* and *cahoots,* anyway?

Jake said, "Hey, Mom, Grandma wants to take us to lunch at a nice new restaurant." He looked at her. "What's it called again?"

"The Cottage Inn, dear. Everything is made from scratch, and is simply delicious."

Well, nothing disturbing or suspicious about that stilted, overrehearsed exchange, right? On the other hand, I'd been wanting to try the new eatery, which also specialized in desserts to die for, so if they had a hidden agenda, I did too.

"I'm game," I said.

Mother was studying me. "Brandy . . . perhaps you'd like to put on something . . . more . . . *presentable.*"

I looked down at myself. What was wrong with jeans and a rugby? The Cottage Inn wasn't a fancy restaurant.

"Yeah," Jake said. "Maybe a dress? And you're a little smeary." He pointed to his eyes and crossed them—nice touch.

So my mascara could use some attention. What was it to Jake?

"*Fine,*" I sighed. "I wouldn't want either of you to be ashamed of me."

This was where Mother and Jake were supposed to assure me that they weren't at all ashamed . . . but didn't.

Dutifully I trudged upstairs, thinking, *You want presentable, I'll show you presentable.* I changed into a Ralph Lauren denim shirtdress I'd gotten 75 percent off because somebody stole its leather belt (not me!). I slipped on short brown Lucky Brand cowboy boots—legs left bare showing off the last of my summer tan—and picked out (from the tangle of purses on my closet floor) a small cross-body green parachute-material bag by Nicole Miller.

(Regarding big, heavy, leather designer purses: I get crabby just toting my airport bag from one gate to another—why would I want to lug a monster purse around *all day?*)

At my round-mirror Art Deco dressing table, I reapplied make-up, then—convinced any further spackling would be counterproductive—headed downstairs.

Sashaying into the dining room, I smirked at the nonbelievers. "Now, is this presentable or is this presentable?"

Jake was grinning. "I knew you could do it, Mom."

Mother nodded. "Indeed, dear. You will make a *splendid* impression."

For what? On whom? The restaurant owner? The other diners? Somehow I couldn't imagine my fashion sense being a topic of discussion.

"Can we go?" I asked. "I worked up an appetite, looking this good."

Suddenly, Sushi began dancing excitedly in front of us.

"What's up with her?" Jake asked.

Mother sighed. "Your mother said a *no-no*."

Jake frowned. "All she said was, 'Can we go?' "

Sushi's excitement escalated, stopping just short of jigging on her hind legs and doing a back flip.

"The no-no word is *G-O*," I explained, "because she wants to *G-O* with us."

Now Sushi began twirling in a circle, as if chasing the tail she couldn't see.

"I hate to break it to you," Jake said, smirking, "but that dog can *spell*. Anyway, she can spell *go*."

And Sushi began to punctuate her canine choreography with barks.

"Oh, dear," Mother sighed. "Now we have to appease the little rascal, and we'll be late to lunch."

I frowned. "We have a reservation?"

"Oh, yes. This bistro is very hard to get into because it only opened recently."

Which was typical of a small town with limited cuisine . . . although I doubted any restaurant in Serenity could ever be worthy of the designation "bistro," much less "cuisine."

I was shaking my head. "We're out of turkey, and I can't think of anything else on hand that Sushi really likes."

"I brought some beef jerky along," Jake offered, "in case I got hungry on the bus."

"Probably not the best thing for her," I said, "but it'll have to do."

He dug into the duffel bag by his chair, then handed Sushi a stick of the stuff. Rocky, stretched out contentedly in a stream of sunlight, smelled the treat, and gave a low ruff, and Jake tossed him a piece, to keep the peace.

Mother, standing, emitted a Nero Wolfe–like "Satisfactory," but *I* knew we wouldn't be sure if the bribe had taken until completing a full inspection of the house upon our return for tooth marks and/or piddle. (Sometimes I didn't find Sushi's latest little "gotcha" for days.)

We hurried out to the battered Buick and climbed in, Mother riding shotgun, Jake in back. I had a little trouble coaxing the car to life, but after a symphony of sound effects worthy of Golden Age radio—a rattle, a clank, and a couple of backfires—we were backing out of the drive.

I took Mulberry Avenue, so Mother could view the still-grand homes set back from the street, porches decorated with pots of colorful fall mums, towering trees in full autumn glory, some beginning to drop their leaves on the grass in paintlike splashes of red, orange, gold.

Jake said, "I've read some of your books."

Mother twisted her neck. "*Have* you, dear? How do you like them?"

"Oh, they're pretty cool for something by old people—'specially the one I was in—*Antiques Maul?* Only—"

"You wish *I* had written more of the chapters?" Mother prompted, rotating her head Linda Blair–style.

"No, Grandma. I was going to say that *sometimes* you *seem* to not be telling the, uh, whole truth . . . exactly."

A diplomatic way of calling her a liar.

"Goes for you, too, Mom."

Us liars.

With a cracking swivel, Mother returned her head to its forward position, then blew out a *pshaw*. "Jake, dear, sometimes a writer must embellish the truth just the teeny-weensiest bit."

"Why?"

"Well, in order to make a book more interesting or advance the plot, we take what's called 'artistic license.' "

"Didn't you have your license revoked?"

She frowned at Jake in the mirror (I was smiling). "That was my *automobile* license, dear."

"I mean," Jake said, "take that part at the Old Mill when—"

"Honey," I interrupted. "Some people haven't read that book yet . . . you don't want to spoil it."

"Oh. Yeah. Sorry."

"Anyway, the unreliable narrator is a well-accepted literary device."

"Well, then," Jake said with a shrug, "I guess you and Grandma are doing great."

We had arrived in the quaint downtown—snugged on the bank of the mighty Mississippi—four blocks long, three wide, consisting of everything a little burg such as ours might need, modern buildings blending well with structures of the past in a sort of aesthetic stalemate.

The Cottage Inn, neither a cottage nor an inn, was located on Main Street on the first floor of a recently regentrified Victorian building.

Main Street had free curbside parking, and I kept circling the block to find an open space—if I took a metered side street, Mother would start digging in her purse for slugs instead of coins to feed the meter. And I was pretty sure city hall was on to her.

Jake leaned forward from the back seat. "Mom, you better call on that magical feather of yours."

He was referring to my Indian spirit guide, Red Feather, who was great at getting me parking places. (I was working on winning on the lottery, but so far, no dice. Perhaps I needed to actually buy a lottery ticket for that to work out.)

"Red Feather," I murmured as we again approached the Cottage Inn, "parking place, please. . . ."

Suddenly a middle-aged man in an unzipped navy Windbreaker, sides flapping like wings, came running out of the restaurant, jumped in his car, and took off, leaving me a space right in front.

Mother said, "I bet the poor soul doesn't even know where he's headed."

"Probably just got the sudden urge to leave," I said, "in the middle of his meal."

"Spooky," Jake said.

I claimed the spot, we exited the car, and entered the eatery through an antique etched-glass-and-wood door. The restaurant had retained its original wood floor and tin ceiling, but had added a German/Swiss theme of stenciled walls, blue-and-white-checked tablecloths, and mismatched secondhand-shop wooden dining sets.

The entry area—where we stood waiting to be seated—was a bakery with a glass display case filled with homemade pies and cakes and cookies, sweet enough to give your diet amnesia.

A young woman greeted us, menus in hand. She had a heart-shaped face, dark hair neatly pulled back, and was wearing a red gingham full-skirt jumper over a white dotted-Swiss blouse. Thanks to our reservation, we were ushered swiftly away from those tempting treats.

The dining room was packed with patrons—mostly women, but a few families, farmers, and businessmen, talking and laughing between bites of delicious-looking homemade meals, their voices drowning out the polka-style background music, which was muted already, thankfully.

Since the restaurant was full, I couldn't see where the waitress was going to put us; the only chairs left were at a table for four, where a male patron was already seated, busy texting on his cell.

When it became clear we were going to have to eat with a stranger, I almost protested . . . but he *was* good-looking. Or maybe *he'd* protest at the intrusion. . . .

But Mother shushed me, saying, "Dear, I'd like you to meet Bruce Spring."

Good Lord! Was Mother playing matchmaker

again? Was *that* what this luncheon was about? She knew I had just started dating Brian Lawson, the current chief of police. But *I* knew she didn't entirely approve of Brian. . . .

The man stood, smiling. Perhaps mid-thirties (judging by his line-free face) with prematurely white hair (judging by the black eyebrows), alert sky-blue eyes, prominent nose, and sensual mouth, he was wearing an expensive black tailored suit jacket over a shirt the color of his eyes, and designer blue jeans. He had a great tan. As he extended a hand toward me, a diamond ring winked on one finger while a gold Rolex watch glimmered on his wrist.

"I'm very pleased to meet you, Miss Borne."

"If this was my mother's idea," I said, "I do apologize. Mother . . . shall we go?"

Mother was struck temporarily (and atypically) mute, but Jake blurted, "Mom . . . that's *Bruce Spring*," as if I should have known. Then, responding to my blank stare, he added, "You know! Host of *Extreme Hobbies?* And *Witch Wives of Winnipeg?*"

"Oh," I said, nodding. "Reality TV. I'm afraid I don't watch it." I had enough reality in my life as it was.

In case you're wondering, I knew I was being boorish; but I'd been bamboozled by not only Mother (which was to be expected), but my own son!

Still, that was no reason to take it out on a stranger.

Extending my hand, I said, "Nice to meet you, Mr. Spring."

His grasp was firm. "I apologize, Miss Borne . . ."

"Brandy."

". . . Brandy. I thought you knew all about this meeting."

"Now, children," Mother said, including Bruce Spring in her collective brood, "that was just my silly, eccentric sense of humor. I thought Brandy would get a charge out of running into a celebrity at one of our little local eateries."

If Bruce Spring was a celebrity, I was Lady Gaga.

"And I must admit," Mother rambled, "that in retrospect it would have been wiser to discuss our potential business with Brandy on the way here in the car. But we got talking about other things and—"

"And besides," Jake said to Bruce Spring, "we didn't think Mom would come if we told her."

Bruce's eyes were fastened on me in an intense but friendly manner, as we stood there by the table, awkwardly frozen on our feet. "Whatever the case, Miss Borne . . . Brandy . . . I hope you'll stick around. I'll buy you lunch and make you a *Godfather* offer."

"One I can't refuse, huh?" I shrugged. "Well, I *am* hungry." I pulled out the chair across from him, and plopped down.

"Fine," he said with a white smile against the Hollywood tan. He waited until Mother had settled next to him on the right, and Jake on the left, before returning to his chair.

While I studied a menu, Mother made small talk.

"Bruce, dear," she said, looking coyly over the

top of her menu, " 'Spring' seems an unusual last name. Whatever is its origin?"

The TV star, uninterested in his menu, said, "It's really Springstein. For obvious reasons, I thought it wise to shorten it."

Mother's eyes widened behind the thick lenses; in that green pantsuit, she looked like a surprised bullfrog. "Wise indeed! One mustn't get on the wrong side of the Boss!"

The waitress returned for our order.

Since "Bruce, dear," was paying, I began with a cup of homemade spinach and cheese soup, followed by turkey and mashed potatoes with chives, topped off by French apple pie with cinnamon ice cream. I'd actually gotten a little too thin of late and could indulge. Mother ordered just the soup (bowl), and Jake, a cheeseburger (rare) with American fries, plus chocolate layered cake. Our host wimped out with a small garden salad, sans dressing.

After the waitress left, Bruce got down to business.

"I've just stepped down from hosting shows on Discovery to act as both on-air talent and a producer for the new Extreme Interests channel. My current mission is to find fresh talent to feature in reality shows. Extreme won't have a single focus, but will look at various hobbies, sports, and professions . . . but 'extreme' examples."

"We write books," I said, "and have a booth at a local antiques mall. That doesn't strike me as very extreme."

He raised a forefinger, politely indicating I

should wait. "I happened to catch Vivian on CNN a few weeks ago, and thought she handled herself very well."

A barrage of reporters and camera crews had shown up on our doorstep to cover the startling news that Senator Clark had fathered a love child (me) in the early days of his political career. Mother, thinking they'd come to cover us about the string of murders we had solved in Serenity over the past year or two, had babbled on incoherently until realizing her mistake.

Mother took a dainty sip from her water glass, pinkie extended as if dining with royalty. "Unlike some theatrically trained performers, I have no difficulty appearing before the camera. One simply dials it back a shade, as it were."

Gag me with a spoon. And my soup spoon was handy. . . .

"You're a natural, all right," Bruce said, with a straight face. Was he an escapee from an asylum, I wondered? A very cute one with a great tan? "You are very much at ease in front of a camera—which is important."

Relieved that I was out of the mix, I said to the producer, "Hey, if you want my blessing for Mother to appear on one of your existing shows, I think that's just peachy."

Reaching for my water glass, I managed not to add, "We could use the money." Or that it would also keep Mother busy and out of trouble.

Bruce gave me the kind of smile a runaway gets from a guy she just met outside the bus depot. "Not an existing show, Brandy, but a *new* one. And not just Vivian, but *you*."

Mouth full of water, I nearly did a spit take. I was doing show biz shtick already!

I managed to swallow and say, "You can't be serious. I have the stage presence of a potted plant."

Mother, eyebrows hiked above her thick eyeglass frames, said, "Why not? I have a lifetime of stage experience, and can carry a potted plant around with me, if I so choose."

Really? She had trouble lifting Sushi.

"Be that as it may," I countered, "what kind of show could possibly interest an audience in us? I'm not into eating worms, or jumping off a cliff. And if a bachelor handed me a rose, I guarantee I'd bleed to death from the thorns."

Okay, maybe I *had* watched a *little* reality TV. . . .

Jake piped up. "Mom, just listen to the pitch, will ya?"

The pitch? So Jake was showbiz now, too?

I sighed and sat back, arms folded. "Okay. Why not? As long as it doesn't involve Donald Trump, I'm listening."

Bruce, elbows on the table, hands folded as if in prayer, said, "The reality show I have in mind will be about antiques—similar to *Pawn Stars, American Pickers,* and *Auction Hunters*—but with a heartland *twist* . . ."

He made us wait for it.

". . . murder."

Mother clapped her hands, like a little girl getting a pony for Christmas. "I love it already!"

Bruce continued. "It will be called *Antique Sleuths,* and—"

Mother, her giddy grin turning to a frown, interrupted, "Could you call it *Antiques Sleuths*? 'Antique' makes it sound as if Brandy and *I* are antiques, and that hardly applies to either of us."

"Fine. *Antiques Sleuths* it is." Bruce, having lost his momentum, asked, "Where was I? Oh, yes. *Antiques Sleuths*, starring Vivian and Brandy Borne, who run an antiques store, and—"

"We don't *have* a store," I interrupted.

"We'll get you one," Bruce said, with just the teeniest bit of irritation.

"Rent or buy?" Mother asked.

"We'll lease a building, with an option to buy, if the pilot is picked up. You'll have a budget, to be determined, to fill that store with items to supplant what you already have in your booth."

"But what's the format?" I asked. "If it's reality TV, we can't solve murders. There may not be any more in Serenity, and anyway, the police are unlikely to cooperate."

"And," Mother said, "a few of my investigatory techniques might not be anything I'd want recorded by a camera crew."

Not a few—most.

"We understand that," Bruce said. "We'll do periodic little minidocumentaries on the murders you've already solved . . . which will increase your book sales, I might add. The format of the show will be about 'sleuths' in the sense that people come in with antiques that you evaluate. On-the-spot evaluations, or you can research those pieces that are outside your existing areas of expertise."

I said, "We just sit around and wait for customers to bring stuff in?"

Bruce grinned. "When we announce this show, people will be lining up to haul in their latest finds. It's basically the *Antiques Roadshow/Pawn Stars* format. If it goes, we'll only be shooting thirteen weeks a year . . . and the rest of the year, you'll just be two very famous TV personalities with an antiques shop that customers will flock to. Just selling T-shirts alone will make you girls very, very flush."

Mother banged the table with open palms, startling the silverware. "Then it's settled. . . . I'm in. Bruce, I assume you have a standard contract? Naturally, our legal representation will want to see it. I'll give you the contact information. In other words, have your people talk to my people."

Mildly amused, the producer turned to me. "Vivian's given her answer—what about you, Brandy?"

"Oh, I'm in," I said with a smile.

Not just because doing the pilot would keep Mother happily occupied, but because *not* doing the pilot would make her unbearable to live with. Besides, I'd take perverse pleasure in subjecting millions of viewers to her antics.

And I certainly wasn't bothered by playing second fiddle. My participation would be relegated to playing Ethel Mertz to her Lucy Ricardo.

Our food arrived, and the conversation thereafter consisted of Jake asking Bruce questions about his other reality shows, and Mother giving advice on how they could be improved. By the time dessert was finished, the producer looked thoroughly exhausted, and I wondered if he was having second thoughts.

Bruce informed us that tomorrow we'd be meeting with our new show's line producer, Phil Dean, who was also the director of photography.

With that, we parted company, Bruce staying behind to settle up with the bill.

Climbing into our car at the curb, Jake said, "Know what? We should do some, uh, what do they call it? Location scouting. You know, for the antiques shop?"

Mother, fastening her seat belt, said. "No need, dear. I already know just the perfect place."

"Where, Grandma?"

"Why, the murder house, of course."

A Trash 'n' Treasures Tip

Location, location, location! When starting an antiques business, your store should be in a high-traffic area, easily accessible, with good parking. A notorious murder having once occurred there is optional.

Chapter Two

Chop Talk

Mother's news that the perfect location for our antiques reality TV pilot was "the murder house" got the following response from me: "You're going to have to be more specific—we have plenty of those in our little burg lately."

"Yeah," Jake said to me, "ever since *you* came back."

He was in the backseat of the Buick, with me behind the wheel, and Mother riding shotgun.

"That's not very nice!" I said to my son, glancing at him in the rearview mirror. "Anyway, that's just a coincidence."

"Yes, dear," Mother said to Jake. "National crime statistics have finally caught up with our sleepy little town."

Or had they? Maybe me moving back in with Mother had created a kind of perfect psychoneurotic storm, making me a lightning rod for the deaths that had happened here in the past few years.

Silly as that might sound, at the very least I'd been a catalyst for Mother's tenacious sleuthing—and an unwilling catalyst, at that. Mostly unwilling, anyway. Now and then I did get caught up in Mother's *Murder, She Wrote* melodramatics. . . .

But all I wanted right now was a nice, quiet week with my son, free from talk of murder and mayhem—was that too much to ask? And for that son not to needle me with gratuitous digs?

Mother, twisted around in her seat, was saying to Jake, "Anyway, murder is nothing new in Serenity."

His eyes were bright; nothing like a little mayhem to get a boy's attention. "Really? No kidding?"

"Kid you not, kiddo. Why, have I ever told you about the ax murder that happened here when I was but a young lass?"

"Must you?" I moaned. "Maybe he's not interested."

"*Ax* murder!" Jake blurted. "Wow, none of you guys' murders were ever *that* cool. Go on, Grandma, go on. Who hacked who?"

"Jake!" I blurted back. "Will you *listen* to yourself?"

My son's grandmother (okay, great-grandmother) gazed back at him with an unconvincing frown. "Your mother's quite right, dear. That's who hacked *whom*. . . ."

She took a deep breath, summoning the concentration of Olivier about to perform Hamlet's soliloquy.

"It was nineteen-fifty—and one of the hottest summers on record. A person could literally fry an egg on the sidewalk. Though why one would want to, I couldn't say. Not terribly appetizing."

She did so love to set the stage.

"I was eight," she went on, "still in pinafores and bloomers, when—"

"Wait a minute, wait a minute," I interrupted. "Pinafores and bloomers in 1950? And if you were eight in 1950, you'd have been born, when? 1942?"

"That's not relevant, dear."

"So then you had Peggy Sue when you were in junior high?" I gave her an evil grin. "How old were you really? Twelve? Thirteen?"

"Oh!" Mother clapped her hands and beamed the phoniest of smiles. "Here we are, home already. . . . Jake, darling, I'll tell you all about the ax murder later . . . *without* unwanted interruptions."

Wheeling the car into the drive, I smirked. "What a great bedtime story *that'll* make."

"Come on, Mom," Jake chided. "Can't be that gory. Nothing compared to *Saw* or *Friday the 13th*."

I suppose, actually, it wasn't—as ax murders go. On the other hand, that long-ago murder had been real, not special effects. But by the time Mother exercised her "artistic license," there would surely be buckets of blood.

Inside the house, on the foyer floor, we quickly found a "welcome home" present from one of the two dogs in residence: a little brown carrot. And since it wasn't a bratwurst, the culprit was obvious.

Yet Rocky was the canine that trotted over, hanging his head, while Sushi remained curled up oh-so-innocently on the Queen Anne settee.

"Really?" I said to her, hands on hips. "You're going to let *him* take the blame?"

Next to me, Jake offered, "I'll get a paper towel," and disappeared into the kitchen.

Mother, stepping over Sushi's latest indiscretion, said to me, "Dear . . . don't get too settled—we'll be off in a moment, as soon as I use the little girl's room. A mature woman's bladder is unmerciful, as you'll one day learn."

"Where are we going?" I asked. While *my* bladder was merciful enough, my stamina wasn't; I could use a nap.

She waggled a finger. "We must pay Andrew Butterworth a visit, lovey, straightaway."

Mother had been watching a lot of British TV mysteries lately, and had adopted many of their expressions. At least she was sparing me the hoity-toity English accent she sometimes fell into, when in sleuth mode.

I sighed. "I don't suppose we could give him a call, and let him know we're coming . . . ?"

She laughed merrily. "Don't be a silly goose."

Mother was strictly a drop-by kind of gal, which I accepted because 1) there was no arguing with her, and 2) I derived a wicked pleasure out of seeing people's faces when they unwittingly opened their door onto Vivian Borne's shining countenance.

Leaving Jake behind to play with the dogs—and forestall further "presents"—Mother and I headed back out to the Buick. This time it took more than a little coaxing to get the beast going . . . but soon we were once again tooling toward the downtown.

On the way, Mother filled me in on the details of Andrew Butterworth's life since the death of his father. Like most residents of Serenity, I knew quite a bit about the ax murder, but very little of the aftermath.

Seemed after being acquitted of the murder, Andrew (at the suggestion of his lawyer) left Serenity for a military school in the east, where he finished high school, then entered college.

But the day he turned twenty-one, Andrew inherited half of his father's fortune—the rest going to sister Sarah, unmarried and living in Chicago—and dropped out of college. He took off for Europe, finding a new life in the south of France, only occasionally returning to his hometown to check on his rental properties . . . which included the so-called "murder house."

For many years the notorious Butterworth family home remained vacant, boarded up, but in the 1970s, the property had been rented by a series of businesses: a hippie "head" shop; then (after the hippies got busted) a camera store; next (when the camera store *went* bust) a greeting card shop; and (most recently and successfully) a mystery bookstore.

Considering the house's history, Scene of the Crime made both a clever and tasteless name for the shop, which was run by an eccentric woman named Mary Beth Beckman (and if Mother thinks you're eccentric, you are *way* eccentric).

But now the bookstore, too, was gone, the

lease having run out. Andrew had refused to renew it, much to Ms. Beckman's displeasure at having her thriving business interrupted. Rumor had it that Andrew was disgusted that Mary Beth had exploited the unsavory history of the house for gain and profit. This was not hard to believe since an ax was part of the store's logo, and little ax pins had been offered in a point-of-purchase display at the register.

Mother and I had had several successful book signings at Scene of the Crime, and were sorry to see the store leave that prime downtown location. While Mary Beth Beckman did manage to relocate her store in a strip mall, her business took a severe hit.

"According to the rumor mill," Mother said, and she would know as she was head miller, "Andrew kicking that bookstore out of the house where the murder happened was a virtual admission of guilt, after all these years."

"Well, that's ridiculous," I said, turning right on red. "Anyone in Andrew Butterworth's place wouldn't like having that tragedy dredged up for fun and profit."

"I know, dear, I know. And don't look at me like that—that was one rumor I had *no* part of spreading." She leaned toward me with narrowed eyes behind her magnifying lenses. "But the same can't be said for Mary Beth *Beckman*. . . ."

We cruised along Main Street, passing the trendy shopping block of Pearl City Plaza, which signaled the end of the business section, and began the slow-but-steady climb up West Hill.

At the base of the hill were a few moderate

homes—including the former bookstore/ "murder house," a two-story white clapboard with a cement front stoop—but as we ascended, the residences became bigger and better, increasing in grandeur, and value, commensurate to their view of the scenic river.

At the top of the hill was an impressive array of mansions, many built in the 1800s by city founders—lumbermen, bankers, and pearl button makers—exquisite examples of Baroque, Queen Anne, Gothic Revival, Greek Renaissance, each a work of art determined to outshine the other.

But among the old mansions were a few "newer" models dating to the early twentieth century. One such home had Mother pointing to it, going "Ooo ooo," like Gunther Toody on the old *Car 54* television show. (Before my time, but Mother has the DVDs.) (Yes, I watched them with her. They're darn funny.)

"*That's* Andy's domicile," she said excitedly. Her vocabulary always got tonier in this part of town. "That Prairie House on the left . . ."

Andrew Butterworth's residence wasn't as flashy as its towering neighbors, but the low-slung, sprawling structure with hipped roof, broad eaves, and long bands of windows providing indirect light, had a quiet elegance more in harmony with the woodland bluff.

I knew a bit about American architecture from my college days, including that the Prairie style grew out of the Midwest at the turn of the last century as a rejection of the fussy, overdone, tasseled, velvet-and-floral Victorian decor so popular at the time.

The Prairie style was all about *natural* form and function, a simplicity that touched the souls of those who felt like stripping away artificiality in both their homes and lives.

For my taste, the approach was too austere, and I preferred what Frank Lloyd Wright had built on (figuratively and literally), which was to use Prairie as his foundation, but add Art Deco touches.

I found an open space across from the house. The steep angle of the street was one of those rare instances where a parking brake proved its worth. Traffic was nonexistent and both Mother and I took the house in as we slowly crossed. Whatever I might think about the Prairie style, this was an impressive, well-maintained "domicile."

We climbed three wide cement steps, walked a short distance, then up three more steps buttressed on either side by four-foot tan brick walls topped with squat-square cement planters showcasing an array of autumn flowers.

There was no porch to speak of, though cement paths, confined by more brick walls, led off in either direction, giving one a feeling of being at the beginning of a maze.

We stepped up to the front door, which, instead of a modern doorbell, had a round metal plate with a handle, which Mother cranked. On the other side of the door, a bell went *ding, ding, ding*. Who needed electricity?

Mother had to crank the handle once more,

but finally the door swung open, revealing a man who just had to be Andrew Butterworth.

He was under six feet with the physique of a man much younger than his late seventies. He had a full head of silver-gray hair combed in a side part, a tanned and chiseled face, with dark eyes, long eyelashes, straight nose, and sensual mouth. Mother—recently on a Tyrone Power movie kick (DVDs again)—said Andrew resembled the actor, or would have had Power lived longer than his mid-forties. And she was spot-on.

But what was most surprising about Butterworth's handsome face was his expression: he actually seemed pleased to see us.

Trust me, having accompanied Vivian Borne as she dropped in on many an unsuspecting host, this was hardly our standard reception.

Wearing a multicolored pullover sweater (European, I'd bet), sleeves casually pulled up, and tan slacks, Andrew Butterworth stepped forward on bare feet to extend a hand to Mother.

"Vivian!" he said, his smile showing off deep dimples and straight white teeth. "What a lovely surprise." His hand went to me. "And you must be Brandy."

"I must be," I managed, finding his grasp firm and friendly.

"Andy, dear," Mother cooed. "It's not my habit to just drop in unannounced on people. . . ."

It wasn't?!?

(**Editor to Brandy**: *Please use either one question mark or one exclamation point, not both and not in multiples. That is incorrect and unnecessary.*)

(**Brandy to Editor**: *Incorrect maybe.*)

Mother was saying to our host, "But I hope you don't mind us stopping by, Andy, out of the blue like this."

"No, no, of course not," he said, seemingly sincere. "As a matter of fact, Sarah and I were just discussing having you over for tea."

Mother jumped—just a little. "Oh! Is Sarah here, too?"

He gestured vaguely behind him. "Yes, out on the veranda. She's visiting for a few weeks before going back to Chicago."

"What *luck!*" Mother gushed. She turned to me as if she'd just been handed a gigantic lottery check. "Brandy, you're going to get to meet Sarah!"

"Great," I said, making my upper lip reveal my teeth in what I hoped resembled a smile.

Then, as Andrew stepped aside, Mother strode in like a general sizing up conquered territory.

I followed her into the entryway of a vast open room with a low dark-wood beamed ceiling, then bumped into her when she stopped abruptly.

"Oh, Andy, *darling!*" she gasped, clasping her hands before her as if the Virgin Mary had just materialized on breakfast toast. "This Arts and Crafts decor! It's simply perfection!"

I winced. There it was: the British accent. Her way of seeming "posh."

"Yes," Andrew was saying, "and, you know, it's all authentic Stickley."

He meant the furniture.

"Right-oh," Mother gushed, managing not to add, "Wot wot," or "Pip pip." Then another gasp escaped her heaving bosom. "And is that *Fulper* pottery?"

Our host nodded, apparently somewhat bemused by the Serenity native's sudden accent.

"*Brilliant!*" Mother enthused.

(Truth be told, Mother had not mastered British idiom as well as she thought. For a long time she was convinced that "Mind the gap" meant not shopping at that particular clothing chain.)

Regarding the Fulper pottery that had sent Mother into spasms of ecstasy, I had to admit the collection of vases displayed on a nearby Stickley sideboard was lovely, the patina adding a warm glow to the brown sheen of the furniture.

I was beginning to rethink my prejudice against the staid Arts and Crafts vision, at least the way Mr. Butterworth incorporated it, remaining true to the architecture of the house but cleverly inserting other periods and styles for diversity and interest. It was as if he used the warm, brown wood as his canvas on which to add different textures and splashes of color.

From the unenclosed entryway, Mother and I were led down a red-gold-and-green oriental runner to one of several seating areas, each designated not by walls, but by muted-colored rugs and arrangements of furniture—chairs, couches, standing lamps, and end tables.

The section we were currently walking by showcased a few Native American artifacts, such as a collection of arrowheads in a small glass case on an end table, and a colorful Indian blanket thrown casually across the couch.

Continuing along the runner, other cozy areas we passed held some surprises, like the large silk-screen picture above the central fireplace—blue, diamond-studded high heels on a black back-ground—which I recognized as Andy Warhol. (The original, I bet.)

Andrew had a little trouble steering Mother toward the double doors at the end of the vast room, which led to the outside, Mother's head doing a 380-degree turn, not wanting to have missed a single stick of Stickley, or objet d'art.

But finally we stepped out onto a wide ve-randa, which was partially covered by wooden slats, the patio confined by a low wall that did not obstruct a spectacular view of the Missis-sippi River, its surface sparkling like diamonds in the midafternoon sun.

Seated in a white wicker chair, at a matching round table, was a woman I took to be Andrew's sister, Sarah. As we approached, she pushed back the chair and stood.

She was a large woman—big-boned, not heavy—and at least six feet tall; while she wasn't pretty, she also wasn't unattractive . . . what Mother would sometimes call "a handsome woman." Sarah—a year older than her brother—also looked young for her age.

Wearing tailored black slacks, a beige silk blouse under a canary-colored cardigan, and expensive-looking black patent flats, she glided toward us, graceful for her size, offering the same warm smile as her shorter brother.

"My dear Vivian," she said, formal but friendly, "how delightful to see you once again."

Before there could be any response, the woman wrapped her arms around Mother, who flinched from the bear hug. She had a bad back, after all—particularly when it came time to load up antiques.

Sarah, releasing Mother, turned twinkling eyes toward me. "And you must be Brandy, about whom I've heard so much."

When people say such things, usually in a much less proper a manner, I've learned it's best not to inquire as to what they've heard.

"Very nice to meet you," I said.

From the sidelines, Andrew made an exaggerated motion with one hand. "Come! Sit down at the table . . . have some tea. I'll get extra cups. . . ."

While he disappeared, we girls settled into waiting wicker chairs, making small talk about the beautiful fall weather.

Returning with the cups, Andrew took the remaining seat while Sarah poured tea from a silver pot on a tray. She added the requested lump of sugar for Mother, and cream for me.

After a dainty sip, Mother said, "You've heard about Pickles?"

"Yes," Sarah said, frowning sadly.

"And Wheaty," Andrew added.

Mother sighed. "Seems as though all of our childhood chums are passing on to their final reward."

Couldn't anyone just say "died," anymore? And with this talk of "chums," I was starting to wonder if maybe Mother had been *thirty-two,* not twelve at the time of that ax murder.

Mother stretched her arms across the table in a V, grasping the hands of her friends. "But *we're* still here, aren't we? The Three Musketeers?"

"Yes, indeed," said Sarah.

"*And* Sam Wright," Mother added as if having forgotten a fourth Musketeer.

But neither brother nor sister said anything, and a momentary glumness seemed to settle in.

Wright, who also lived on West Hill, was the deacon of a church we occasionally visited. A nice enough man who I didn't feel deserved such a chilly reaction from our hosts at the mere mention of his name.

Mother went into damage control, fingers fluttering. "Remember the pigeons?"

Sarah put a hand to her chest. "Oh, my *yes!*" she giggled. "Weren't we just *terrible!*"

Andrew chuckled. "I bet the senior class thought twice before picking on freshmen after *that.*"

I was expected to ask, so I did. "What happened?"

In a nutshell (and guess what nut imparted this info): After underclassmen had suffered a year of bullying courtesy of the high school seniors, Sarah, a freshman, and Andy, ninth grader from junior high (as it was called back then), filled the high school auditorium the night before graduation ceremonies ... with pigeons. Mother, a precocious seventh grader, was involved because *she* knew where to get the birds.

Sarah, laughing, said, "The audience fared

the worse by far—at least the seniors were wearing mortarboards!"

The prank, I figured, happened just a few months before Archibald's murder, after which brother and sister's world would be turned upside down—Andrew leaving for a military school after the trial, Sarah going east to live with relatives. Neither would ever marry, as if the shadow cast by their father's murder had somehow stunted their futures.

As the trio continued their sentimental journey, an amazing thing happened: faces softened, lines lessened, expressions and gestures seemed more juvenile than geriatric. The three seniors seemed to physically regress in age, years falling away as they shared good times—and, perhaps, other, as yet unspoken secrets.

After the reminiscing ran its course, Sarah finally said, "Tell us what you've been up to, Vivian."

Since Mother's answer might take a while, I poured myself another cuppa, as we British sleuths are wont to say.

"Well, my dears," Mother said, no trace of UK affectation now, "I know neither of you has spent much time in good old Serenity lately, but surely you've heard about my theatrical endeavors."

"Oh, yes," Andrew said. "On a business trip home, I caught your bravura-starring performance in *Everybody Loves Opal* a few years back."

She nodded by way of a bow. "And perhaps you've heard of the female prison theater group I had organized a few months ago, while temporarily—if erroneously—a guest in the county hoosegow?"

"Actually, yes," Sarah said, nodding herself now. "Andrew sent me a clipping from the *Serenity Sentinel,* which said the inmates performed for the town, and that the play was such a success you were thinking of taking it on the road to other cities."

That is, jails and prisons.

"That's right," Mother said, and took a long sip from her teacup.

"Did you?" Sarah asked.

"Did I what, dear?"

"Take the play to other cities?"

The briefest glance between brother and sister told me they also knew about that, as well, and were gently teasing.

Mother, who didn't catch that, shifted in her chair. "Well, we were a big hit in Des Moines. And a smash at Eldora."

"But a bust in Ft. Dodge," I said. "Or bust *out,* anyway—two of the players escaped, and that was finis for the Serenity Jailbird Players."

Mother frowned, not so much at me as the memory. "They *at least* could have waited until the end of the last act!"

Brother and sister laughed warmly.

Mother quickly switched gears. "Perhaps you heard about my most recent march on city hall. Did you know that those city government nincompoops wanted to tear down our beautiful old stately courthouse and—"

"Yes," they interrupted simultaneously, "we heard." (In case *you* didn't: the nincompoops

sought a modern building with air-conditioning.)

Mother looked a little miffed. She leaned
forward, put her elbows on the table, tenting
her hands. "Well *here's* something you *don't*
know—because it just happened a few short
hours ago . . ."

A nice segue to the purpose of our visit. Had
she been heading here all the while? She really
was, in her way, a fine actress.

". . . Vivian and Brandy Borne are going to
have their very own reality television show."

This brought a gasp from Sarah, and raised
eyebrows from Andrew.

"Look out, Guy Fieri!" Mother shouted. "Make
way, Kardashian clan!"

Andrew seemed confused by this news, but
Sarah gushed, "How marvelous! But how did
this happen? Is it because of your notoriety in
solving murder mysteries as of late?"

So they knew about that, too.

"Partially," I said, beating Mother to the
punch, hoping to apply the best spin. "But it's
mostly because of our interest in antiques."

"Yes," Mother jumped in, "we quite often
'solve the mystery' "—she made air quotes—"of
an antique's pedigree. What is the darn thing?
Is it trash, is it treasure? Where did it come
from? When was it made? How much is it worth?
The show will be called *Antiques Sleuths* . . . isn't
that clever?"

Both Andrew and Sarah nodded, smiling,
perhaps politely, but smiling nonetheless.

Mother's frown struck me as a little too studied, or anyway the forefinger she edged alongside her face did. "There's only one problem," she continued, "which is finding just the right location for the show, and for our new antiques business."

"You see," I explained, "if the pilot doesn't sell, we'll still want to stay in that location."

"And *carry on*," Mother said, back to her faux Brit accent.

I said, "We need somewhere quaint, with a lot of color and character—an interesting local location for the show and our shop."

Sarah was nodding pleasantly, but Andrew had narrowed his eyes—something dark passed over his face.

"You want to use the old family house," he said flatly.

Mother shook her head, as if saying no, but her words contradicted the gesture: "Well, of course that *had* crossed our minds, Andy, dear . . . being located near Pearl City Plaza, and all of the other antiques stores! That would be ideal."

Andrew's sky-blue eyes turned ice blue. "Not possible."

Sarah touched his arm. "Now, Andrew . . . don't be hasty. The house *is* vacant at the moment." She added enigmatically, "After all, we are in Vivian's debt."

Andrew pushed back his chair, stood. "No. That structure is nothing but a reminder of everything I've spent a lifetime trying to forget. Nothing good has ever come of it or from it. Vivian, Brandy, I'm afraid you're too late. I've already made my mind up to have it torn down."

Sarah gazed up at her brother with eyes as soft as his were hard. "Andy, dear," she said gently. "It's half *my* house, too."

Her brother said nothing, glancing away.

Then Sarah said to Mother and me, "Would you mind waiting inside?"

Abandoning our tea, we left the siblings to determine the fate of our store's location. And our show's.

In front of the fireplace, Mother studied the Warhol painting.

"What's so special about *high heels?*" she asked. "I could've painted *that* in my sleep."

"Mother?"

"Yes, dear?" She was still studying the painting the way a dog watches TV.

"What do Andrew and Sarah have against Samuel Wright?"

Mother tore herself away from the Warhol. She lowered her voice and for once underacted: "He was the main witness for the prosecution at the trial—although a hostile one, being a close pal of Andy's. Of *all* of ours."

I whispered, "What information did Wright have that was useful to the prosecution?"

"That he had seen Andy chopping wood around the time of the murder, when Andy was supposed to be fishing . . . and shortly before the ax went missing." Her eyes wandered back to the painting. "Of course, then *my* testimony blew that nonsense out of the water. Or muddied it, at least." Who was telling the truth? After so many years, did even Mother know? An impressionable girl, perhaps with a crush on an older boy, might make herself believe anything.

The patio doors opened, signaling our hosts had concluded their confab.

"We've decided that you may lease the house," Sarah announced, smiling.

Andrew's steely expression seemed to state otherwise, but no words emerged from him to contradict his sister.

Sarah raised a finger. "But understand, Vivian, Brandy . . . any renovations or expenses to the property will be your responsibility."

"But of course!" Mother responded. "As a matter of fact, the show's producer has a budget for improvement."

There was an awkward silence, after which a glum Andrew said, even more awkwardly, "I suppose you'll want a key."

"Yes, thank you, thank you, my dear friends," Mother said, no longer underplaying. "You won't regret this!"

"I hope not," Andrew said, and went back out on the veranda.

A Trash 'n' Treasures Tip

To ensure repeat customers, stock your antiques store with unique merchandise. I suppose Mother's dress shield autographed by Frank Sinatra qualifies.

Chapter Three

Chopped Liver

Shortly after arriving home from our afternoon visit with the Butterworths—and while Jake was taking both dogs out for a walk—I used the landline on the little table near the kitchen so that Mother, getting ready to prepare dinner, could overhear my call.

"Hello, Mrs. Lange," I said. "It's Brandy."

There was a pause while the woman processed my name. Then: "Why, Brandy, how nice to hear from you!" She was a plump, pleasant widow of about sixty who reminded me of Aunt Bea in the old Andy Griffin reruns.

(**Vivian to Editor**: *Brandy has gone and done it again! Confused poor Andy with Merv!*)

(**Editor to Vivian**: *We'll change it in the editing process.*)

(**Vivian to Editor**: *I hope so. We can't afford to*

alienate any more readers. But I do wish we had an actual Merv Griffin reference in the book—I did so love those wonderful sportcoat linings he liked to show off!)

Mrs. Lange was saying, "Joe will be thrilled that you've called, Brandy. I'll get him—he's upstairs."

Joe, an only child and self-styled oddball, had been a friend since high school when we were thrown together as lab partners in biology class, and I had to learn to either tolerate his nerdy eccentricities or throw him out a window.

"Before you do," I said quickly, "do you mind if I ask . . . is he back on his meds?"

Joe had served in the Middle East and came back traumatized. He went to the same mental health clinic as Mother and me, but come summer, he had a bad habit of going off his meds. He would put on his old fatigues, pack up his survivalist gear, and go live in a cave at Wild Cat Den State Park until fall (ostensibly protecting the hikers and picnickers from terrorists). Occasionally he would sneak home at night to collect food left out by his mother.

Mrs. Lange, relief in her voice, said, "Oh, yes, I'm happy to say that Joe's back on his medication again."

"That's nice."

A relief is what it was.

I gave a thumbs-up to Mother, who was stirring batter in a mixing bowl, and she nodded, giving me the go-ahead.

"Mrs. Lange," I said, "the reason I'm calling is

that Mother and I have some work for him to do for us—a bit of remodeling."

"Well, that's wonderful! He does so need to get out of the house."

Meaning *she* needed him to get out of the house.

Mrs. Lange continued. "There *is* one small issue, though. . . ."

I waited. How bad could it be? Actually, fairly bad—like the time he knocked me in the noggin out at Wild Cat Den, mistaking me for a terrorist.

"The pills haven't *quite* taken full effect," she said. "He's still talking, well . . . military."

"Not a problem," I assured her. I had gotten quite good at deciphering his Marine-speak. Even fully medicated, Joe would sometimes ask a waitress the ETA (estimated time of arrival) of a cheeseburger.

I asked her to call him to the phone.

A full minute passed before Joe's baritone voice barked, "Lange here."

With little fanfare, I filled my friend in on the pending reality TV pilot show, and how we wanted to use the old Butterworth home, but that repairs would be necessary. Which was where he came in.

"You'll be paid, of course," I concluded. "Are you interested?"

"Affirmative."

"Civilian clothes."

"Negatory."

"Come on, Joe. Consider it a spy mission."

"They shoot spies. Khakis mandatory."

This was Joe *on* his meds, huh?

"Okay . . . but leave the artillery at home."

"Affirmative." Then: "Coordinates?"

I gave him the address, and told him to be there in the morning at nine, when the show's producer and cameraman would be doing a walk-through.

"Roger," he said. "Oh-nine-hundred."

The phone clicked dead.

I wandered into the kitchen, wondering if I'd done the right thing in contacting Joe. Despite Sushi's pedigree, I had a bad habit of taking in strays—Rocky a case in point. I perched on a red 1950s step stool to watch Mother bake cookies, like I was still just a little kid.

Mother was Danish, but there was some Norwegian in there as well, and this recipe was her nod to them.

NORSK SMAA BROD
(old Norwegian Cookies)

BATTER:
½ cup butter
1 cup sugar
2 eggs
4 tbsp. sweet cream
3½ cups sifted flour
1 tsp. soda
1 tsp. cinnamon
¼ tsp. ginger
1 tsp. vanilla
1 cup raisins, chopped

GLAZE:
1 egg white, beaten
4 tbsp. sugar
5 tbsp. shredded almonds
1 tbsp. cream
1 tsp. cinnamon

Cream butter and sugar. Add eggs and cream, beating well. Add flour sifted with soda and spices. Then add vanilla and lastly, chopped raisins. Chill thoroughly. When ready to bake, roll small pieces of dough into pencil-slim lengths to form circles. Spread glaze over top of cookies. Bake 12 minutes at 350 degrees. Makes five to six dozen.

Mother always made some of the cookies with chocolate chips, because little Brandy didn't like raisins, no matter how finely chopped (ditto for big Brandy), but she did so reluctantly, saying this substitution was a slap in the face to good Norwegians everywhere. (Sorry, Norwegians, but I'm a chocolate gal. Anyway, the weather in Norway is so cold, the occasional slap might be beneficial.)

While Mother readied what she called her "trademark pot roast" for dinner (not worth a recipe), I set the antique Duncan Phyfe table in the dining room with our green-jade (is that redundant?) Fire King dishes. I loved the large plates, which had raised surfaces to keep the foods separated, just like the plastic ones in our old picnic basket.

(**Vivian to Editor**: *There is* nothing *wrong with my pot roast! Brandy is out of line disparaging this dish, which won first prize at the 2009 Iowa State Fair.*)

(**Brandy to Editor**: *It won, all right . . . after person or persons unknown doused all the other entries with Tabasco sauce.*)

(**Vivian to Brandy**: *I resent your insinuation, and would remind you that we have slander laws in this country.*)

(**Brandy to Vivian**: *In a print work, it's libel, not slander, and anyway the truth is the best defense.*)

(**Editor to Vivian and Brandy**: *Ladies, we've been down this road before—no more authorial discord. Write any comments you might have about each other in pencil in the margins of the copyedited manuscript—not in the body of the work. Unfortunately, in the last book, such squabbling made you both look foolish.*)

(**Brandy to Editor**: *Point well taken.*)

(**Vivian to Editor**: *A No. 2 pencil?*)

I prepared my contribution to the meal, a garden salad, then wandered into the living room, where through the picture window I could see Jake and the two dogs coming up the front walk.

I had to laugh because a tuckered-out Sushi was getting prodded along by Rocky, who was right behind her, nudging her in the rump with his nose. Sushi was too tired to growl or otherwise complain.

Inside, Sushi rolled onto her back, her

tongue lolling, submissive and exhausted. But when Rocky trotted off toward the kitchen, she clambered onto her feet and back into the game, to see what was cookin'. Meanwhile Jake replaced the leashes on a hook by the door.

"Every squirrel and his brother was out," he complained, which explained why he seemed a little winded. He held up a blue plastic bag. "Where does this go?"

"There's a can by the garage marked DOGGIE DO-DO."

He made a face. "You *are* a girl, Mom. Oh, hey! Know anybody who drives a red Toyota?"

I thought for a moment. "No . . . why?"

" 'Cause I swear one was tagging along while I walked the dogs."

"Tagging along?"

"Yeah, going real slow. It was kind of creepy."

"Did you see the driver?"

He shrugged. "Naw . . . but the plates were Illinois."

I shrugged. "I'm sure it's nothing."

There were plenty of red Toyotas around. And lots of folks from neighboring Illinois, across the river, worked and played in Serenity. Or maybe somebody was looking for an address. Probably nothing.

And I put it out of my mind.

The following morning at oh-nine-hundred-ish, Mother, Jake, and I piled into the old Buick, and a quick five minutes later pulled up in front of the murder house (*would we always call it that?* I wondered).

We were dressed for work: Mother wearing

her old painting clothes—slacks and top (once gray) splotched with a Jackson Pollock rainbow; Jake in a pair of old jeans and a Da Bears sweatshirt left behind on his last visit (now a little too small); and me sporting torn overalls and faded plaid shirt (I decided to pass on a country-bumpkin straw hat).

Joe had beaten us there, of course, standing at parade rest on the front stoop, wearing beige fatigues, nary a grenade nor Glock in sight, I was pleased to note.

Jake, in the car next to me, whispered, "You *sure* that screwball is okay?"

I whispered back, "That screwball is a friend of mine."

"I know. But is he *okay?*"

I shrugged. "I guess we'll find out."

We climbed out of the Buick, but Jake still had misgivings. "Mom, didn't that guy knock you out in one of those caves at Wild Cat Den?"

"That was last summer. He's better now."

"Do you know *anybody* who isn't on medication?" he asked.

I just gave him a look. "Why, would you like to be?"

Mother called out to Joe. "Ahoy there, matey! Permission to come aboard."

"He's a Marine, Grandma," Jake said with the superior smirk of the young.

"Yes, and the Marines are a part of the United States Navy, in case you didn't know." She giggled like a schoolgirl, possibly summoning memories of Marines she'd dated. " 'From the halls of Montezuma to the shores of Tripoli!' "

I asked, "Anyone else here, Joe?"

Meaning our producer or cameraman.

"Negatory."

Mother went *tsk-tsk*. "That's showbiz folk for you—they just don't have the discipline we denizens of the stage possess." She sighed, weight of the world. "Well, we might as well go in."

Producing a key, Mother worked it in the lock of the ancient front door, and in another moment our little group was stepping inside, where we were greeted by darkness and the musty smell of a house vacant for too long.

"The electricity probably isn't on," Mother said.

I tried a nearby wall switch, and she was correct.

"Jake," I asked, "would you raise all the shades?"

"Sure."

He did, and sunlight flooded in.

The downstairs floor was typical of a clapboard turn-of-last-century house: small foyer, open parlor/sitting room to the right, library/den to the left, and center hallway leading back to the kitchen and formal dining room. Since no stairs to the second floor were visible from where I stood, they most likely would be off the kitchen, leading up to three (possibly four) bedrooms and a single bathroom.

The austerity of the home, with its rooms smaller than the norm for their era, confirmed what Mother had claimed about its long-deceased owner: that the wealthy Archibald Butterworth had been a skinflint who denied his two children the luxury they might have enjoyed.

Mother, hands on hips, surveyed the area like a sergeant might a beachhead. "Well, we certainly have our work cut out for us."

"Roger that," Joe said.

The prior renter, Mary Beth Beckman, had apparently packed her bookstore belongings and left in a hurry, and with no consideration for any future renter. Trash was scattered everywhere: discarded pizza boxes, diet soda cans (with a large pizza? why bother?); wadded-up wastepaper. The carpet was stained and littered with cat hair.

Jake crinkled his nose. "Yuck. If I wanted to deal with this kind of mess, I coulda stayed in Chicago and cleaned my room."

Mother huffed, "Apparently that Beckman woman has no pride *or* breeding." Then, to no one in particular, but everyone in general, she commanded, "Pull up that loose carpet over in the corner—I want to see what's under there."

Joe, accustomed to taking orders, walked briskly across the room, bent, grabbed a loose piece of carpet, and yanked it back.

Mother went over for a look. "Just as I thought," she exclaimed, her tone positive now (not "negatory"). "A parquet floor. Joe! More."

She unleashed a Sgt. Bilko-style nonsense command, "*Hay yah hay ruuup!*"

And Joe hopped to it, uncovering a larger section of flooring, revealing an intricate geometric design—a surprising slice of extravagance in the otherwise dreary house.

"Oh, goody-goody," Mother said happily, clapping her hands, a child given her birthday wish. "What *production* value!"

Production value, I would learn, was anything that didn't cost you much that made a TV show or movie look like it had spent some money.

"I doubt the *floor* will make it into any shot," I said. "Besides, some of it looks to be rotting away."

Mother frowned, her birthday wish already failing to come true. "Nonsense! All we have to do is replace a few questionable boards here and there—and"—she pointed to the wall separating the two front rooms—"knock that out to make one large room."

"I hate to be a Debbie Downer," I replied, "but I believe that's a supporting wall."

I had taken a CAD course in architecture at our community college, thinking I might become the next Frank Lloyd Wright. I never did, but I knew a supporting wall when I saw one.

A voice from the foyer spoke. "I'm afraid your daughter is correct, Mrs. Borne. The wall stays . . . much as my cameraman might wish it gone."

Bruce Spring gestured to the man with him. "I'd like you to meet Phil Dean—best shooter in the reality game. His hand-held is better than Steadicam."

That sounded impressive, though I had no idea what it meant.

Phil, early forties, was muscular, with thick dark hair tinged with silver at the temple, a salt-and-pepper beard, and intense dark eyes. He wore scuffed white Nikes, torn Levi blue jeans, and a wrinkled black polo shirt with the production company's logo on the pocket; he also lugged a black Sony HD camera—the kind newscasters used.

Phil's casual attire said, "I'm the worker," while Bruce's polo shirt, tailored slacks, and Italian shoes, reminded, "I'm the boss."

Mother skirted around the pulled-back carpet and approached the men.

"Bruce, daaahling," she drawled, going Hollywood, the British accent a distant memory, "it's a delight seeing you again."

As if it had been ages, not yesterday.

To the cameraman she cooed, "I just know we'll do a simply maaahvulous show together, Mr. Dean."

Mother extended a languid hand. The cameraman hesitated, perhaps not knowing whether to shake or kiss it, finally settling on the former.

Then he said, "Mr. Dean is my father. Call me Phil."

"And I am Vivian"—she let out a brittle Katharine Hepburn laugh—"the star of our fledgling production."

Further introductions were made—Joe, Jake, and myself. None of us used a Hollywood accent, if that's what Mother had been doing, and I whispered to her to knock it off before I kicked her in the theater seat.

"Vivian," Bruce said, glancing around, "correct me if I'm wrong . . . but isn't this the Butterworth murder house? We did an episode about that unsolved crime on *Heartland Homicides.*"

"Yes," Mother said, grinning like a skull. "This

is indeed the infamous murder house. What better home for *Antiques Sleuths?*"

Then she clamped a hand over her mouth, and glanced around like she was looking for the other two monkeys. She withdrew her palm and stage-whispered, "Of course, we mustn't refer to it as such—*ix-nay on the urder-may!* A condition of the owners, you see . . . they're the family connected to the crime. *But!* . . . people in the know will, uh . . ."

"Know," I said, crooking my finger for her to come over for a private conference.

"What is it, dear? We have important Hollywood people here—let us not be rude."

"Not be rude? 'Rude' doesn't cover what you've done. You duped your old friends up the street into providing this house for our show when you *knew* Bruce Spring was involved with that documentary on the murder. They're going to be furious!"

That *Heartland Homicides* episode had brought national attention to the crime and stirred up local interest.

"Fiddlesticks," she said. "We're not going to do anything about that case on *Antiques Sleuths,* are we? Bruce won't be hosting that show, *we* will be."

"No," I said tightly. "He'll just be producing it." I held up my hands in surrender. "They're *your* friends. If you think you can get away with this, fine by me."

Bruce and Phil had already begun a walkthrough of the house, and we returned to tearing out the parlor carpet. Then after about fifteen minutes, the two men reappeared. Bruce seemed pleased, Phil not so much.

"Well?" Mother asked them anxiously. "What do you think of our enchanted cottage?"

Bruce smiled. "Well, the house is perfect. Lots of character. It'll make a great set." He turned to his shooter. "Phil?"

The cameraman shrugged. "It's cramped, will be hard to light, and will basically make my life a living hell. Otherwise, it's perfect."

"Come on, man. It's not that bad."

"What does it matter what I think?" Phil said sourly. "You're going to do what you want."

An embarrassed silence draped itself across the room.

Bruce, forcing a smile, said, "Would you excuse Phil and me for a moment?"

And turning his back on the cameraman, he walked away. After a beat, Phil glumly followed.

"No *problemo!*" Mother called after them. "As a theatuh director, I am well aware that one must often work out creative differences between . . . Oh. They've gone. Too bad. I was going to give a wonderful example of how it's done."

I'll give one: the time Mother donned dual hats in *Everybody Loves Opal,* and director Mother constantly yelled at actor Mother, and vice versa.

(**Mother to Brandy**: *I did not yell at myself. That would be unprofessional and undignified. But I did give my character the occasional stern talking-to. Sorry, Editor—couldn't find a pencil.*)

Right around then I noticed that Joe and Jake had gone AWOL.

Hearing faint voices above, I went into the kitchen—where snoopy Mother was eavesdropping on Bruce and Phil in the dining room—and found the stairs leading up. Jake's voice came from a bedroom: "Okay, I'm in. We'll go fifty-fifty."

"Negatory," Joe said. "*I'm* doing the grunt work."

"But *I'm* the one who'll get in deep doo-doo if *she* ever finds out."

"Sixty-forty. It's my caper. Also, I have the contacts who would pay premium shekels for this sort of thing."

Jake sighed. A pause. "All right, all right. I don't care what anybody says—*you're* normal, all right. You must be, to drive that hard a bargain."

"What's going on?" I asked from the doorway.

Jake jumped, but Joe whirled toward me in a threatening karate stance.

Couldn't I ever learn not to surprise a Marine?

"Whoa!" I said, palms up. "I'm a friendly, remember?"

Joe uncoiled, stood, maintaining an uneasy parade rest.

"Well, what's up?" I asked again. "Am I the 'she' you'll get in deep doo-doo with, if I find out?"

Jake said, "No, no . . . we're just talkin' about selling my baseball cards. Dad's ex gave me a couple of valuable ones that I want to peddle with the rest of my collection."

My son couldn't lie any better than I could.

"What's this about a 'caper'? And 'premium shekels'?"

Joe said, "Baseball cards are collectibles," as if that answered everything. I was about to press them further, when shouting broke out below.

From the sound of it, things had gotten physical between Bruce and Phil.

Yet it was a woman doing most of the yelling.

Guess what woman.

"Joe!" I barked. "Can you serve as an M.P.?"

"Affirmative."

To Jake I said, "You better stay here."

"No way!" he shot back. "Somebody's mixing it up down there, and my money's on Grandma."

We hurried down the stairs, through the kitchen, and into the parlor.

Where it wasn't Mother who was yelling, after all—rather, a heavy-set woman in black sweater and slacks, the house's former renter, Mary Beth Beckman herself, arguing loudly with Bruce Spring.

What the devil was the heavyset bookseller doing back here? Had she come for her pizza boxes?

Mary Beth—turning nearly as red as the scarf around her neck, tendrils of gray hair doing a Medusa number around her tomato of a face—thrust a threatening finger at the producer. "Perhaps Andrew Butterworth would be interested in knowing that the host of *Heartland Homicides* is involved here—the host slash producer who produced that documentary episode on his father's murder, practically accusing *him* of it!"

Bruce, unfazed, countered, "Maybe he would be interested in knowing it was *you*, Miss Beckman, who contacted me in the first place. I'd never heard of the Butterworth murder or Serenity flipping Iowa, either, before you called me!"

Actually, he didn't say "flipping."

The bookseller's mouth yawned open, then clamped shut, like a gate.

"Besides," Bruce went on, "what makes you think he *doesn't* know I produced the documentary?"

The woman laughed once, humorlessly. "Because you're *here*, in this *house!* If Andrew Butterworth knew you were involved, he'd have never granted permission for you to shoot here!"

I moved deeper into the parlor. "What's all this about?"

Mother, an interested bystander in this little tit-for-tat, scowled at me for busting in. She did love a good fracas.

"My dear," Mary Beth addressed me in a highly patronizing manner, "I don't think you have any idea who this Bruce Spring individual really is—which is to say, a liar, a conniver, and a breaker of promises . . . especially where *money* is concerned. Anyone who does business with him had better have an iron-clad contract and a regular Perry Mason for a lawyer."

We had neither. (Mr. Ekhardt, our family attorney, now ninety, had been Serenity's Perry Mason for many years, but now was prone to falling asleep in court.)

Jake, with Joe in the parlor entryway, came forward. "Bruce Spring isn't any of those things, lady. He's a reality TV *genius!*"

That might be overstating it, but I'd learned long ago not to criticize my son's heroes—real or fictional.

"And besides," my son went on defiantly, "who invited *you?*"

Mary Beth, momentarily befuddled by the boy's pluck, recovered, and huffed at everyone in general, "Well, don't say I didn't *warn* you!"

She wheeled and left, slamming the front door.

"Who *was* that ol' windbag?" Jake asked.

"Just a poor, sad, delusional woman," Bruce answered quietly.

I looked at the producer. "*Did* she contact you about doing a documentary on the Butterworth murder?"

He didn't answer for a moment, then sighed. "Well, she did bring the crime to my attention, back when I was hosting *Heartland Homicides* for A & E. But she wanted an executive producer's credit, a hefty fee, and royalties. Which was ridiculous." He gestured dismissively. "I counteroffered an associate producer credit and a flat fee, but she turned it down."

"So you made the documentary without her," I said, a statement not a question.

Bruce spread both hands. "Hey! I didn't *have* to pay that woman anything—no one has a claim on a *true* crime."

Mother was nodding. "That's right, dear. One cannot copyright history."

I gave her a suspicious look. "How did Mary Beth even know about this? About the show, and the Butterworth 'murder' house being the set, and . . . you just couldn't keep it to yourself, could you?"

Mother's eyes flitted like a butterfly, landing nowhere. "Well, I may have mentioned it to, uh . . . one or two of the girls."

Bruce said, "You were supposed to keep all of this to yourself, Mrs. Borne. We like to handle the rollout of productions ourselves, and—"

"Pish posh and tish tosh," Mother said. "Let us no longer speak of unimportant things."

Bruce frowned. "What's that—Lewis Carroll?"

"No," I said wearily. "Just Mother."

She clapped her hands once. "Let's forget *all* about that unpleasant woman and get down to work. How do we proceed, Mr. Producer? With the renovations, that is. What is your vision?"

More to the point, I asked, "And what do we use for money?"

Bruce withdrew his wallet from a front pocket. "This cashier's check should be enough to cover everything," he said. "Repairs, new fixtures, and what-have-you."

"Yippee!" Mother said.

She really did.

Bruce added, "Of course, I'll need receipts for everything." He handed Mother the check, who looked at it, then gave a low whistle.

I took a gander, too. So much for Mary Beth's claim that Bruce was a welsher.

(**Mother to Brandy**: *Dear, do you have any under-*

standing of the term "welsher"? **Side Note to Editor***: Sorry, still out of pencils! Why don't you send me some? I believe they would qualify for "media mail.")*

(**Brandy to Mother***: No, I don't know the history of the term "welsher." Anyway, what did happen to all the pencils? I think you deliberately threw them away.)*

(**Mother to Brandy***: The term is quite derogatory to the Welsh . . . and we have some readers across the pond in Wales, like that lovely correspondent, Gwenllian Cadwalader. Gwenllian, I do apologize for my daughter's ignorance.)*

(**Editor to Vivian and Brandy***: I* am *sending you a box of pencils—*FedEx—*and I expect you to use them!)*

I said to Bruce, "There's something I don't understand—why would your production company put money into a house it doesn't own?"

"That money is in the budget already," he said. "You see, usually we build a set, then tear it down after. In this case, everything stays, which is to your benefit. You'll be able to continue using the house for your antiques business."

"Cool!" Jake said, then, looking around, asked, "Where's Phil?"

Mother said, "I saw him slip out. I'm afraid our DP went AWOL."

"Well, that's a SNAFU," Jake said, " 'cause we gotta have *him*—he's worked on all the big reality shows."

Bruce raised reassuring palms. "Not to worry—I'll have Phil back on board as soon as I go back to the hotel and smooth his ruffled feathers."

"Then perhaps you best do so now," Mother

suggested. "It's never wise to let hard feelings fester. In the meantime, we'll carry on," her British accent momentarily returning.

As the afternoon wore on, we expected Bruce to return with a placated Phil, but when five o'clock arrived with no sign of either, we hauled the last of the downstairs carpet to the curb, then locked up the house.

I offered Joe a lift, but since he lived not too far away, my friend opted to hoof it (or, rather, march) home.

Tired and dirty, our hearty little band—Mother, Jake, and me—climbed into the Buick and headed back to the Borne homestead.

Where, greeting us in the foyer, were two dogs, practically cross-eyed with the need to go outside.

Quickly, I put Sushi and Rocky out back on their respective chains, and noticed that the yard could use some "sprucing up." So I grabbed the plastic pooper-scooper and set about my work, being careful where I stepped. (The alternative was helping Mother in the kitchen cooking our dinner, the much-dreaded liver and onions that she alone liked.)

Jake came flying down the back porch steps. "Mom?"

I knew what he wanted. "Don't worry," I told him. "There are plenty of cold cuts and cheese slices in the fridge. Fresh bread on the counter, too."

He smiled. "Awesome." He frowned. "But how do we make that liver disappear?"

I smiled. "That's what dogs under the table

are for—just keep your grandma busy talking about herself."

"Which is only the easiest thing in the world," he said, still grinning. Then, "Say, Mom? Do you still have a bike?"

"Yeah, but the tires are flat. Why?"

"Oh, I just thought I might ride around while I was home. Decent weather. Where is it?"

"In the garage. You'll have to dig through Grandma's junk to get to it." I raised a warning finger. "If you get scratched from anything rusty, you'll need a tetanus shot."

Jake, heading for the stand-alone garage, called over his shoulder, "Had one last year, remember? When I went digging for my old snow sled?"

After dinner and kitchen cleanup, I went upstairs for a nice, long bubble bath. Jake, having found my old bike, was outside in the drive, fixing the flats. Mother was busy at the dining room table, constructing a model of the Butterworth house by stacking two medium-sized cardboard boxes on each other, and using single-serving cereal boxes, toilet paper tubes, and Popsicle sticks to construct how she wanted the interior to look.

You had to hand it to the old girl—she was theater through and through.

After my soothing bath, I got into my jammies, and crawled into bed, joining Sushi (curled by my pillow) and Rocky (stretched out at the foot), both looking contented after their unexpected under-the-table feast.

Settling in with a book (I'm an e-book fan only on planes), I may have read for an hour, or only a few minutes, I couldn't say. But when I awoke next the lamp by the bed was still on, and I was in a half-conscious state, my eyes merely slits, when Sushi's little furry face came into focus, and she began to whistle.

At least it seemed like she did, until the cobwebs in my head cleared, and I realized it was only that silly whistling ringtone on my cell phone from the nightstand.

The caller was Jake, and the time, 1:45 A.M.

I bolted upright. "Where are you? Tell me you're in your room and calling on your cell."

"No, I'm not."

"What is it?"

"Mom, you gotta come. Right away." His voice sounded small and distant.

"Where are you?"

"The . . . the murder house. Something's happened. Please. Please hurry."

"What is it?" I was out of bed, shoving my slippers on.

"There's a body."

"Body?" I was trying to process it. "You mean . . . a dead one?"

"Oh, yeah."

"Whose?"

"I . . . I can't tell." His voice cracked. "It's all . . . all chopped up."

A Trash 'n' Treasures Tip

Modest pricing of merchandise creates rapid turnover and repeat customers. High prices create stagnant stock and less foot traffic, which means less money in your pocket. On the other hand, some items, like a certain Smiley Face clock, don't sell no matter what tactic you try.

Chapter Four

Chop Till You Drop

Note from Brandy: The first half of this chapter is written by Jake, because my son can explain better than I what happened to him at the old Butterworth house during the wee morning hours.

Hi. Jake here. But you already know that. I'm not a writer, but then Mom isn't really a writer either, and this is, what? Her seventh book? Anyway, it would be cool if you cut me some slack.

Speaking of cool, how cool is my mom, not making me eat that gross liver and onions crap? Is that okay to say, crap I mean? I don't know what the rules are. But dinner is a decent place to start my story, because after I fixed myself a baloney and cheese sandwich, careful not to let

Grandma see me doing it, I went outside to fix the old Schwinn. I pumped up the tires and got the chain back on its track and it seemed like it was working okay.

By the time I got back in the house, Mom was already up in bed with the dogs. I said good night to Grandma, who was busy at the dining room table making one of her art projects out of cardboard and Popsicle sticks. I didn't ask what the project was because she might tell me, and that could take a while.

Upstairs I could smell the dog farts all the way into my room. Can I say that? Farts? Really, I should have asked for some kind of guidelines. Anyway, dog farts. Mom and I must have fed them way too much liver under the table.

You know, this writing is hard. I have spent a whole paragraph on dog farts and they really don't have anything to do with anything. The farts, I mean. The dogs, either.

Anyway, I got in bed with my clothes on and pretended to go to sleep. Then at half-past midnight I tiptoed out of my room and listened to make sure Mom and Grandma were conked out. They were. Both snoring like they were competing for first place. So I snuck down the stairs and out to the bike, climbed aboard, and pedaled away. The Schwinn rode great. Old School is the best sometimes.

I was all set to meet Joe at one hundred hours. That's how a military nut says one in the morning. We were meeting at our RV, and I don't mean recreation vehicle. RV stands for Rendezvous Point in Joe-speak. Why it isn't RP, I couldn't tell you. Our RV was the old murder house.

You're probably wondering why I was sneaking out "at all hours" (as Mom would later call it) on this mission (as Joe put it).

So I'll tell you.

Yesterday afternoon, while I was pulling up that gross old carpet in the murder-house library, I discovered a few loose floorboards. When I pried them up, I found . . . I should probably do some suspense thing here, right? Okay, wait for it, wait for it . . . an old ax under there, covered in dust!

Well, I just about peed my jeans!

(**Mom to Jake**: *Honey, I am trying to stay out of your way here, and really you're doing just fine. But do remember that we have a number of older readers, some with an aversion to bad language, so you'll need to watch what you say.*)

(**Jake to Mom**: *But I did watch my language. Would you rather I use the* other *"p" word?*)

(**Mom to Jake**: *Forget I said anything. You're doing great.*)

Anyway, I knew right away that this ax must be the long-ago murder weapon, hidden away after that Scrooge- type character got chopped up way back when. I knew all the gory details from listening to Grandma, but I didn't take the thing out right then in front of everybody.

Why not?

Well, earlier Joe mentioned if we *did* happen to find the ax, which wasn't ever recovered, that he knew some nutty guy out east who collected murder memorabilia. I guess it was murder memorabilia from famous murders, because just an everyday murder thing wouldn't be that collectible. This collector, Joe said, would pay megabucks for something like the actual Butterworth ax.

So I didn't tell anybody but Joe that I found the ax, and cut him in on the deal, because I wouldn't have known the thing was valuable if he hadn't told me. Seemed the fair thing to do. Mom and Grandma have a different opinion, but I've seen them snatch plenty of antiques out from under the noses of other collectors.

But it did spook me and make me feel weird about it when Mom interrupted Joe and me talking upstairs about my discovery. Doing the right thing by Joe meant I was doing the wrong thing by everybody else.

Now if you think I was just being greedy, I don't blame you. My dad makes good money with his investment company. And I get a decent allowance, better than any of my friends, though Dad does expect me to buy *everything* out of it, even clothes, which kind of sucks. Can I say that?

I mean, do you know how much an Apple iPad with Wi-Fi+3G and 32 gigabytes costs? Seven Benjamins and change! Saving that out of my allowance would be possible, if I didn't mind waiting till my sophomore year in college. Only thing is, I wanted it *yesterday*.

(**Grandma to Jake**: *Dear, while you're doing splendidly telling your little story, although rather prone to discursion (like your mother), might I suggest* *that you please try to stay on point and be succinct, like your grandmother?*)

(**Jake to Grandma**: *Gotcha.*)

Anywho, I was late getting to the RV because halfway there my transport wimped out on me. Not the bike, which was rad, but the tires went flat again, and I had to ditch the bike and haul butt on foot!

As a result, my ETA was twenty minutes off, and I expected to find one p.o.'ed Marine standing on the porch.

(**Mom to Jake**: *Honey, again, please keep in mind our mixed readership and refrain from using such terms as "p.o.'ed."*)

(**Jake to Mom**: *Again—I didn't have to use initials. Do you want me to tell my story my own way or not?*)

(**Mother to Brandy**: *Dear, leave the boy alone and stop trying to suppress his native narrative style. If our readers know how to interpret those initials, they will likely not be offended. Nor will they if they don't. Do please continue, Jake. . . .*)

Well, Joe was *not* waiting on the stoop, so I figured he was running late, too. Only then I noticed that the front door was open a little, which was weird because I was the one who had a key. I lifted it from Grandma's jacket pocket. (Sorry, Grandma.)

(**Grandma to Jake**: *Quite all right, dear. I would have done the same thing at your age.*)

(**Brandy to Mother**: *You would do the same thing at* any *age. And thanks for giving my son a free pass for stealing!*)

So I went on in the house, switched on my flashlight, and called out to Joe, but he didn't answer. I kept calling out his name because I didn't want a replay of what happened to Mom in that cave when she surprised him. Then I went into the library room, where I figured I'd find him, since that's where the ax was hidden. And where I left it.

But Joe wasn't there, and the ax wasn't either! The floorboards had been pulled up and the chopper taken out, leaving just its outline in the dust. It had been hidden there a long time so that outline was real distinct.

I can't tell you what I said when I saw the ax was gone because it might offend sensitive ears, like my mom's. But I *can* tell you it flipped me out and I was kicking myself for trusting Joe, who I figured had beat me to the punch and taken the ax all for himself.

So I ran out of the library and headed to the back of the house, just to make sure that crazy sneak wasn't around somewhere, and the next thing I knew, I was on my butt sitting on the kitchen floor, after slipping in something gooey.

On the way down I dropped my flashlight, and it was on the floor now, shining at something that I couldn't make out at first. It seemed to be a leg, but that couldn't be right, because it wasn't attached to anything. Like a mannikin leg.

Then I saw the blood and realized it was a real leg that belonged to a real man, only it wasn't attached to anybody anymore.

I scrambled to my feet, almost slipping again, but got up and got the hell out of there, and I won't soften that, Mom, Grandma, because I already *did* soften it.

The next thing I know I'm outside, losing the baloney and cheese sandwich I'd eaten after dinner, which I guess was better than barfing liver and onions.

Was that Joe's leg in there? I didn't know, and I wasn't about to go back in and find out, not by myself, anyway.

Then I called Mom on my cell.

That's about it.

Brandy here. Nice job, Jake! (The writing, I mean—not sneaking out of the house!)

After receiving Jake's distress call, I threw on a robe, slipped my phone into a pocket, and rushed into the hallway, where I ran into Mother, also in robe and pajamas.

"What is it, dear?" she asked anxiously, her eyes wide without benefit of her magnifying glasses. "Your phone doesn't usually whistle in the middle of the night."

"It was Jake."

"Isn't he in his room?"

"No. But he's all right. He *is* in trouble, though. I hate to say it, but *your* kind of trouble. *Our* kind of trouble. . . ."

Quickly I filled her in on my brief conversation with Jake, as we hurried down the stairs, where I grabbed the car keys off the marble-top

Queen Anne table by the front door. In another moment we were flying out, in robes and pajamas and slippers, heading for the Buick.

The streets were deserted, thankfully, because I drove like a maniac—even Mother couldn't have topped my performance behind the wheel. We arrived at the murder house in less than five minutes, bumping up over the front curb, practically parking in the yard.

I could see Jake on the cement stoop in the glow of a streetlight, and he came swiftly down toward me as I ran up the walk, my heart pounding. Nice to have a child be so glad to see you. Just not under these circumstances. . . .

"You're all right?" I asked, out of breath.

Jake threw his arms around me, hugged me tight, and at this odd moment I realized for the first time that my son was now almost as tall as I.

"I'm okay," he said, his voice muffled against my chest. "But . . . whoever is in *there* isn't."

"Did you call the police?"

He pulled back. "I was waiting for you."

Mother, having joined us, gave her grandson a smile that seemed only a trifle demented. "Good decision, dear. This will give me an opportunity for a quick look-see—Brandy?"

I shook my head. Unlike Mother, I had no stomach for murder tableaux, and I warned her, "Don't you dare compromise the crime scene."

Mother, already heading toward the house with the glove-compartment flashlight, shot back, "Not any more than our local-yokel boys-in-blue will, when they get here!"

"I'll give you five minutes," I said, "and then I'm calling 911."

Jake and I sat on the top step of the stoop. At first we sat silently, just glad to be together, and well. I hadn't yet gone from relief that my son was safe to parental indignation (like Roger had the other day); and Jake didn't want to push me there.

Finally I asked him to tell me his story, and he did. When I heard he was to have met Joe here, I said, "My God, my God—that's not *him* in there, is it? It's not . . ."

"I don't think it's Joe."

"What makes you say that?"

"The leg? The pants on it—they weren't khakis."

"Ah. Right." Then I said, "I'm going to have to call your father."

"Oh, yeah," he sighed. "Don't I know it."

"And he'll want to take you back to Chicago. Right away."

Jake twisted toward me. "But he can't—not 'right away,' anyway."

"Why's that?"

He gave me the tiniest of smiles. "I'll be a material witness—you know, can't leave town, and so on and so forth."

Had he been reading our books, or just watching *CSI* reruns?

Mother reappeared, and we craned our necks to look at her. It was then that I noticed what she had on her feet—my last Christmas's gag gift: a pair of big moose slippers, the antlers flopping as she stepped toward us, black beads in the plastic eyes rolling around crazily. Those could make some wild footprints at a bloody crime scene.

"Well," Mother announced, a deep sigh coming all the way up from the moose (mooses) (meeses). "At least it's not Joe Lange."

"We already knew that," I said. "Who is he?"

"He used to be the producer of our TV pilot—Bruce Spring."

Jake drew in a startled breath. "You're *sure* about that, Grandma?"

She nodded. "Unless someone else in Serenity wears the same brand of expensive Italian loafers."

Agape, I said, "I can't believe it—who would do such a vicious thing? It's terrible!"

"You're telling *me?*" Mother said, hand on hips. "There goes our TV show!"

I got to my feet. "That's all you can think about? Are you really that cold-blooded and selfish and old—"

"Let's not be unkind, dear," she said, raising a hand like a traffic cop. "Anyway, sentimentality won't help that poor man now." She unleashed a particularly melodramatic sigh, this one causing the moose feet to wiggle their eyes. "I am afraid there is something else. . . ."

"What?" Jake and I blurted.

Mother crooked a finger at me.

I looked at Jake. Pointed at him as if he were Sushi. "Stay."

"Don't worry," he said glumly, still seated on the stoop. "I've seen enough for one night."

I followed Mother back into the electricity-free house, her flashlight beam slicing through the darkness, leading us into the parlor, where the beam circled the room, then landed on a slumped figure in a corner.

Joe.

In one piece, at least, but otherwise the news wasn't good. Still in fatigues, he was seated with legs drawn to his chest.

And clutching an ax, its blade darkly stained.

"Oh no," I whispered.

Had my friend finally well and truly lost it? Could he have committed such a mad, savage deed?

I clutched Mother's arm. "You don't think he's . . . dangerous? I mean, would he do anything . . . to us?"

She focused the center of the light on his face; the eyes didn't blink. "I don't believe so, dear. He's in shock."

"Mother, we have simply *got* to call the police. We've delayed too long already. We're not the most popular citizens they serve and protect, you know."

"I suppose you're right," she said with reluctance, as if I'd insisted we leave a fun-filled gala. "Besides," she added, "I've made all of my observations."

"Such as?" I couldn't help asking.

"Such as"—the beam circled Joe again—"if your friend had killed our producer, he would have *much* more blood on his clothes."

* * *

Officer Mia Cordona was the first to arrive, squad car lights flashing—but sans siren, out of consideration for the slumbering neighbors, I supposed. Not that either Bruce Spring or Joe Lange were in any hurry. Mother and I met her at the curb.

Mia, whose curvy, raven-tressed, dark-eyed beauty remained undiminished by the masculine uniform, scowled at us. "A murder, and you two call it in. Why am I not surprised?"

Mother smiled understandingly and said, "Frown lines are so unbecoming, dear."

"Never mind," she snapped. "Fill me in."

We had once been good friends, Mia and I, but events of the last several years had strained that friendship beyond its capacity.

I let Mother do the honors, which she performed with surprising (for her) succinctness, submerging her Sarah Bernhardt instincts within a clipped, Jack Webb just-the-facts manner.

Mia listened intently, then spoke into her shoulder communicator, calling for backup, and to get the PD's two-person forensics team out of their warm beds, plus the paramedics— the latter in deference to Joe.

Mia asked where Jake was, and I pointed to our Buick where I had insisted he wait; while I couldn't keep him out of this mess, I could keep him out of the cold, the plummeting temperature tightening its grip on the night, making our breaths plume.

Mia muttered, "I suppose I can fathom Vivian involving the boy . . . but *you*, Brandy?"

I wondered how much time I'd serve for smacking an officer, but only said, "If you'd been listening, you'd know neither Mother nor I involved Jake in anything more than helping clean up this house, many hours ago."

"Let us not bicker, girls," Mother chimed in. "Now is not the time for animosity. After all, there's a dismembered producer in the house waiting for processing! Not to mention an ex-Marine with a bloody ax."

What could Mia say to that? I certainly had nothing.

A second squad car arrived, parking at an angle in the street, blocking it off, not that the nonexistent traffic minded. Officer Munson, a lanky middle-aged man with a hound-dog face, climbed out and joined our little group, Mia bringing him up to speed.

By now, the flashing lights of the police cars had attracted the attention of neighbors, who peered out of windows, some coming out in their nightclothes, braver souls, or at least snoopier ones, moving down to the sidewalk to see better. Lights came on in all the houses across the way but one.

"I don't want Joe to get hurt," I told the officers. "Let me help—I understand his illness. I'm sure I can convince him to go with you."

Munson and Mia exchanged troubled glances, then senior officer Munson said, "All right, Ms. Borne. But if he gets violent, we're stepping in."

"I understand," I said. "But you don't know that he's your perpetrator, remember. As Mother pointed out earlier, he doesn't have enough blood on him for that."

Mia winced in quiet irritation and Munson just gave me a glazed nod. "You follow us in," he said.

"Please . . . let me go in first."

The two cops exchanged glances again, but Munson said, "Well . . . all right. But anything we tell you to do, you do at once, got it?"

"Got it."

Mother touched my arm. "Good luck, dear. Will you be all right without me?"

"I'll try to manage."

"As you move into your thirties, dear, sarcasm will only read as bitterness."

"I'll keep that in mind."

My eyes went to Jake in the Buick, who was leaning forward in the front passenger seat, watching us intently. I gave him a nod and a re-assuring smile.

The distant wail of a paramedic truck signaled that time was short before the handful of gawkers would become dozens. I told Munson and Mia what I had in mind, admitted it was a little strange, but said it should work.

And we headed into the house.

As I stepped through the front door, Munson and Mia on my heels, I started to sing loudly.

" 'From the Halls of Montezuma,' " I sang, loud as a bullhorn, " 'to the shores of Tripoli! We fight our country's battles, in the air, on land, and sea!' "

I kept repeating those lyrics because that's all

I knew of them, from the old Bugs Bunny cartoons. By my third time through, the officers had Joe spotlighted with their mag lights.

He hadn't moved, remaining seated with his legs drawn up, still clutching the ax. But his vacant, staring-straight-ahead eyes were now focused on me.

"It's Brandy," I said, moving slowly toward him. "Put down your weapon. We have surrendered. We'll be given all the rights of the Geneva Convention."

Behind me, Munson muttered, "What the—?"

Joe's grip on the ax tightened, and the officers drew their guns, which gave me a start. Fine for them to be armed, but if Joe charged, I was in the front line.

But then my traumatized friend relaxed his grip, and lowered the ax slowly to the floor.

He got to his feet.

"Corporal Joseph E. Lange," he said, standing erect. "United States Marines, serial number 747608012."

"Okay, soldier," Munson said, almost gently. "Turn around, hands behind your back."

Joe complied, and the officer cuffed him.

I sighed in relief.

Mia whispered to me, "That was tense. Could've gotten ugly. Thanks, Brandy."

High praise from anyone on the PD, and a rare kind word from my ex-friend.

With Munson in the lead (and holding on to Joe's arm), we left the house, stepping out of darkness into what seemed like day. I had to squint from the glare of the emergency lights, a paramedic truck having added its beacon to the bunch.

There were other, lesser lights as well, from cameras and cell phones, pictures taken by the ever-growing crowd, soon to be launched on the Internet.

Someone grabbed my arm, startling me.

Police Chief Brian Lawson—my on-again-off-again-currently-on-again boyfriend—looked disheveled in his rumpled tan slacks and wrinkled blue shirt under a Windbreaker, as if having thrown on his work clothes from the now-previous day. His thick sandy hair, however, was neatly combed.

"Come with me," he said brusquely, the puppy-dog brown eyes colder than I was used to seeing them.

"What?" My eyes traveled past him to the Buick, front seat empty. "Where's Jake? And Mother?"

"They're in my car. Yours is blocked in. You can get it tomorrow."

"I only *have* one car!"

"We'll get it back to you tomorrow. Come along."

"Where are you taking us? To the station?"

"No. Home."

"Really?" I smiled a little, relieved to avoid that ordeal. "Well. That's fine. That's great."

We were at Brian's unmarked car now, Mother and Jake sequestered in back.

I touched his arm. "Thank you, Brian, for

being so considerate—letting us get some rest before taking our statements."

His smile was blandly businesslike. "You're only going home in deference to your . . . attire. But don't count on getting any sleep just yet. This night isn't over."

And opening the door of his unmarked car, Brian deposited me in back with Jake and Mother.

We rode home in silence. Jake fell asleep against my shoulder, while Mother wore an expression of concentration as if trying to remember her lines in a play—probably deciding what she *was* and *was not* going to share with Brian.

Inside the dark house an awakened Sushi and Rocky sniffed us over—Rocky bestowing Brian a low growl—before both trotted back up to bed.

Lucky them.

Mother turned on a few lamps, then Brian flipped on the bright ceiling lights.

I asked him in what I hoped seemed like good humor, "What are you trying to do, turn my living room into an interrogation chamber?"

When he didn't answer, I shrugged, then tended to Jake, who'd stretched out on the Queen Anne couch. I got my son a throw pillow and crocheted blanket and tucked him temporarily in. Then I sat next to him—with his legs up and over my lap—while Brian took an armchair across from us.

Mother had disappeared, saying she was going to make a pot of strong coffee, but there was a lot of banging coming from the kitchen for such a simple task.

Brian withdrew a pad and pen from the pocket of his Windbreaker jacket, and began to question Jake. Tired as I was, I stayed alert to look after my son's best interests, in particular that he didn't incriminate himself.

Midway through Jake's "interview," Brian stood and began pacing back and forth in front of the picture window, his reflection showing in the darkened glass. If any neighbors were watching, they were getting quite a show.

Brian then moved on to me. But since I didn't have much to tell—certainly with no intention of revealing that we had delayed calling the police while Mother conducted her own preliminary investigation—my interview was concluded in under ten minutes.

That left Mother to be grilled. She was still in the kitchen, the clanking of dishes and cups having brought the dogs down again, hoping for a wee-hour snack.

"Mrs. Borne," Brian called out. "Please come in here."

Only the *ding* of the microwave answered.

"*Now,* Vivian."

In another moment, Mother appeared with a large tray containing cups of steaming coffee, and an assortment of bakery goods—scones, tarts, and Danish strudel.

Placing the tray on the marble coffee table, she said, "I do hope this will suffice, Chief Lawson. I didn't have any doughnuts on hand."

"Contrary to the cliché, Vivian," Brian said, words clipped, "not all officers eat doughnuts, and I happen to be one of them."

"Oh, well, then you're really missing out," Mother said, shaking her head. "Have you ever tried Casey's General Store doughnuts? Fresh every morning! Get there early enough and you can have one hot out of the oven. How would you like your coffee? Milk? Sugar?"

Brian's cheeks were blossoming a dark pink. "Mrs. Borne. Will you please stop fussing and *sit down!*"

"No need to be rude. I was just trying to be a good hostess. It isn't every day that we have the Serenity Chief of Police in our home."

Just every other day, it seemed.

"Even," she added, sweet as any doughnut on the planet, "if he *is* only the *acting* chief. Or is the term 'interim'?"

"Mother, please," I said, wearily. "We're all tired. Let's get this over with."

Jake, stretched out on the couch, his legs on my lap, raised his head off the cushion. "Grandma, face the music. I wanna get to bed before I graduate."

Mother smiled at her grandson. "All right, dear. Your wish is your grandmother's command. No need to prolong this in any way. We should get right to it. Deal with it head-on. Straightaway." She plucked up a coffee cup and scone, then took the armchair vacated by the pacing Brian. "Shoot!" she said.

Somehow Brian managed to blink away that assault of words and say, "I'd like to pick up at the point where you entered the Butterworth house and examined the crime scene."

Mother, taking a sip of coffee, choked, then managed, "Well, what blabbermouth told *you?*"

"Not *this* blabbermouth," I said.

"Me neither," Jake added.

Mother's eyes narrowed to normal size behind her buggy glasses. "Then *who* done it?"

"Why, *you* done it, Vivian," Brian said with a nasty smile. "Just now."

Mother, setting her coffee cup on an end table, stood, the scone falling from her lap to the floor where it was instantly gobbled up by a vigilant Rocky.

"If you are going to resort to trickery," Mother said, drawing herself up, "I refuse to answer any further questions—not without Wayne Ekhardt present."

That was the octagenarian lawyer I mentioned earlier.

"Fine," Brian said tersely, snapping his little notebook shut. "I'll expect you both at the station tomorrow—today, that is, before noon."

"That's inhumane," Mother said. "You know I need my beauty rest, followed by my morning beauty regimen!"

He waggled a scolding finger at her. "Noon," he said. "With or without lipstick."

And he turned on his heel, heading for the front door.

"Brian?" I called. "A word, please? Outside?"

"Sure."

The purple-pink rays of dawn were just beginning to chase the night away as we stood on the porch facing each other.

"Did you have to be so hard on Mother?" I asked.

"Hard on *her*? If that meddling old biddy compromised that crime scene in any way—"

"That 'meddling old biddy,'" I reminded him, "has solved more major crimes in the past year than your police department did in the previous decade."

"That's not true and you know it," he snapped.

"No, actually it is true. I researched it. And *why* did you insist on conducting our interviews now? After all we'd been through! Couldn't that have waited?"

"You think I was being mean, don't you? A real jerk."

"A perfect deduction if I ever heard one."

Those brown eyes softened. "You know why I took your statements now? To *protect* you."

I stared. Then it dawned on me: Brian's insistence on driving us home; all the lights on in the living room; his high-profile pacing in front of the picture window.

I said, "You don't think Joe did it, either, do you?"

"No."

"Because there wasn't much blood on his clothes, like Mother said?"

He nodded.

I frowned. "And that means . . . ?"

"The killer is still out there."

I touched his arm. "Brian . . . I'm sorry I got all over your case like that."

His face softened. "Apology accepted. Normally having you all over my case isn't that bad." Then: "Brandy?"

"Yes?"

"Stay out of this one."

"Understood."

He cocked his head. "Not exactly a promise."

"I *will* try."

"This one's different. This is a damn *ax* murder. Nasty, scary stuff. You've got precious cargo on that couch in there. Protect your son and yourself by letting me and my guys handle it."

"You make a lot of sense."

His grin had frustration in it. "You really know how to hedge, don't you? See you tomorrow."

I remained on the porch until Brian's unmarked car disappeared, then turned to go into the house . . .

. . . but not before noticing a red Toyota drive by.

A Trash 'n' Treasures Tip

Shoppers can "smell" a dying business, making them less apt to buy, so owners must stay upbeat and friendly. Mother plasters our merchandise with cute little signs, like the one she put on a porcelain rabbit: HARE TODAY . . . GONE TOMORROW.

Chapter Five

Choppy Waters

After Brian left the house around four A.M., I was too tired to follow Mother and Jake upstairs to bed, and wound up crashing on the hard Queen Anne couch. My head had barely hit the throw pillow before I was out and dreaming nonsensical gibberish.

When an incessant pounding wouldn't stop, I tried working the noise into my dream, but finally gave up, forcing my eyes open. The clock on the mantel said seven.

Three hours of delirious sleep. What more could a girl ask of life? How about another three hours or maybe six? I turned my back to the knocking.

But the banging at the front door only continued.

Could Brian have returned for more questioning, and/or to return my car? If so, he was way out of line coming back so soon.

My spine was stiff, every bone in my body creaky, every muscle annoyed at me, and the only way I could stand was to roll off to the floor, then get to my knees and take it from there.

"All right, all right," I hollered. "I'm coming! Sheesh."

Hobbling like a geriatric patient in search of a lost walker, I eventually reached the door. Sushi and Rocky were already there, yapping and barking, respectively, having been roused from their slumber as well.

Pushing the dogs back with one leg, growling at them for a change, I cracked the door, and looked up into the angry face of my ex.

Jake must have called his father before going to bed and told him everything. Because I hadn't yet.

"About damn *time.* . . ." Roger said tersely.

Realizing I was a mess, a zombie with hair askew and sleep-puffy features, I resignedly let my former husband in, then followed him into the living room, where he wheeled to face me. He was wearing a tan leather jacket, brown tailored slacks, and expensive shoes. His idea of casual. He looked great. And greatly annoyed.

"I should have known better than to let Jake stay here," he snapped, his gray eyes cold, rugged face haggard from a four-hour early-morning drive—which had given him plenty of time to get worked up into a lather.

Too tired to defend myself, I said nothing.

He went on. "I'm gone—what?—less than twenty-four hours? And already you're mixed up in another murder!" He gulped air. "Involving our *son! Well?* Say something for yourself!"

I started to cry. Softly at first, little choking sounds, then louder, like a braying donkey.

It wasn't a stunt. I wasn't using my female wiles to get out of a jam. After all, braying-donkey snort-sobbing isn't exactly flattering. In addition to being exhausted, I had finally been hit by the tragedy of the night before—and, yes, guilt for putting Jake at risk, even if indirectly and unintentionally.

The dogs didn't like what they'd been hearing and let Roger know that he was a very, very bad man for upsetting me like this—Sushi delivering a sharp warning bark, like little gunshots, while Rocky, hair on his back standing up, emitting a long, low, truly threatening growl.

My weeping also brought Jake and Mother rushing downstairs.

Jake, in his rumpled clothes from last night, his hair sticking up on one side like a ragged Indian feather, looked accusingly at his father and said, "What did you do to *Mom?*"

While Mother, in robe and moose slippers (had she worn them to bed?) answered, "Why, being a big *bully,* of course. You should be ashamed, you, you, you *brute!*"

Roger spread his hands. "Don't turn this around on me! I'm just beside myself about what happened."

Mother huffed like Jack Benny, "*Well!* If you're beside yourself, *both* of you should feel ashamed. Just imagine how *we* must feel. We *lived* it! You just *heard* about it."

He pointed an accusatory finger at her. "This fiasco has your name written all over it, Vivian."

"Dad," Jake told his father, "*I'm* the one who snuck out of the house last night and got myself into this mess. Be mad at me if you want . . . but don't take it out on Mom. Or Grandma, either."

Roger, exasperated, shouted, "I'm *not* taking it out on your mother! Or your grandmother, either."

"That's exactly what you're doing," Jake said defiantly.

Frowning, Roger said, "Don't talk to me like that—I'm your father!"

Yeah. Go *there.* Like *that* ever worked on any kid.

Jake folded his arms and looked away.

Exasperated, my ex put hands on hips and shook his head. His expression bore a brand of confusion known only to the male sex, particularly fathers. "Since *when* did *I* become the bad guy?"

Mother shrugged. "That's just the way it is around here, Roger dearest—you should be used to it by now. You are on *our* turf. Could I interest you in a cup of coffee?"

His eyes and nostrils flared. "No! Jake, get your things together. I'm taking you home. Right this instant."

"I can't go home, Dad," Jake said with a shrug. He jerked a thumb back at himself. "I'm a material witness. Right, Grandma?"

"That's correct, darling," Mother said. "You can't leave until the police allow."

Roger's forehead was tight and his eyes bulging. "Well how long will *that* be?"

Recovered from my crying jag, I sniffled. "A couple of days, maybe."

"You're most welcome to stay in the guest room," Mother offered cheerfully. "Our house rules are very liberal."

"Yeah, I noticed," Roger said, grimacing. "No, thanks very much, Vivian. But I'll find a hotel."

"Suit yourself," Mother said with a shrug. "Now, who wants breakfast?"

"I do!" Jake said. "Will you make me Yummy Eggs?"

Roger closed his eyes. He might have been wishing he could disappear. Or maybe that Mother would.

"Adam and Eve on a raft in a storm!" Mother replied, like a short-order cook. "Comin' right up. . . ."

(Yummy Eggs recipe: see *Antiques Maul.*)

While grandmother and grandson disappeared into the kitchen—the dogs, too, choosing the possibility of food over protecting me—Roger trudged over to the QA armchair by the picture window and sat down, dejected.

"It's not fair," he muttered. "Everyone gangs up on me. Even Sushi. And who the hell is that other mutt?"

"Rocky. Tony's dog. We're sort of dog-sitting."

"Ah, your old boyfriend's dog. No wonder it wanted to take a bite out of me."

I crossed to stand in front of him. "Rocky's a police dog. Best keep that in mind."

"He doesn't *look* like one."

Meaning a K-9.

"Don't let that fool you," I said. "Make a wrong move and you'll see. He'll take a bite out of crime."

Rocky could fetch a gun and climb ladders. I'd seen him do it (*Antiques Knock-Off*).

Roger grunted. "I best behave, then. . . . Brandy?"

"Yes?"

"*You* don't think I'm a bully, do you?"

"Of course not." Well, maybe a little. What man isn't, under the right (or wrong) circumstances? "You're just a good dad who cares about his son."

"I love him to pieces," Roger said, a tremble in his voice as he hung his head. "I don't know what I'd do if something ever really—"

I touched his shoulder. "I understand. But please remember . . . I love him, too."

For the record? Roger was a decent man. Okay, maybe a little controlling. But then, hadn't I been looking for a father figure, someone *to* take control? He was the knight in shining armor who whisked me away from boring Serenity and maddening Mother, to live in his castle in a high-end Chicago suburb. I was just a small-town Cinderella trying to fit in, busying myself with motherhood, charity works, and playing the exemplary executive's wife. But I was too immature, and the ten-year difference in age between us became an ever-widening chasm. And in the end I screwed things up.

I said, "Have breakfast with us."

He swallowed and smiled a little. "Okay."

Despite the morning's inauspicious beginning, we had a surprisingly pleasant breakfast around the Duncan Phyfe dining room table. I had Yummy Eggs, too, while Roger and Mother opted for French toast coated in corn flakes and smothered in rich maple syrup. No recipe for that, I'm afraid—strictly a "by guess and by gosh" process, as Mother put it.

After the meal, Roger headed out, taking Jake with him; my ex had rushed here in a hurry, without packing any clothes or toiletries, so he needed to buy a few things.

Roger's Hummer was barely out of sight when the current man in my life, Chief Brian Lawson, pulled up in my battered Buick, followed by a squad car driven by Officer Munson. Brian hopped out and moved quickly up the walk. He was in a navy shirt with a white tie and brown slacks, his badge pinned to his belt, a revolver on his hip.

I met him at the front door, still in my robe from last night. "Good morning."

"Morning. I was just going to leave your car keys in the mailbox here. Didn't mean to wake you."

"You didn't. I've been up a while. Would you like to come in? I think there's some breakfast left."

He shook his head. His smile was friendly but reserved. "I have to get back. But I do need to say something."

That sounded a little ominous.

"Okay."

He let out a weight-of-the-world sigh. "I'm trying to keep this murder under wraps for the time being. Sort of a press blackout."

"Oh. Why is that?"

"Bruce Spring is a national media figure. A reality show host and big-time producer, getting hacked to pieces in a house where the same thing happened sixty years ago?"

"It'll attract attention." I let out my own weight-of-the-world sigh. "Just like that media mess last summer." (*Antiques Knock-Off.*) "Are we gonna have to go through junk like that again?"

He nodded glumly, a hand on the handle of his holstered weapon. "Probably. But I'm trying to keep that fuss from kicking in till we've had a few days to investigate. Last thing we need right now is a media circus."

"But as soon as it gets out that Bruce Spring's been murdered—"

He raised a hand. "His real name was Bruce Robert Springstein. I'm listing him as a murder victim named Robert Springstein. And the dismemberment aspect of the crime I'm keeping hush-hush for now."

"What about Spring's people at his network?"

"I've questioned that cameraman, Phil Dean, and he's cooperating. He called the network president, who agrees that keeping this matter low-key at the outset is the right approach."

It wasn't a "matter," it was a murder.

I said, "But it *will* get out. . . ."

"Sure it will. Only, with a little luck, not before we've got our killer. We're holding Joe, but you and I both know he's almost surely not the perp. Still, it may give the real killer a false sense of security."

I nodded. "All right. I'll do everything I can to keep a lid on this."

He pointed at me, right at my face. "You do everything you can to keep a lid on your *mother*." Then he touched my nose with his fingertip, almost playfully. "She's the most likely to leak this."

I could only smile at the truth of that. "I'll see what I can do."

For a moment I thought he might give me a little kiss, but he didn't. Just nodded, and went back to Officer Munson's squad car. Maybe he didn't kiss me because Munson was around.

Maybe that was it.

Back inside, I looked at the couch and then at the stairs, wondering where I was going to go back to sleep, because that was the plan. And like all best-laid plans . . .

Mother, also still in her robe, strode in and, top sergeant style, ordered me into the music/library room where she stored an old grade school chalkboard.

"No time to waste, dear," she said, wheeling the board out from behind the ancient upright piano. "The cat will be back soon, and we mice must play—*detective*, that is."

I took a seat on the piano bench.

With a piece of white chalk, Mother began to write, and I caught a little nap. Her "*Brandy!*" woke me, and I almost tumbled off the piano bench. My eyes showed me Mother stepping back to survey her work.

MURDER OF BRUCE SPRING

Suspect	Motive	Opportunity
Joe Lange	the ax	yes
Phil Dean	ill will over work problems	?
Mary Beth	bore grudge over documentary	?
Andrew B.	perhaps found out Bruce produced documentary	?
Sarah B.	same as above	?
Driver in red Toyota	?	?

Frowning, I asked, "How did you know about the red Toyota guy?"

Mother, replacing the chalk on the ledge of the board, said, "Jake told me while you were talking to Brian on the porch."

I said, "Jake could have imagined being followed, you know."

"Yes." Mother nodded. "It might just be the overactive imagination of an impressionable lad at work here"—she raised a finger—"*but* . . . Jake spotted the car a *second* time."

"When?"

"When he and I were waiting in the police car at the murder house. A red Toyota was parked at the curb, about a half block away."

And I had spotted it a third time.

But for now I'd keep that to myself. Mother

was ablaze, and splashing more gasoline her way wasn't such a good idea.

"Still," I said, "it *could* be a coincidence. We're a small town and seeing the same car now and then is no big deal."

"Isn't it?"

"We don't even know how many red Toyotas there are in Serenity. Uh . . . did Jake see the driver last night?"

"Not clearly. But he *did* think it was a male— or a big-boned woman. Ask yourself, dear, why would someone be sitting in a car at that time of night?"

Why indeed? I stood. "What if somebody's out to kidnap Jake? Roger's got money, you know."

We'd had a kidnapping scrape with my son last year.

Mother narrowed her eyes and shook a finger. "Then the plan has been *foiled,* dear, because Roger is here now, looking after Jake. What better bodyguard than a boy's own father?"

Maybe it was me who had the overactive imagination. In any case, I'd better inform Roger about our red Toyota stalker, if Jake hadn't already.

"I don't think," I said, gesturing to the board, "the red Toyota belongs on the suspect list."

Mother arched an eyebrow. "I disagree, dear. That car *was* at the scene of the crime."

"Well, a red Toyota was. We can't be sure."

"A red Toyota with someone sitting in it. In the middle of the night. No, dear, our mystery man with the Japanese ride is definitely a suspect. Wouldn't that make a simply *wonderful* title for this adventure?"

"It's not an adventure, Mother. It's a crime, a tragedy, and anyway, it doesn't fit our title scheme."

"But after *The Girl with the Dragon Tattoo*, shouldn't *we* be updating? I think *The Man with the Japanese Ride* has a wonderful sense of mystery."

And she wheeled the chalkboard behind the piano, out of sight.

In the living room, Mother used the downstairs landline to call our lawyer, to set up a time when Mr. Ekhardt could meet her at the police station, where she was expected to give a statement. Meanwhile I went upstairs for a quick shower.

A word about Mother and cell phones. They didn't mix. She had one, yes, but for emergencies only; hers is a voice-mailbox-full, ring-tone-off affair, usually out of juice. Only recently had she learned to text, a painful one-finger process to watch. And when reminded to take the phone with her, Mother's frequent comment was "Perhaps I don't wish to be found!"

Half an hour later, dressed in DKNY jeans, a Norma Kamali for Walmart black hoodie, and gray Lucky Brand boots, I felt darn near human.

"Ah, there you are," Mother said as I came down the stairs.

I did a double take. She looked fabulous, wearing a new Breckenridge autumn outfit: orange and gold leaf-patterned jacket, gold top, and rich brown corduroy slacks. Her silver hair, newly washed, full and wavy, was pulled back in a youthful ponytail. She wore full make-up, her complexion radiant, cheeks rosy, lips a pretty pink, and looking as if she'd had a full night's sleep instead of a few hours. Even at her undisclosed, somewhere-past-seventy years of age, Mother was still quite the Danish strudel.

Only one aspect of her appearance was a little over the top.

"Kinda heavy on the mascara," I advised her, wiggling a finger.

"I hardly used any at all, dear," she replied.

Behind the magnified glasses, her eyelashes looked like a pair of tarantulas, moving their many legs every time she blinked.

She said, "It's the glaucoma drops that make my eyelashes grow. Isn't that wonderful?"

Always a silver lining with Mother.

She was saying, "And thanks to my genes, you'll probably get the disease, too! So you have wonderful long eyelashes in your future, dear!"

Something to look forward to. That and blindness.

I got off the subject. "Okay. So where are you off to?"

Meaning where did I have to take her (otherwise she might get behind the wheel, since her philosophy was "They can't take your license away when you no longer have one").

"To the police station," she was saying, "for questioning by your latest chief-of-police boyfriend."

If she thought dressing to the nines would soften Brian up, she was woefully misinformed. That only worked when I did it, and not always then.

I asked, "Do I have to wait for you at the station? There's something I wanted to do myself this morning."

"No, dear. I'll catch the free ride home."

By which she meant the gas-converted trolley, sponsored by local merchants to encourage shoppers to part with their money downtown and not at the mall.

Shortly, I was dropping Mother off at the modern red-brick building that housed both the police station and fire department. My parting shot was "Take it easy on Brian, Mother." Hers was an indignant "Really, dear! *I'm* the one facing the third degree."

While still at the curb, I made a quick cell call to make certain arrangements, then tooled north out of town on the picturesque, woodsy River Road, which ran parallel to the mighty Mississippi, its surface today dark and choppy.

After about fifteen miles, a well-worn sign pointing to Wild Cat Den State Park popped up, and I turned left onto a blacktop road. A few miles later, I glided by the old Pine Creek Grist Mill, its giant wooden wheel slowly turning, churning the water.

Against a woodland backdrop, the trees of late fall more skeletal than leafy, a log cabin at last came into view, the residence of park ranger Edwina Forester. I'd always thought of her as Miss Park Ranger, but she was "Eddie" to her friends, and I was one of those now, thanks to our connection to Joe Lange.

I pulled the Buick up to a hitching post, then hurried up the stone walk, where Eddie, expecting me, was coming out the front door.

The fortyish former Marine and one-time truck driver was wirily muscular with short brown hair, an average-looking woman, devoid of make-up. Her eyes, however, were anything but average—intelligent, piercing, not missing a thing.

As per my instructions, Eddie wore her former olive-green service coat with sergeant stripes and matching slacks. One hand held her cloth garrison cap.

"I hope this works," she said, briskly brushing by me. "Are you sure you don't want me to take my own wheels?" She had a Ford Ranger truck. (What else?)

I said, "I'd rather discuss our strategy on the way. I can bring you back."

She shrugged. "Fine by me."

By the time we hit the city limits, we had a plan.

"You know," Eddie said casually, "I should've busted you for all that champagne years ago. You and . . . what's her name?"

"Tina." My BFF.

The summer before I got married, Tina and I made a habit of skipping college classes on really nice days, and imbibing in the alcohol-free state park. And by "alcohol-free," I don't mean the alcohol was free. . . .

"But what the hell," the ranger went on. "I happen to be partial to champagne myself."

I glanced at her sideways.

"I know," she said with a grin. "I look more like the hard stuff type."

I returned the smile. "Guess we should've invited you to the party."

We were downtown now and, in another few minutes, I wheeled into the parking lot of the new county jail, situated across the street from the historical wedding-cake of a courthouse, and adjacent to the police/fire station.

Mother, generally a champion of old buildings (and lost causes), had campaigned tirelessly for the modern jail, after having spent time herself in the original ancient, crumbling, bug-infested facility. She felt the prisoners deserved better—especially Vivian Borne.

We climbed out of the Buick, then headed up the walk of the two-story, octagon-shaped building, which might have been a medical center or private business, having no wire fence or outside guards. Only the small windows running along the second floor suggested the building's real purpose.

We went through double-glass front doors and into a large room with beige-colored walls and industrial gray carpeting; down the center were two rows of bucket-shaped chairs, back to back, and beyond that, a walk-through metal detector. We could have been in an airport waiting area—complete with vending machines—except for the bulletproof window to our right, behind which a male deputy monitored computers in the adjacent room.

Eddie approached the window, then spoke into the glass-embedded microphone.

"Sheriff Rudder, please."

The male deputy, young, pockmarked, with a blond crewcut, started to protest even before looking up.

"The sheriff is busy—oh! Hello, Ms. Forester."

She raised her eyebrows. "Sheriff Rudder in?"

"Ah . . . yeah. I'll see if he's available."

"Please."

It wasn't long before the steel-gray door next to the window opened and Serenity's sheriff stepped out.

Tall and burly, oozing confidence, he reminded me a little of John Wayne, if I really squinted. Walked like him, too, kind of a sideways stride, as he approached us. Style or corns? Who could say?

"Eddie," he said, pleasantly, "what can I do for you?" Then he noticed me, tucked behind her. "*She* with you?"

"That's right, Pete."

His eyes narrowed. "What's this about, anyway?"

I let Eddie do the talking. "We'd like to see Joe Lange."

"Why?"

Eddie gave the sheriff a friendly smile. "We think it would be helpful to let him know he still has some friends in Serenity."

"Is this her idea?" He nodded toward me.

"Might be," Eddie said, then quickly added, "but either way, I happen to think it's a good notion. As you know, I've dealt successfully with Joe before, when he got, well, delusional."

Meaning the cave and me, and the knock on my noggin.

Rudder grunted, rubbed his chin. "The boy *is* rather agitated. We have him in a pod."

A pod was a separate area, away from the general jail population, usually reserved for psych cases. And quite comfortable accommodations, according to Mother, who should know.

I asked, "Has Joe's psychiatrist been to see him?"

Rudder shook his head. "Won't be till this afternoon."

Eddie pressed: "If Joe *is* agitated, my speaking with him—as his superior officer—will calm him down. And Brandy's presence will help, as well."

The sheriff mulled this over. Then: "All right, five minutes. But will ya do me a favor?" He was addressing Eddie. "Make it clear we don't need his rank and number anymore. If he doesn't stop repeating that, I'll *end* up in a pod. In a jacket that buttons up in the back."

"You got it, Pete. Thanks." Eddie held out a hand.

Which the sheriff grasped. "I'll send out a deputy to take you in."

And Rudder disappeared back through the steel door.

A few minutes later, a deputy named Patty, who I knew from when I'd visited Mom—arrived via the same door. She was in her forties, rather plain, with short dishwater blond hair and a bored attitude that said she got all the crappy assignments.

The deputy led us to a wall of small lockers, where I deposited my purse (Eddie didn't have one), and then we went through the metal detector, the brass buttons on Eddie's military coat setting the thing off. But Patty waved her on.

I set the thing off, too, with my keys, which I'd stuck in one pocket, so back to the locker I went.

After clearing me through the scanner, Patty—using a plastic security card—unlocked the door that led into the inner jail. We went through two more locked doors before arriving in an area consisting of three separate visitor's stations, small rooms similar to those reserved for safe-deposit customers at a bank.

With only one chair in front of the Plexiglas window, Eddie took it, putting on her military cap, which rode her head like a child's paper boat.

I stood unobtrusively behind her, while Deputy Patty retreated outside the cubicle, closing the door, allowing us some privacy.

I noticed one nice improvement in the tiny room: no more silly phone.

The minutes crawled by and just as I was about to say, "I guess he won't see us," the door on the other side of the glass opened, and—escorted by a burly guard in navy shirt and slacks—Joe entered.

My friend was wearing an orange jumpsuit

that hung on his too-thin frame like a scarecrow's secondhand threads. His face looked pale, and he seemed withdrawn, even subdued (possibly from antipsychotic drugs)—and anything but agitated at the moment.

When Joe recognized Eddie, his eyes lit up, and he snapped to attention, giving her a crisp salute.

"At ease, Corporal Lange," the ex-sergeant said. "Take your seat."

Joe did, the chair on his side screeching like fingernails on a blackboard as he pulled it out and back.

"Corporal," Eddie said, "I need a full report of what took place last night."

Without hesitation Joe replied, "At one hundred hours, I went to the old Butterworth house, where I was to meet Brandy's son, Jake. After waiting fifteen minutes, I tried the door, and found it unlocked. I entered. Inside I discovered that the ax Jake and I had found that afternoon was gone from beneath the floorboard. I went looking for it. My recon led to the kitchen."

His eyes seemed to glaze over.

"Go on, Corporal."

"That's all I remember, Sergeant. Until I arrived here."

He looked at me. "Is . . . Is Jake all right?"

"Yes," I said. "A little shaken up. But fine."

"Corporal," Eddie said, getting his attention back, "did you know that a dead body was found in that house?"

Joe nodded. "I heard the scuttlebutt."

"And you can't tell me anything about it?"

He leaned forward, "I'm sorry, Sarge, I can't tell you anything more."

Can't, or won't?

"You were found with an ax in your hands, Corporal. Do you remember picking up that object? Or someone handing one to you?"

"No, ma'am."

"No memory of that at all?"

"No, ma'am."

Eddie sighed. "All right, Corporal. That will be all." The ranger stood, and so did Joe, giving her another salute.

I whispered in her ear. "Uh, remember— name and serial number?"

"Oh. Oh, yes." Eddie said, "Corporal, one further order. . . ."

And she fulfilled the sheriff's request.

As Joe was being led away, he stopped and looked back. "Sergeant? I *do* remember one other thing."

We waited for what we hoped would be an important detail.

"The Medivac never came," he said sadly.

In front of the station, on the sidewalk, I asked, "What did Joe mean by that? Medivac?"

Eddie shrugged. "It means he did see the body—a comrade down—and called out for a medical helicopter."

I raised my eyebrows. "Which means Spring was already dead when Joe got there. . . ."

A crisp nod from Eddie. "Way I see it."

I dug out my keys. "I'll take you back to the park."

Eddie gestured with a hand. "No need. Got

some business at the courthouse. I'll get a lift from there."

"You sure? I can wait. You did me a favor. . . ."

She smiled. "Go. That's an order, Private."

I grinned at her and nodded, heading back to my car, feeling better about Joe's innocence.

Somewhat.

A Trash 'n' Treasures Tip

Shop owners need to find new ways to reach buyers, i.e., sending mass e-mails to current customers that offer them a discount for bringing in a new customer. (We put flyers in people's mailboxes until the postal inspector told us to stop. Buzz kill!)

Chapter Six

Chop Around

Dearest ones! Vivian speaking (writing) once again, coming to you direct from the heart and the heartland.

To my great dismay, I have once again been relegated to a token chapter in the middle of the book. :(This I feel is a tactical error, not to mention unfair, considering that my fan mail has now exceeded Brandy's.

The young woman has tried to placate me by insisting that being in the middle is preferable, even providing a treat for readers—like the creamy center of a Twinkie or the fluffy frosting of an Oreo (Double-Stuf). She seemed sincere when she suggested this, or perhaps she was just hungry.

But what if one doesn't care for the fattening likes of Twinkies or Oreos? There are those who consider such delectables mere junk food, callous conveyers of empty calories.

(**Vivian to publisher's legal department**: *Please make sure that I may say the above without engendering legal action from the good folks at Hostess and/or Nabisco. You might remind them that "delectable" is a compliment.*)

But, dear reader, that's not the *worst* of it. :< My word limit has been reinstated, in reaction to my chapter in *Antiques Disposal* running just the teensy weensiest smidge long, having to be split into two chapters. (Which Brandy and even our editor accused me of doing on purpose!)

Now I ask you, were William Faulkner, F. Scott Fitzgerald, or Ernest Hemingway ever restricted to word-count limitations? Did anyone complain when Leo Tolstoy turned in his manuscript of *War and Peace*? (Well, readers still complain, but we're talking editors here.)

I grant it's possible some editor found the occasional need to rein in Norman Mailer and Truman Capote, but then the former was an egomaniac and the latter a trifle eccentric, and really both were just terrible show-offs, a couple of regular Chatty Cathies.

(Again, legal department?)

At any rate, I will have to be on my guard to prevent myself from going on and on, exploring this discursive topic and that one, inadvertently using up my quota. I am on the alert!

It was about ten-thirty in the A.M. when Brandy dropped me off at the police station. I strolled through the open-air atrium with its fruit trees in full fall foliage, then strode into the red-brick building with the confidence of an amateur sleuth who had led this simple small-town police department to the solution of so many a major crime.

The small waiting area was empty but for me, of course, and a few mismatched chairs, an over-worked Coke machine, and a sad-looking rubber tree plant. I had arrived before my attorney, Wayne Ekhardt, which was not surprising, because Wayne hasn't been moving quickly for the last decade or three.

I marched up to the bulletproof glass and announced myself to a female dispatcher, whose auburn hair brushed her shoulders. Her dark blue eyes were keen behind red-framed glasses.

"Vivian Borne to see Brian Lawson," I said formally. "And I'm expecting my lawyer, momentarily."

She nodded, businesslike. "When you're both here, I'll contact the chief. Until then, please have a seat."

Her name was Heather and she was a recent hire, taking the place of the former dispatcher, Evelyn, who'd been dismissed for giving me inside information.

Rather a sad state of affairs, really, and just plain sad—over the years I had lost so many moles in the PD, dispatchers mostly, some dispatched into the ranks of the unemployed, others transferred away from my supposed "bad influence" to another department or precinct.

So far I had been unable to find any weakness of Heather's to cultivate; but as everyone has an Achilles' heel, I'd keep trying with her.

(Mine is Godiva chocolates—big box assortment. Write that down.)

Evelyn's heel had been the painkillers she needed to stay alert during late nights at work, so I from time to time had generously shared my own prescription left over from my double hip replacement. Perhaps "generously" is the wrong word—I was careful not to administer too large a dosage.

(**Legal department to Vivian**: *We advise dropping the previous paragraph.*)

(**Vivian to legal department**: *I disagree! No one can prove that really happened, and I doubt Evelyn would cause any trouble. Everyone says I'm an unreliable narrator—why can't we take advantage of that?*)

I selected a chair near the neglected rubber tree, then removed my cuticle scissors from my purse, and began to expertly cut away the dead leaves, giving the plant some much needed TLC. :)

I just love emoticons, don't you? What will these imaginative kids think of next? Here are a few of my very own emo-creations (feel free to use them).

$$$$ (show me the money)

&-o (where's my left eyeglass lens?)

3 (soft as a baby's bottom)

@:-] (I got a new hat!)

+_+ (a little tipsy)

You're welcome!

I was nearly finished with my plant pruning when Wayne entered the station. At least, he *tried* to enter, his frail body struggling to keep the heavy glass door from snapping him in two like a twig.

I jumped up to assist.

"Why, thank you, Viv," he said, breathing hard, once safely inside. "That wasn't really necessary, but it was very thoughtful."

"Anything for a dear old friend," I said. "And thank you for meeting me at such short notice."

Wayne, pushing ninety, slight of stature, his head covered with more liver spots than hair, wore a navy pinstriped suit that by now was too large for his shrinking frame. He carried a hefty briefcase, the overall effect that of a boy (albeit a wrinkled one) playing dress-up in his father's business attire.

Taking Wayne's arm—as if he were steadying me when vice versa was the case—we made our ponderous way over to Heather, who told us the chief would be out shortly.

Rather than take five minutes doing an impression of Tim Conway's Old Man walking back to the chairs, we stayed put.

"Now, Wayne, dear," I warned, "when we get in there, I must ask you to follow my lead."

He gave me a sideways glance. "Do I have a choice in the matter?"

I squeezed his arm and he smiled, or was that a wince? "Oh, octagenarians *do* say the darnedest things."

The door to the inner world of the Serenity police popped open and Brian Lawson—wearing a navy shirt with white tie and tan slacks, badge clipped cutely to his belt—gestured for us to enter. His expression seemed troubled. I hoped he wasn't having a bad morning.

Soon he was leading us down the now-familiar beige-tiled hallway—the PD had become something of a home away from home for me of late—passing police photos on the wall of by-gone days (I would pause to straighten this one and that one as we progressed).

Near the end of the hall, we paused in front of a door marked INTERVIEW ONE, which Brian opened for us, and we all went in.

The small room was chilly, with the same beige walls and tiled floor as the hallway. Wayne and I sat in plastic chairs at a metal table, which was bolted down (what with all the thieves they interviewed here, this probably prevented pilferage).

A little tape recorder was on the table. Brian leaned in, turned the machine on, then spoke.

"Chief Brian Lawson. Interview with Vivian Borne. Attorney Wayne Ekhardt present. Wednesday, November fourteen, ten twenty-three A.M."

He cleared his throat. He remained standing, arms folded. Which is very defensive body language, according to *Reader's Digest.*

"Mrs. Borne, after you left your daughter Brandy and her son, Jake, on the porch of the old Butterworth house, you entered the crime scene. What did you do inside?"

I smiled pleasantly. "I refuse to answer on the grounds that it might tend to incriminate me."

Wayne closed his eyes. Was that a gesture of frustration, or the start of a nap?

"Vivian," Brian said patiently, "I'm only seeking information that may prove vital to the case. You are not a suspect. But you are a material witness, and have a responsibility to share what you know."

Well, dear reader, I'd watched enough *NYPD Blue* reruns to be hip to such police chicanery.

I looked down my nose at the chief, which wasn't easy to do since he was still standing. "Must I remind you that I haven't been read my Miranda rights?"

Wayne's eyes remained closed. You tell me.

"Vivian," Brian said less patiently, "I repeat— you are *not* a suspect."

I folded my arms across my chest. "Then turn off that tape recorder."

"Fine," Brian said, sighed, and did. "*Now* will you answer the question? What did you do after you entered that house?"

"Thank you for turning off that machine. But I *still* refuse to answer on the grounds that I might incriminate myself."

Bruce looked at Wayne. "Mr. Ekhardt!"

Wayne opened his eyes.

"Would you *please*," the chief said, "advise your client that it would be in her best interest to cooperate."

Wayne pulled himself up into his suit, darn near filling it. "I'm afraid she *is* within her legal rights, Chief Lawson."

Maybe he hadn't been napping!

The chief glared at me. "So *that's* how it's going to be?"

"I refuse to answer on the grounds that—"

"Damnit!"

The veins stood out on his forehead, and he snatched the recorder from the table and shoved it in his pocket.

"There's no sense in continuing this charade," he snapped. "Thanks for wasting my time!"

"No problem," I said with my sweetest smile.

He thrust a finger in my face. Most rude, really, particularly considering that I was his girlfriend's mother. What kind of impression was that to make?

"Vivian, you know we're trying to keep this thing under wraps, to give us a head start on finding the murderer."

"Yes, Brandy said as much."

"We haven't released *any* information as to the grisly details of the murder. You need to keep that to yourself, for the time being. Do you understand, Vivian?"

"Certainly."

"In other words, keep your big mouth shut!"

I touched my bosom, cut to the quick. "And here I thought you were angry that I *wasn't* talking today! You should make up your mind . . . *Interim* Chief Lawson." I rose. "Good day."

Outside the interview room, I whispered to Wayne, "I think that went swimmingly, don't you?"

The lawyer appeared to roll his eyes in response, although I couldn't be sure, because his eyesight at this age was on the hinky side.

The chief, you will be outraged to learn, did not do us the courtesy of showing us out. Rather, he left that to a twenty-something policeman I didn't know, whose badge read HORTON. As he escorted Wayne and me to a back exit, Officer Horton was cute and polite and would have made a fine new interim chief.

Along the way I wheedled some information out of the newbie.

"I understand Phil Dean, the cameraman, has returned to California," I remarked casually.

"No," Horton said. "We haven't given him permission to leave Serenity yet. He's a material witness."

"So am I!"

He gave me an odd smile.

I said, "I hope he isn't stuck out at the Holiday Inn. They're remodeling, you know, which must be unpleasant for him."

Officer Horton, unlocking the exit door, remarked, "No, he's moved to the Grand, downtown. He was afraid the media might track him down when this hits."

The old hotel had been remodeled by way of fantasy "theme" suites.

"But you know the media!" I said. "They won't have any trouble checking around and tracking him down."

"Maybe, maybe not," Horton said. "He's registered under a phony name, at our suggestion."

"What name would that be?"

"Dean Phillips," the young cop said without thinking. "Hey, I didn't tell you that, lady."

A new snitch in the making!

"Well, he'll enjoy the Grand," I said. "I hear the Tarzan suite is something to *yell* about!"

Horton smiled pleasantly, but his expression

was strained. It was probably occurring to him that he shouldn't have talked so freely around me. Poor baby.

Outside, I parted with Wayne, the attorney shuffling off toward his Lincoln Town Car in the police parking lot—good Lord, that man should not still be driving! **<:0**

Shaking my head in worry, I hurried off toward the Grand Hotel, five blocks away.

The eight-story Victorian edifice, built in the 1880s on a beautiful bank of the Mississippi, had fallen into disrepair some years ago, its clientele running to down-and-outers and renters-by-the-hour. But the old girl, slated for demolition, was saved by the wealthy female publisher of the *Serenity Sentinel,* giving her a face-lift—the building, that is, not the publisher (although rumor has it the publisher had one done around the same time, too).

The hotel's face-lift, however, cost considerably less than its new owner's—three million clams. People came from all around the Midwest to spend a night or two in a fantasy suite—such as the Grecian temple room with its marble statues and waterfall, the way-out moon room with its space-capsule bed, or the valentine-arrayed bridal suite for honeymooners (wedded or not, here they came).

I arrived in the opulent lobby unsure of how to go about finding Phil Dean. The desk clerk would likely be warned to fend off anyone asking for Dean Phillips.

So I wandered into the glass-and-chrome bar to ponder my next move, and quench the thirst I'd worked up not answering Chief Lawson's questions.

I slid onto a stool and ordered a Shirley Temple from a pretty, spiky-haired barmaid, then smiled at the only other customer in the place, who sat nursing a Scotch on the rocks, three stools down.

Phil Dean himself.

I couldn't get away with such a coincidence in a fictional work, but because this is a true story, I have no option other than to report this happy happenstance. ;)

The trimly bearded cameraman, wearing gray sweats and Angels baseball cap, didn't seem to recognize me all gussied up and out of my DIY painter's duds.

I slid a stool closer. "Well, well, I'll be darned, if it isn't 'Dean Phillips.' "

He blinked at me.

I touched my bosom. "It's Vivian Borne!"

"Oh. Yeah. Hi. Sorry, I'm . . . I'm a little out of it about now." His eyes were bleary and bloodshot, maybe from lack of sleep or possibly the hooch.

I slid onto the stool next to him. "I quite understand. Terrible tragedy about your friend Bruce." I went *tsk-tsk* and shook my head sadly.

Phil didn't reply, looking down into his glass.

"He *was* your friend, wasn't he?"

He squinted at me, like I was poor television reception that he was trying to bring into focus. "Well, sure. I mean, he was my boss. We worked on a lot of projects."

I shifted on the stool (if bars would just make

these things more comfortable, more mature women like myself would hang around and class up the joint).

"I just came from the police station," I said, "where I got the good old-fashioned third degree."

"Really? They gave you a hard time?"

"For what good it did them. I gave them the Fifth back for their trouble." I leaned toward him, intimately. " 'Twas I who found the body!"

Not sure why I said " 'twas." I guess I thought it might lend something. Not sure it did.

"You, huh?" he said, vaguely interested. "Didn't know that."

The barmaid delivered my drink.

He gave it a look. "Is that a Shirley Temple?"

"Yes! Have you ever tried one? They're delicious, and one can drink a dozen of them without losing a single brain cell. Of course, you get your share of exercise walking back and forth from the loo!"

He just kind of looked at me. I admit I was having difficulty modulating my approach. Sometimes I get a little British-sounding, when I'm excited or anxious.

I leaned closer. "But I'm afraid I did have to mention to them that you and Bruce had a small argument the afternoon before he was killed."

I was lying as convincingly as only a skilled thespian or sociopath can (not necessarily mutually exclusive categories). :)

He frowned. "You told the cops that?"

I waved off his concern. "But I assured the

constabulary that it was just the kind of typical friction people so often experience when working closely together."

He said nothing.

I took a dainty sip of my drink. A bit heavy on the grenadine. "I mean, that *was* the case, wasn't it?"

He didn't answer for a moment. Then he shrugged. "It was no big deal. I was unhappy with the location—small houses are hell to shoot in. Bruce knew that, but just figured he'd stick me with any problems." Another shrug. "That was my beef."

I took another dainty sip. A bit stingy with the maraschino cherries, too. "Doesn't sound like anything worth dismembering anybody over."

He swiveled toward me, eyes narrowed. "What the hell is this, lady?"

"Nothing to worry about, dear," I said, patting his knee. "I merely have a proposition for you."

Perhaps I shouldn't have touched his knee, because he had a rather stunned look. :O

I laughed girlishly. "A *business* proposition, you silly goose."

His expression seemed skeptical. "Really? What kind?"

I looked around the bar, which had begun serving lunch. "Let's find some privacy."

We slid off our stools and, taking our drinks, headed to a far cozy corner, where a brown leather couch and several overstuffed chairs were mostly hidden behind a Japanese silk screen.

Parking our glasses on a coffee table, Phil plopped down on the couch. I sat beside him, perched on the edge, angled his way but not crowding him.

"First, let me ask you," I said. "What do you think our pilot's prospects are at this point in time?"

He blinked, as if by "pilot" I was referring to a plane ride.

"You mean *Antiques Sleuths?*" he asked. "Probably just a little deader than Bruce."

"That's a shame. Is that a certainty?"

He thought it over. "Well, the show was Bruce's baby, his concept . . . but it may depend on how the publicity goes. Your local cops won't keep the media off this thing forever, you know."

"Oh, I know. And the publicity might keep the show alive . . . don't you think?"

"I'm a tech guy, Mrs. Borne. I don't really know for sure. . . ."

"Make it 'Vivian.' So this is my proposition, my idea. Why don't we go ahead and put together a project ourselves? In the remaining days that you're here, I mean. And it does look like you may be stuck in Serenity for a while."

He eyed me warily. "What kind of project?"

"It might be a pilot for a different series, or else footage that could be used to spice up the eventual pilot that we might yet make. You'd be the producer yourself, this time."

That had him interested. "Go on."

"Surely you've heard that I have quite a reputation for solving crimes—with my daughter as my little helper."

He nodded slowly.

"And I intend on finding Bruce Spring's killer. Toward that end, I've compiled a list of suspects and together we can interview them on high def."

His laughter had a hollow ring. "You have to be kidding—why would any suspect, or anybody else, for that matter, cooperate with something like that?"

"Sir, despite a certain whimsical bent to my nature, I assure you I *never* kid about murder."

He shook his head. "Maybe so, but lady, you're nuts if you think a potential suspect would agree to a taped interview."

"What if the suspects don't know what the interview is *really* about?"

"How would that work exactly?"

My shrug was grandiose. "I'll tell them we're doing a little piece for Iowa Public Television. Something called"—I painted a picture in the air with a sweep of a hand—"*Fireplaces of Serenity*."

"Would anybody believe a program like that existed?"

"Well, they did *Doorways of Ft. Dodge* last season, and *Tulips of Pella* the season before that."

"Okay. So that gets us into their homes. Under false pretenses, but in."

"Who's to say we're *not* doing a fireplace documentary? Then, after shooting a short little bit on the history of their stupid fireplace, you'll step outside for a smoke or something . . . You *do* smoke?"

He nodded.

"Wonderful! So you step outside, leaving the camera running. Inconspicuously, of course." I drew a breath. "Then, while you're gone, I'll just move the conversation to the murder—where they were at the time of, and so forth. Later, we can intersperse the interviews with reenactments of the murder, and at the end of the pilot, I'll announce who the killer is!"

His eyes were wide. "That would be cool, actually, though I'm not sure what it has to do with antiques."

"The murder was in an antiques shop, wasn't it? Think outside the box, man!"

Phil nodded, but also frowned. "Using what's essentially hidden camera technique to tape a subject is on *very* shaky ethical grounds. . . ."

Goodness gracious! Since when did anybody from Hollywood ever worry about being ethical?

"We're *not* hiding the camera," I insisted. "It'll be right there in plain sight!"

"It's still a trick. And the footage won't be usable."

"Why not?"

"Because everybody you interview has to sign a release—which, even if they sign, will not cover the secret footage. Unless . . ."

I liked the sound of that. "*Unless . . . ?*"

He was scratching his bearded chin in thought. "I can work up a release on my laptop that just says, 'Serenity Documentary' on it. That should cover us."

"You're thinking like a Hollywood producer already!"

He reached for his drink and finished it. Then he said, "Might work. But what if you *don't* solve the murder?"

Oh, ye of little faith! I shrugged. "Then our pilot will be about an *unsolved* mystery case. They didn't find out who killed Laura Palmer in the first episode of *Twin Peaks,* did they? That *Killing* series went a whole silly season without solving the darn thing!"

Phil was smiling at me. "Well, this may land me in jail even without committing a murder. But why not? It's a shot at saving our show, and what else do I have to do, stuck here in fly-over country?"

Like wherever he was, he wouldn't be sitting in a bar with a drink about now.

He asked, "When do you want to start?"

"How about now?"

"Right now?"

"Why not? What else is there to do in fly-over country?"

He grinned. "That was a dig, wasn't it, Vivian?"

"Maybe a little. Can you get that release form typed up and run off?"

"Sure. The hotel has a business center. Give me half an hour." He got to his feet, but with a little difficulty. +_+

"Assuming you're up to it, that is," I said.

"Oh, I'm up to it. But I may regret this when I sober up." He threw a ten spot next to our empty glasses, paying for my drink. "By the way, am I on your suspect list?"

Of course he was.

"No, certainly not, dear," I answered angelically. **O:)** "I would never keep company with a murderer."

Three more Shirley Temples and two trips to the ladies' room later, I saw Phil—now professionally dressed in black polo shirt and dark jeans, sans cap—returning to meet me out in the lobby. He was loaded down with the camera, tripod, and black gear bag, the releases tucked away in the latter.

Soon we were settled in his Ford rental car, me riding shotgun, the equipment in the back. Our first stop was to interview Andrew and Sarah Butterworth, just a short distance from the hotel on West Hill. We arrived at their mansion a little before noon.

Parked at the curb, Phil said uneasily, "Maybe we should've called. What if they're not home? Or refuse to see us?"

I gave him a short laugh. "They're always home, dear. And as far as refusing to see us, why we'll be seen and inside before they have the chance."

"In other words, we're just gonna barge in?"

"They won't know what hit them. I'm afraid I can't help you with your gear, dear—I'm not union."

He gave me half a smile for that jest before loading himself down like a native bearer on safari.

We climbed the wide cement steps to the low-slung sprawling home, me in the lead, Phil trudging behind. Then I cranked the round metal plate of a doorbell.

Sarah answered. The tall, big-boned woman was wearing tan wool slacks, a brown cashmere turtleneck, and a surprised expression.

"Why, Vivian! Of all people. . . ."

"Wonderful to see you again, too, Sarah," I said as I pushed by her.

"What . . . who is your friend? What is that *equipment?* Is that a camera?"

"As you've probably heard, Sarah, darling," I said, talking a mile a minute now, "my antiques reality show has been put on hold due to the untimely death of its producer. But in the meantime, I'm switching over to *another* pet project of mine with our cameraman, Phil Dean—Phil, Sarah, Sarah, Phil—best shooter in the biz, our Phil. We're not missing a beat, going right into production on a special for Iowa Public Television entitled *Fireplaces of Serenity* . . ." Once again I painted the air. "Don't you just *love* it! Of course, I thought of you and your *unique* fireplace first. Hello, Andy, I was just saying—"

White-haired Andrew, wearing a light blue pullover sweater, navy slacks, and an annoyed expression, had materialized as if from the ether (or a nearby room).

"I heard," he said coldly, "and I *don't* love it. Vivian, we're not interested."

Phil and I had made it through the entryway and to the grouping of mission furniture with Native American artifacts. Since Andy's words had an air of finality, I summoned my theatrical talents, sank down in a chair, and whipped up a few tears. :'(

(That approach worked for Brandy with Roger, didn't it?)

"You have no idea," I sniffled, "how *terribly* disappointing it is to have my reality show face probable cancellation even before it's been shot, much less aired. I am trying to fill my time with creative endeavors, to ward off despair. All I'm asking are a few moments with my old dear friends—is that so much to give to a *loyal* Musketeer?"

Andrew still looked resolved, but Sarah's expression had softened, and she put a hand on my shoulder.

"No, of course not, Vivian," she said soothingly. "And we *do* understand your disappointment—don't we, Andy? It's just that we're not comfortable being on camera."

I dabbed my eyes with a hankie from a pocket. "But I'll be doing most of the talking."

"No surprise," Andrew said.

This atypical unkindness I ignored, pressing on: "And the interview won't take but a short while." I spread both hands, the hankie waving. "You know the high quality of Iowa Public Television, yet how *seldom* Serenity has been featured! Think of how proud our local residents will be to finally be showcased. And the rest of the state will learn something about our proud community! Oh, I know it's a far cry from a national show, but I've got to start somewhere . . . do *something* . . . to save face, and my sanity."

If that didn't move them, I should stop treading the boards.

Sarah and Andrew exchanged looks. Hers seemed to say, "What do you think?" His seemed to say, "It's the only way we'll get rid of her."

"All right," the man of the manor said with a resigned nod. "You have one hour."

"You won't regret it," I lied, jumping up, swinging into director mode. "Phil, set the tripod over there, with a nice wide angle of the fireplace. I'll be seated to the left, angled slightly. Our guests to the right, facing me. We can go in later for some closer shots. Let's get them miked up. Oh, and where are the releases for them to sign?"

Soon we were all in place and, most important, with papers signed. Phil positioned himself behind the tripod, looking into the camera's viewfinder.

"Let me know when you're ready, Vivian," he said.

"Why, Phil, I was born ready!"

Everyone but me sighed. Strange.

"On one," the cameraman said. "Three, two, one."

I gave the camera my best smile. "Hello, my fellow Iowans! This is Vivian Borne, bringing you a special presentation—*Fireplaces of Serenity!* With me are local businessman Andrew Butterworth and his sister, Sarah, visiting from Chicago. We are filming in the lovely Butterworth Prairie Arts home, in front of a most unusual fireplace."

I turn to my guests. "I say 'most unusual' because of the center placement, which makes the fireplace the focal point of the room." I gestured with a hand. "I understand that only *local* materials were used to build it—the large stones culled from a nearby quarry, accented by smaller ones from the Mississippi River. And the timber for the mantel was indigenous, as well. What else can you tell our viewers, Andrew?"

Andrew said blandly, "I rather think you said it all."

"Oh, did I? My bad!"

Sarah was giggling. I considered her officially won over!

She said, "Vivian, you did say you'd do most of the talking, but, really dear, try to save *something* for us."

"I *do* apologize." I looked at Phil, who wore an oddly shell-shocked expression. "Let's go again."

"Three, two, one," he signaled.

This time, after my introduction, I threw the ball to Sarah first.

Blah, blah, blah.

Then tossed it to Andrew.

Blah, blah, blah.

After five minutes of this twaddle, I thanked my old friends for allowing me into their home and to take up a few minutes of their precious time.

Then I again addressed the camera. "But the Butterworths are not the only bearers of a fantastic fireplace here in Serenity. Stay with us after the break for another thrilling heartland hearth!"

I smiled broadly and held it.

Then said, "Cut!"

Sarah was frowning. "Vivian, why the commercial break? You said this was for public television."

"Ah, it is," I said, thinking fast, "but it's one of their special pledge programs, with breaks to raise funds. That fireplace of yours is going to really light up the phones!"

Andrew, shifting in his chair, said, "Are we done?"

"I'm afraid not," I said. "Phil is going to do a number of close-ups of the fireplace, and then some close-up reaction shots on all of us."

Sarah nodded. Andrew just sat there.

Phil addressed me: "Mrs. Borne, do you mind if I take a break?" He smiled at our hosts. "Okay if I step outside for a smoke, before doing the rest? Filthy habit, I know. . . ."

"Not at all," I responded on cue. "I wouldn't mind having a word or two with my friends in private."

After Phil disappeared, leaving the red eye of his camera on, I looked from Sarah to Andrew and back again.

"I just wanted to say how sorry I am about what happened"—I grimaced—"down the street."

Andrew sat stone-faced.

Sarah, once again, was the more gracious of the siblings. "You were hardly responsible, Vivian."

"Not directly," I said, shaking my head, "but you both put your trust in me, allowing me to use the house, and all I've succeeded in doing was open old wounds." I let out a deep, regretful breath, then added, "And with this second murder, you just *know* tongues will start wagging again."

Arching an eyebrow, Andrew said, "I'm afraid there's nothing we can do about that. Except ignore it."

I said, "I suppose one way to silence those tongues will be to have an alibi. You do both have an alibi for Tuesday night?"

Sarah looked stunned, like I'd slapped her in the face with a mackerel.

Andrew asked angrily, "Why in the world would *we* need alibis? Neither one of us ever even *met* the man."

I sat forward and my voice was gentle, and again I looked from one to the other. "Were you aware that Bruce Spring was the producer of our show, the same man who put together that odious documentary about your father's murder? I *wasn't* aware, I assure you, until after the fact."

Andrew stiffened. "Yes. We were informed of that."

"How, might I ask?"

Sarah, who had gone rather pale, said, "We received a phone call from that Beckman woman. She's *odious* herself."

"We considered," Andrew said, "calling you and withdrawing our consent for the use of that house. We frankly would have discussed that with you, probably today, if the . . . the murder hadn't occurred."

Murders didn't actually "occur," did they? Someone had to make them happen.

"The fact that you knew about Bruce Spring's involvement," I said, "before his murder? That puts both of you in a rather delicate position."

Sarah fumed, "Are you implying that we have a motive?"

I raised my palms in gentle surrender. "Not me, of course, but others might—like the police. Have you heard from them yet?"

Andrew stood abruptly. "I think we're at the end of this farce."

Sarah stood as well. "Yes, Vivian. Please go."

I sighed. "So then you *have* no alibi . . . that *is* bothersome."

"We do have one," Sarah said indignantly. "We were here, all evening. We had a late dinner, then watched an old movie on Turner Classic, which didn't get over until midnight. At which time we went to sleep."

"Then you are . . . each *other's* alibi? Oh, dear. I'm afraid that won't put the naysayers to rest."

"Ready for those pick-up shots?" Phil asked, returning.

And I told him we wouldn't be needing any.

Back in the rental car, I asked Phil, "How much of that did you hear?"

"All of it. I only pretended to go outside."

"Then you know how weak their alibi is?"

He grunted. "Each other? And watching an

old movie on cable doesn't help. They could easily have seen it before, and all they have to do is check the listing."

"So no alibi at all, then," I said.

"I know you would like to have cleared them," Phil said, "being your friends and all. But look at the bright side—we got some *killer* footage."

"Yes we did!"

And I gave him a ^ *5*.

But the high of the five lasted only momentarily, because Phil was right—these were indeed my friends, and I'd had to play a sneaky trick on them. Even for *moi.* :(

I would like to continue on with my story, dear reader, but I approach the limits of my word count. So the exciting information revealed by our other interviews of suspects— including the revelation of vital clues—will have to be imparted to you in some other fashion, probably a banal, unexciting one.

(**Brandy to Mother**: *All right. You can have another chapter, but on two conditions.*)

(**Mother to Brandy**: *The first being?*)

(**Brandy to Mother**: *There will be a chapter of mine between your two.*)

(**Mother to Brandy**: *Excellent idea, dear! Variety is the spice of life, to coin a phrase. Let the reader's suspense build in anticipation of returning to my narrative stream.*)

(**Brandy to Mother**: *I was thinking more along the lines of giving the reader a break.*)

(**Mother to Brandy**: *Very droll, dear. And the other condition?*)

(**Brandy to Mother**: *Enough already with the silly emoticons.*)

(**Mother to Brandy**: *You do drive a hard bargain, dear, but I accept.* **:p** *Last one, I promise.*)

(**Editor to Vivian and Brandy**: *Have the pencils arrived yet?*)

A Trash 'n' Treasures Tip

Shop owners should periodically rearrange existing merchandise, which allows customers to discover something they may have missed on their previous visit. But no matter where we move it, Mother's autographed photo of Sonny Tufts just never attracts a buyer.

Chapter Seven

Chop Chop

It was approaching lunchtime when I parted with park ranger Eddie in front of the jail, feeling more convinced than ever that Joe Lange had not killed Bruce Spring. Clearly Joe had come upon the producer dead, and then gone into combat-related post-traumatic shock, picking up the ax reflexively.

I got into my car, looking forward to an egg salad sandwich (so simple, so good), when I spotted Mother several blocks away, walking briskly toward Main Street. She had a spring in her step and determination in her jaw, and God help the good people of Serenity. And the bad ones.

She must have finished with her interview at the police station, and was now about to unleash herself upon the unfortunates on her suspect list. I might have offered her a lift, or joined in on her interviews, but *she* was the self-styled sleuth, not me. I was just a woman who had a date with an egg sal' san'.

I pointed the Buick's nose homeward, and was cruising through a green light when a Lincoln Town Car ran the red and nearly sideswiped me. (I would use an emoticon here, but I have my standards.)

At large in the large Lincoln was our attorney of record, Wayne Ekhardt, his head barely visible above the steering wheel. It might have been a chimp driving. If that image wasn't disturbing enough, the elderly lawyer continued on through the intersection, unfazed, apparently not realizing his near miss (no such thing as a near miss—they're all near *hits!*).

I made a mental note to make sure in future to build some time/distance into Mother's schedule and mine, whenever she had the ancient barrister in the mix.

By the time I was tooling along Mulberry, one of the main arteries from the downtown to home, my heart (speaking of arteries) had found its way back inside my chest and slowed to a normal beat.

I began thinking about that sandwich again, with its diced celery, hot-and-sour mustard, salt and pepper, and just enough mayonnaise (*not* Miracle Whip) to hold the chopped eggs together. And, on the side, locally produced Sterzing's potato chips and tiny gherkin sweet pickles. Ah, life's simple pleasures. . . .

Salivating, I was a block from home when I spotted the red Toyota.

Just up ahead, it was parked at the curb on the right, across from our house and down a little. I slowed, pulled over, then eased up behind it, all the while fumbling for my phone in my purse.

I threw the car in park, jumped out, and snapped a picture of the car's back plate. Then, faster than you could say "gotcha," scurried to the driver's side and grabbed a second photo, this time of the driver.

He was a squat, balding, puffy-looking guy puffing on a cigar, with smoke about the color of his five o'clock shadow trailing out the open window. He hadn't seen me until I was right in his face, which startled him into dropping the cigar in his lap. He did a squirmy little seated dance, trying to recover it.

Around fifty, froggy-looking, wearing a tan raincoat, he used thick fingers to retrieve the cigar, then growled, "Hey! What the hell's the idea?"

"You tell me," I said through tight teeth. I was shaking a little, half of it anger, the other half fear. "Who are you? What are you doing parked across from my house?"

He stuck the cigar in his mouth and spoke around it. "I don't know what you're talking about."

"Don't you? Why are you hanging around here?"

His voice was rough-edged but he was at least

as nervous as I was. "I can park where I want, however long I want. Last time I looked it was a free country."

I showed him my teeth and it was less a smile and more like the way Rocky looked at suspicious passers-by. "You just stay away from me, and my *mother,* and my *son,* and our *house.*"

"I have friends in this neighborhood. I don't know who you are, lady, or what you're talking about."

"Maybe I should just call my boyfriend and have him check you and your story out."

"My *story?*" He laughed roughly, but his eyes were jumpy. "So call your boyfriend already. Am I supposed to be scared? What, is he a bodybuilder or something?"

"No, he's the chief of police."

No laughter now.

"You are way out of line," he said. "You are imagining things. Me being around here has nothing to do with you."

I raised a finger. Not a middle one or anything. I'm much too ladylike for that. It was more like a teacher gesturing for silence in the classroom.

"Fine," I said. "But remember—I've got pictures of you and your car. Just in case I catch you stalking us again."

I didn't give him a chance to respond, just trotted back to the Buick, got behind the wheel, and sat there staring until Froggy and his Toyota pulled away. I watched the red car recede as he put several blocks between us, then disappeared down a side street.

Had I done the right thing by confronting the guy? Or should I have gone straight to Brian? There had been an ax murder, after all. What if Froggy had had a gun? Or an ax? Of course, it's tough chopping somebody up when you are behind the wheel of a car and they're leaning in like a crazed carhop.

Anyway, what was done, was done.

At home I found Jake and Roger back from their shopping trip, seated at the dining room table, chatting over cans of Coke Zero.

"Hey, Mom," Jake said when he saw me. "Where have you been? And where's Grandma, anyway?"

I took the chair next to my son. "We both had errands downtown," I said, keeping it nicely vague. "Grandma won't be back for a while."

"Is she off playin' *Murder, She Wrote* again?"

I smirked. "Well, she's 'off,' anyway."

Looking casual in a light blue polo, Roger kept his tone breezy though his forehead was creased with concern. "Everything all right?"

"Sure. Why not?"

"You look a little . . . tense."

I guess the showdown outside had stayed with me.

"Yeah, Mom," Jake said. "You seem kinda wound up."

I managed a smile. Tried to relax. "Everything's cool."

Jake took a swig of soda. "What's for lunch? We're starving."

"I was thinking egg salad sandwiches," I said,

not giving it much of a sell job, since Froggy had killed my appetite.

Jake crinkled his nose. "Ick. I had eggs for breakfast. Anyway, egg salad is all cold and stuff."

Playing peacemaker, Roger said, "Well, it sounds good to me. Your mom has a great egg salad recipe."

"Let her save it for her bridge club or something," Jake said.

I had never played bridge in my life, but my son had made his point.

"Okay," I said. "But I don't have the fixings for much of anything else."

Jake shot forward in his chair. "I *got* it! It's really, really nice out. Let's go on a picnic to Wild Cat Den."

Without realizing it, my son had set in motion a monster that no one in heaven nor on earth could stop. He had done what Zeus had advised so strongly against—he had released the Kraken.

Sushi.

Having heard the words "go," and "Wild Cat Den"—where I so frequently took her on hikes—she was out from beneath the table, dancing frantically and yipping wildly, as if possessed by a benign strain of rabies.

Roger had a wide-eyed, just-sat-on-a-tack look. "What's with Sushi?"

I explained, a monologue accompanied by an interpretive dance courtesy of the shih tzu.

"Now we'll *have* to go," Jake said, laughing

devilishly, causing trouble on purpose by repeating the "g" word. "But what about Rocky?"

The bigger canine remained stretched out in a puddle of sunshine, oblivious to Sushi's dance of the seven wails.

Roger smirked. "Maybe the big guy only reacts to words like *attack* or *kill.*"

At which Rocky *did* lift his head.

"We'll take him, too," I said. "He could use the exercise."

And it wouldn't be bad to have a police dog along, in case (despite my warning) Froggy again came a-courting.

Soon, dressed for hiking, we piled into the Hummer, Rocky in back with Jake, Sushi on my lap in the front passenger's seat. The size of the vehicle made me feel like we were launching an assault.

Our first beachhead was the drive-through window of KFC, to secure boxed lunches. I reminded everyone that the late colonel was now offering a healthier choice by way of grilled chicken, after which we all selected either Original or Extra Crispy (who says picnic food should be healthy?).

Then, with the food smells turning both Sushi and Rocky manic, we were heading northward out of town along the River Road on a sunny but crisp afternoon, too late in the season for the fall colors to be anything but muted, but lovely nonetheless.

After fifteen minutes we turned left at the well-worn park sign and once again I was gazing at the old grist mill on my right, which somehow hadn't changed a bit since this morning.

As we cruised by Eddie's cabin on the left, Sushi gave a sharp yap. Although blind, she knew very well where we were, and as Eddie always gave her a treat when we stopped by, the little mutt always expected one.

Eddie's truck was parked in the drive, but I lied to Sushi as follows: "She's not home, honey."

Sushi swiveled her furry head my way, fixing her milky white eyes on me with the intensity of Medusa, her jaw jutting as if her inner lie detector had sensed the subtle shifts in my breathing and heart rate. I felt a little guilty, but was not about to ask Roger to go back so I could knock on the ranger's door to request a doggie treat.

Then we were driving through the park's entrance, its long, steel gate swung wide, indicating the playground was open. In another minute we came to a fork in the road with one prong leading onward, the other upward, the park being laid out on two levels.

Seasoned hikers would go onward and to the left, to park their vehicles before starting their hike at the bottom, choosing one of several paths of varying levels of difficulty, all leading to the top. Those who preferred an easier go of it would drive upward and to the right, and let gravity assist them as they hiked downward.

But either way, there came a time when hikers realized that their transportation was at the other end of the journey. At that point it was nice to have several people in your party so that a victim, that is, *volunteer* could retrieve your vehicle.

I suggested to Roger that we go to the lower level, and he complied, following the road to an open area of park benches and tables and grilling pits. Despite the nice day, this late in the season there were only a few others in the picnic area—several teenagers, skipping class from either high school or community college, hard at work throwing a Frisbee, and a family with two kids both under five sitting on a spread-out blanket having a home-packed lunch, while a couple sprawled as far as possible away from the rest on their own blanket, looking at each other with good-natured lust, probably wishing those others weren't around.

We parked next to an empty table in a nice sunny spot, and got out, letting the dogs run free. When they were capering at enough of a distance for us to risk divvying up the food, we did so and dug in, the conversation light and fun, Jake teasing me by telling "dumb blonde" jokes, Roger trying to top him, and me doing my best to pretend to be offended.

Here's one of Jake's: "On a hot summer day, a blonde who looked a lot like Mom was painting her garage wearing a fur coat over a denim jacket. Because the instructions said, 'For best results, put on two coats.' "

Here's one of Roger's: "If a blonde and a brunette fell off a high building, who would hit the pavement first? The brunette. The blonde would have to stop and ask for directions."

I'm sure to anybody else out enjoying this

late-in-the-season sunny day, we looked like the perfect, happy family. And, for the moment, I guess we were.

Sushi and Rocky got wise and came back for a taste or two of chicken, then wandered off on the lush green grass to sniff and leave reminders to other dogs of just who had been out here today. I wasn't nervous about losing track of them—both were good about responding to my voice, and Rocky was staying protectively close to Soosh.

But Jake started getting nervous, with both dogs out of sight. Depositing the remains of his box lunch into the big KFC sack, he said, "Come on, you guys! Let's get a move on."

I took a final bite of coleslaw, then we gathered our trash, stuffed it into that big sack, and made a donation to a garbage can a few yards away.

At the base of the hill were three separate hiking paths, which visitors to Wild Cat Den soon got to know as belonging to the following categories: "Difficult," a steep, rocky climb upward; "Not as difficult," a combination of steep and gradual; and "Pathetic," a meandering trail a little less treacherous than a wheelchair ramp.

We had barely started out when I allayed Jake's worries by calling for the two dogs, who came running, tongues lolling, their happy faces filled with outdoor ecstasy. Wouldn't it be sweet if humans could experience such simple joy?

Sushi was already heading up the "not as difficult" path, which was the one she and I normally took. That held the park's beloved scenic attractions: Steamboat Rock (a boulder shaped like the prow of a ship); Fat Man's Squeeze (a narrow fissure in the bluff wall that was a short-cut upward for the slender hiker); and the Devil's Punch Bowl (a craterlike hole that oozed a pink toxic-looking goo).

Before long, I was huffing and puffing—either I was ready for the pathetic path, or I'd had too much Colonel Sanders (at least I hadn't ordered a "Famous Bowl," that heap of gravy, mashed potatoes, corn, breaded chicken, and cheese described so memorably by Patton Oswalt as "a failure pile in a sadness bowl").

Roger, who had regularly worked out at a health club during our marriage and apparently still did, hadn't broken one bead of sweat. And Jake was already way ahead of us, keeping pace with the dogs.

At Steamboat Rock, Roger gave me a knowing little grin. "Need a break?"

"No," I said, stopping, putting my hands on my knees. "I think I'd like to die standing up."

He took me by the arm and walked me to a weathered wooden bench just off the path.

"Are you working out at all?" he asked.

"Sure."

"What exercise regimen are you on?"

"The one where I sort my closet every three months. How else do you think I got this muscle tone?"

He chuckled. I could always make him laugh. At least up to where my behavior hadn't been all that funny.

"So," I said, no longer winded, "how's business going, anyway? Just making conversation here—no underlying alimony agenda."

That got a smile, not a laugh, out of him. No man finds alimony *really* funny. . . .

"Pretty good," he said.

"Even with the down economy?"

"Even with the down economy," he said, nodding. "Good enough, matter of fact, that I'm thinking about opening an office here in Serenity. There's been a void locally ever since Bob's business went under."

Bob was the late husband of Peggy Sue, my sister (actually, my biological mother, for those keeping score).

I said, "Makes sense. Serenity has its share of wealthy types who like the personal touch."

"That was my take on it. Anyway, if it works out, it could be a branch office where Jake could get his start, and be close to his mom."

"Really?"

He shrugged. "I'm just hoping that someday he'll take over the firm."

Don't count on it, I thought. *Math was never Jake's strong suit.*

But I said, "Well, that's thoughtful. Really nice. Very sweet."

Roger was scuffing at the gravel and dirt with a running-shoe toe as he too casually asked, "Are you, uh, seeing anyone?"

"Well . . . I've been dating Brian Lawson again."

"Ah. I remember him. Is he the chief of police now that that Cassato character is gone?"

"Brian's the acting chief, but I think he'll get the permanent job one of these days."

"Going well between you two?"

"It had been, but, well . . . things get a little strained, from time to time, with Mother's 'sleuthing.' " I shook my head. "Brian gets frustrated with my inability to restrain her. And how I sometimes get caught up in her machinations myself."

He smirked. "I can relate."

"And you, Roger? Are you still with, uh, what's-her-name?"

"I think that's run its course," he said, trying to make it sound like no big deal. "I didn't know you knew about Lori. Got it from Jake, I suppose."

I nodded. "But not in great detail. She younger than me?"

"Older."

"Ah. You were trying for somebody a little more mature this time around. That was sound thinking. I mean, you'd already had a young, raving beauty."

He grinned. "You don't let up, do you? Well, Lori is very pretty. And very nice, very sweet."

"Then what was wrong with her? I got it! She was just after your money."

"No, she's actually very well fixed."

"Oh. So then, she isn't very smart, huh? Looks and loot but a dummy. So sad."

"She's a lawyer."

The only thing I could think of was: "*Jake* didn't like her?"

"No, they get along."

I shrugged. "Then I don't get it. What was missing?"

"I already told you." He leaned toward me, brushed a strand of hair out of my face. "She wasn't any fun."

"Define fun."

He thought a moment. "Well, she never would have served hot dogs to important clients of mine."

"That was pigs-in-a-blanket," I corrected. "An old Borne family recipe, and anyway, I'd forgotten you'd invited them. Besides, they loved them!"

"Lori's a great lady. But you? You make me laugh."

"I do, huh?"

His face was inches from mine.

I kissed him. He kissed me back. It was just a tender little thing that lasted maybe five seconds. But my heart was racing like I hadn't stopped hiking.

"That's another thing," Roger said. "No spontaneity."

"Lori, you mean."

"Lori," he said, and he kissed me.

This one lasted a little longer and things were heating up. That was when I said something that cooled us off.

"I guess I had too much spontaneity," I said.

I was referring to my one-night stand with an old high school flame at my ten-year class reunion. For what it's worth, many a night had been spent crying into my pillow about that big, damn, stupid mistake.

Roger said softly, "I forgave you for that a long time ago."

"You never said."

He leaned back against the bench. Sighed. "Well. Maybe not forgive, exactly . . . more like, I understand it. We were at different points in our life—you, young and wanting to have fun. Me, older and ready to settle down into boring middle age. I only wish . . . nothing."

"What? Tell me, Roger."

"I only wish that you'd *told* me something was wrong."

I said, "I didn't know myself." I shook my head, my hair bouncing everywhere. "Not till it was too late." Then I took his hand and looked right into his eyes. "It's not an excuse, Roger. What I did to you—and Jake—was reprehensible, and I get sick to my stomach when I think about it."

His smile was small but it was there. "Then we won't talk any more about it."

We fell silent.

Then Roger said, "By the way . . . that was a selfless thing you did for your friend, and I'm very proud of you."

Not long ago I'd been a surrogate mother for my BFF Tina (who'd had cervical cancer) and her husband, Kevin.

Roger squeezed my hand. Then we kissed again.

Could we get back together? Would it work this time? Or did I just want him to take care of me?

Hadn't I learned by now that the only person who could really take care of me was me?

"Hey, you guys!" Jake said, wearing a very self-satisfied smirk. "Chop, chop! I thought we were goin' on a hike." He was standing a few yards up the path, the dogs circling around him like he was an embattled wagon train and they were Indians.

Roger and I pulled apart, embarrassed.

Jake jerked a thumb over his shoulder. "I've been waitin' forever for you guys up at Fat Man's Squeeze."

"Okay," I said, "we're coming."

Roger's cell phone buzz-vibrated in his pocket.

"Come on, Dad!" Jake whined. "No business, you *promised!*"

My ex, who was frowning, checked the caller. "Sorry, son, I've just got to take this."

But the signal wasn't strong enough.

"Look," I said, "why don't you go back down to the clearing. You might get a better signal down there. And, uh . . . while you're down there—"

"Bring the Hummer around to the top?"

I shrugged. "Why should we all suffer? If we aren't waiting by the time you get there, meet us at the Bowl."

Not the Sadness Bowl—the Devil's Punch Bowl.

Cell in hand, Roger went back down the path, and I started upward with Jake. But maybe three minutes later, I tired of the steep climb, and got to thinking about how well Roger and I had been connecting.

"Look, I'm gonna go keep your dad company," I told Jake. "See you and the dogs at the Punch Bowl."

"Okay," he said with an evil grin, "but don't you two do anything in public you can get arrested for."

"Try not."

I retreated, my feet lighter now, my journey going downhill but my spirits rising.

Through the trees, I could see Roger at the bottom, walking briskly.

And I stopped in my tracks.

Because he was approaching a familiar vehicle, and it wasn't his Hummer.

Rather, a red Toyota.

I stood frozen there, watching, agape as Roger withdrew his wallet and handed a pile of green money to the cigar-puffing Froggy.

I retreated, quickly catching up with Jake.

A short time later, after Jake, our canine contingent, and I met up with Roger at the Bowl, I said nothing about what I had seen. I kept things light, if not affectionate.

Funny thing—only Sushi sensed something was wrong. On the ride back she didn't yap when we drove by the park ranger's cabin, and instead of facing forward on my lap, she curled toward me, her furry head resting on my chest.

At home, no sign yet of Mother. Jake disappeared upstairs, and I went into the kitchen.

At the sink, as I drew a glass of water, Roger came up behind me, and put his arms around my waist.

Without turning, I said, "So. You hired a private detective?"

He dropped his arms.

I turned.

Looking sheepish, he said, "A bodyguard. Somebody my company uses for background checks in Chicago."

"So you're checking my background now?"

"No. Don't be silly. *You're* a parent."

"Why, yes, I am."

"Then try to see it from my side. That was the call I got at the park—my guy thought he should split, since you—you know . . ."

"Your guy thought. After I confronted him. After he scared me and Mother and Jake. So you paid him off and sent him packing. Some pretty clumsy talent you got there back in the Windy City."

His eyes were moist. "Please. Brandy, please . . ."

Coldly I said, "You didn't trust Jake in my care."

He gestured with one hand. "It wasn't a matter of trust. . . ."

"What *was* it then?"

He shrugged; his eyes were tight, his forehead furrowed. "Just with these damn murders you and your mother have got involved in, it seemed like the responsible thing for a parent to do. You do understand, don't you?"

I did, actually. All too well.

He added, a little defensively, "And as it turns out, I was *right* to take that precaution. There *was* another murder. My God, it's crazy in this lousy little town! It's the apocalypse around here!"

Good place to open a branch office in the investment game.

I said, "Was it Jake who first told you about Bruce Spring's murder?"

He shook his head. "My guy."

Of course. Which explained how and why Roger arrived in Serenity so fast.

"How mad at me are you?" he asked, rather pitifully. "I was only thinking of you and Jake."

"I'm not mad."

Disappointed, saddened. It was no fun to be deceived. I'd taught him that. Now he'd taught me.

Roger risked a shaky smile. "I'm glad this came to light. I hated keeping it from you."

I managed to return his smile, but could think of nothing to say.

He touched my shoulder gently. "I'm going back to the hotel for a shower." He cocked his head. "Will you let me take you and Jake out to dinner later? You can even bring your mother along."

"Sure."

That pleased him.

After Roger left, I went into the music/library room, pulled out the blackboard, and erased the red Toyota from the list of suspects.

Just like I erased from my mind any notion that Roger and I could ever get back together.

A Trash 'n' Treasures Tip

Make the entrance to your store inviting, with eye-catching antiques in the window and interesting merchandise displayed in the front. "Interesting" is a subjective term, of course. My idea of interesting is a mannikin decked out in vintage 1940s clothing. Mother's is a stuffed grizzly bear with bared fangs and claws.

Chapter Eight

Stop and Chop

Yes, my dears, it is Vivian back again, poised to sate your curiosity over the loose ends left dangling in Chapter Six. But first . . . previously on *The Mysterious Adventures of Vivian Borne*—

(**Brandy to Mother**: *There will be no "previously." This is a novel, not a television show. If readers wish to refresh their memories, they can thumb back a few pages and do so. Anyway, it hasn't been long enough for a reader to have forgotten your last chapter, try as they may.*)

(**Mother to Brandy**: *First of all, the intention was to plant the idea in the mind of any producer who might be reading this novel while jetting to Cannes or heading for location in Bermuda that these novels of ours would make an excellent film or television series. Second, you used "previously" yourself, previously . . . refer to Chapter One! Third, to spare the reader the* *trouble of flipping back pages, I should probably include just the itty-bittiest recap.)*

(**Brandy to Mother**: *Fine. Up to you. Of course, you'll be eating into your word count doing so.*)

(**Mother to Brandy**: *Good point. Readers, circumstances require that you fend for yourselves.*)

(**Editor to Vivian and Brandy**: *Where* are *those CENSORED pencils I sent you?*)

(**Vivian and Brandy to the reader:** *We have taken the liberty of editing an offensive word out from our editor's previous note. Doesn't she want us ever to be sold in Walmart?*)

Upon completion of our secret footage session with Andrew and Sarah Butterworth, cameraman Phil Dean and I drove the short distance down West Hill to the murder house, where we hoped to get some outside shots before the wrecking ball came, per Andrew's threat. I still held out hope that *Antiques Sleuths* could be salvaged, but in any case there was a heck of a true-crime documentary my new partner Phil and I could put together.

I did so hope that Phil didn't turn out to be the murderer, because that could require some very complicated post-production negotiations. How helpful would a partner likely be, once you had landed him in the slammer?

Somehow the old Butterworth family home looked even more dilapidated under the unrelenting scrutiny of the afternoon sun. Not just the front door, but the entire yard was rather festively blocked off with yellow-and-black crime scene tape stuck to plastic sticks shoved in the ground.

In places, the tape had snapped—had media locusts moved in, despite Chief Lawson's best efforts?—the ends flapping in the breeze. Through one of these breaches, Phil stepped onto the lawn, camera hoisted on his shoulder.

I positioned myself across the street, watching, ready to give a warning whistle with thumb and forefinger should a police car appear.

Phil had finished with front and side views, and was heading around the back, when I noticed an elderly gent out on the porch of a nearby Gothic Revival house, watering some hardy plants.

I walked over—it was not directly across from the old Butterworth place, rather one house up, up the hill. At the bottom of a flight of cement steps, I gazed up at the open, pillared porch.

I called out, "Well, Sam Wright! How *are* you?"

The deacon of the Amazing Grace Church was a few years older than *moi*—he'd been in the same high school class as Andrew Butterworth—and had once cut a dashing figure; but time had taken its toll, bestowing him a little pot belly, rounded shoulders, jowls, bags, and thinning hair, which he tried unsuccessfully to hide in a comb-over.

Nonetheless, the old boy wasn't hard on the eyes, at least not the eyes of a woman of a certain age. I had even considered dating him after his divorce from Ruth—a scandalous event, considering Sam's close identification with the church. But the ex-wife departed town before I could find out exactly *why* she had left him.

Rumor had it she hated living in the old gothic house, and Sam had no interest in selling the ancestral home.

(Note: A wise woman will always take lunch with the ex of a man in whom she is interested. Best to find out from the most reliable source if he's a philanderer—or even worse, a cheapskate.)

Despite his advanced years, Sam had the energy of a much younger man. But then he would have to, as deacon of the popular, even powerful Amazing Grace Church. (Which was, I suppose, another good reason for nixing any potential Borne/Wright union—a church man's wife plays but a supporting role, while Vivian Borne is at her best in the lead.)

Amazing Grace boasted a large congregation, even bigger than the Methodists, which was saying something in this neck of the woods. The church had been established in Serenity back in the early 1940s by Gabriel Wright, Sam's fire-and-brimstone preacher father. After the elder man's death in the1980s, Sam followed in his footsteps.

Under Sam's steerage, Amazing Grace had only grown in both size and esteem, even possessing political clout, what with so many of the church's members in local government from school board to the mayor's office. Sam had never been a preacher like his pop; he had majored in business in college, and ran the church accordingly, carefully selecting a succession of popular pulpit pounders to keep Amazing Grace lively. But Sam's growing child began questioning its parental Baptist authority and, by the mid-nineties, had severed all ties to its national alliance.

From time to time, Brandy and I would attend Sam's church, especially relishing the wonderful musical services, which were held in a state-of-the-art theater. And we liked the church's practice of giving most of its tithing to help local charities. But the Hell-and-damnation sermons were too much for the Borne women, one on bipolar medication and the other on antidepressants, so we settled elsewhere, at the New Hope Church (or as Brandy calls it, The Church of Mild Admonishments and Common Sense).

Sam, glancing up from his plants, smiled, and called back, "Vivian Borne! Well, don't you look fresh as a daisy."

"Mind if I join you?"

"Please do."

I climbed the cement steps to the porch of the Gothic Revival house, which was fittingly churchlike in appearance if somewhat medieval. A beautiful, gloomy thing to behold, the three-story stone structure had pointed arch windows, cross-gables, and a steeply pitched roof.

I had only been inside a few times, as a young girl, when the rather scary Gabriel Wright allowed Andy and Sarah and me to play with Sam, but we'd been restricted to the damp and cold basement. Since my mother was content to let us kids swing from the rafters, our house soon became the Musketeers' hangout.

Sam, looking fairly jaunty in a light navy

jacket and casual brown slacks, sat in a well-worn rocker, and I took the porch swing, testing it first for strength, as ours had come crashing down last month, leaving me with a black-and-blue polka-dotted posterior.

"I heard you were going in across the street," he said, "with an antiques shop. But after that unpleasantness the other night . . ."

I nodded, swinging just a little. "Unpleasantness" was an understatement, of course, but then Sam would only know what he'd read in the papers, so the ax murder aspect of that "unpleasantness" would be unknown to him.

He was saying, "The whole neighborhood is on edge. But the police have someone in custody, I understand."

"They do indeed. It's been kept out of the papers so far, but I can tell you who it is."

"Not unless you're comfortable doing so, Vivian. It's not really any of my business, and it's hardly Christian to traffic in gossip."

Was that a dig? Didn't seem to be.

"Well, Sam, do keep it to yourself, but . . . it's Brandy's friend, Joe Lange."

"Oh, dear. That poor troubled veteran. He and his mother go to Amazing Grace, you know. She's so very sweet, and he's so very . . ."

"Odd? Yes." I paused for effect. "But I don't believe he did it."

Sam leaned forward in the rocker, and it creaked. Or he creaked. Couldn't be sure. "Really? And how did you come to that conclusion?"

"Well, I can't really say without violating Chief Lawson's request for confidentiality about the crime itself. But let's just say that Joe didn't have *nearly* enough blood on him."

That gave him a start. He sat back, and began rocking slowly. "Well. If Vivian Borne thinks the murderer is still out there, then most likely he is."

"Or *she,*" I reminded him.

I sat forward and almost slid off the swing. I caught myself with a hand on the nearby chain. Good thing, too—my polka dots had almost faded, and it would be a shame to serve up another nether design.

I said, "How would you like to help me catch the killer?"

He blinked, then seemed almost amused. "I'm afraid I'll have to decline, Vivian. Assisting you in your amateur sleuthing is hardly appropriate for a man in my position."

I waved that off and giggled girlishly. "I don't mean anything so overt, Sam! I just thought you might let me know what you remember about"— and I gave this the appropriate dramatic inflection—"the night of the *murder.*"

Sam frowned in thought. "Afraid I don't know anything that would be very useful."

"Well, do try. Please?"

"Okay. Let's see. Probably like everybody else on this block, I was in bed and got woken up by a siren. I thought it might be an ambulance—a neighbor up the street has heart trouble, and six months ago or so was rushed off to the hospital. There were sirens then."

"Of course."

"Anyway, figuring that's what it was, and wanting to offer my help if it was needed, I got out of bed, put on my robe, went downstairs, turned on some lights, and went out on the porch." He paused. "But the ambulance hadn't pulled up in front of my neighbor's house, up the street . . . instead, the flashing lights were across the way in front of the old Butterworth place. And it wasn't an ambulance at all, but a police car."

He stopped rocking, leaned forward. "Like I said, I knew you were renovating the house—rumor was you and your daughter were opening up a shop. There was talk of a reality TV show, too, which sounded unlikely to me. But the paper said the murder victim was a TV producer. Is that the connection?"

"Yes," I said. "We're still hoping to do the show, actually, but first things first. There's a murder to solve."

He shrugged. "More police cars came, and I saw you and your daughter, in your nightgowns or something—is that right?"

I nodded.

"Anyway, I wondered if all the police cars had something to do with the renovation you two were doing."

I said, "Seemed like everybody and their mother were out on the sidewalk before long."

"Oh, yes. I was right there with them—not proud of myself, nothing I hate more than a rubber-necker at an accident scene. Somebody said there had been a murder, they didn't know who, but I knew you were all right, because I could see you and Brandy, and her son, too, right?"

"Yes," I said. "Jake. He stumbled onto the body, shortly after the murder."

"Dear Lord."

"Oh, Jake's fine. He's level-headed, like his grandmother. Did you know the man who was killed?"

He shook his head. "As I said, the paper indicated he was a television producer."

"You've never heard of Bruce Spring?"

"The paper said his first name was . . . something else, I forget what. But, no, that's nobody I ever heard of."

"Bruce Spring was the man behind that controversial TV documentary of a few years back. About the Archibald Butterworth slaying?"

Sam frowned. "Is that right? Killed in the very house where the original murder took place. There's irony for you."

Interesting that a church man wouldn't attribute that to the Lord moving in mysterious ways.

"Did you ever see that program, Sam?"

"No. Oh, I heard about it from well-meaning parishioners, but I wasn't interested. Having all of that filth dredged up after so many years . . . well, it's just hurtful for all concerned. What it must have put Andrew and Sarah through. Terrible. Un-Christian."

I was pretty sure Bruce Spring had been Jewish, so that was kind of a moot point, but I let it go.

I swung a little in the swing. "Well, I *have* seen it. Not lately, but when it first aired. I even watched the rerun."

Sam's frown deepened. Was there irritation in those furrows?

"Did those well-meaning parishioners mention, Sam, that the documentary implies strongly that pious churchgoer Archibald Butterworth was an outrageous womanizer? And that among his conquests was the wife of a certain man of God?"

Sam might have exploded in anger at that; but instead he only laughed once, dryly. "Vivian, don't be coy. Doesn't become you. You mean my *mother*."

"No name was mentioned in the documentary, but . . ."

"But it was 'strongly implied.' " He shook his head. "So what if it were true? Though after all these decades, with the principals long gone, I don't know how you'd prove it."

"Old crimes," I said, "can get new solutions."

"Maybe so. But that murder across the street is a famous unsolved crime—it gets hauled out of mothballs every now and then, and who cares at this late date? I had no idea who this character—what did you say his name was? Spring?—I had no idea who he was, much less that he was in town, and even now I hold no grudge. If that's what you're fishing for."

"Why, Sam, dear, I wasn't fishing at all."

Of course, I had been, and he'd taken the bait, though he'd pulled *me* flapping into the water.

He raised a lecturing finger. "Breaking the seventh commandment—thou shalt not commit adultery—pales in comparison to the sixth."

Thou shalt not kill.

"I'm no preacher man like my father," he said, "but I *am* church through and through. Ask anyone—Sam Wright doesn't just talk the talk. He walks the walk."

I didn't have to ask anyone. His reputation was solid.

I slipped off my rocker. (Brandy! No comments, please.) I offered my hand, and he took it, shook it, as I said, "Thanks for the visit, Sam. My apologies if my questions crossed the line momentarily."

He stood and gently grasped my arm, his expression warm. "You are welcome here anytime, Vivian. And I'd like to see you and Brandy back at church—you're welcome there, anytime, too."

Sam seemed hesitant to let go, so I asked, "Is there something else?"

"I'm not sure I should mention this . . . but there *was* something else I saw that night, earlier."

My ears perked up, much as Sushi's do when she hears a potato chip bag rustle open. "What was that, Sam?"

He let go of my arm. "I spent much of the evening in the living room, reading, and around eleven, when I turned out the lamp, I *saw* someone . . . someone outside, moving through the light of the streetlight."

"Who?"

"I'm sure it was nothing."

"*Who*, Sam?"

He still seemed hesitant. "Andrew."

"Andrew Butterworth?"

He nodded. "Walking up the street in the direction of his house, and in quite a hurry." Reluctantly, he went on. "I didn't mention this to anyone because it probably means nothing—after all, a lot of folks take walks at night, especially older ones. I myself was out for a stroll earlier."

"I understand you keeping this to yourself," I said, "but thank you for telling *me*."

He sighed. "Andrew and I don't exactly have a warm relationship—I mean, I did testify for the prosecution, way back when, which he viewed as me testifying against him . . . when I was just a *kid,* a teenager, who swore on the Bible to tell the truth. . . ."

The old memory seemed to shake him up. He swallowed thickly, forced a nervous smile.

"Vivian, if I were to come out with this information, it would only make matters worse. So sad to think that Andy and I were friends once, that we were *all* friends once." He sighed deeply, then added with a tremulous smile, "But I feel better that *you* know."

"Thank you for sharing that," I said. I touched his shoulder. "I'll let you get back to your plants, Sam. Next time, it'll be a purely social visit."

"Good. I'd like that, Vivian."

I walked back to join Phil, finished grabbing his footage, who was waiting by the rental car.

"Who was that?"

"Someone I wish we'd got on tape," I said.

"Where to next?"

"Mary Beth Beckman."

"Ah. The bookstore lady who Bruce gypped on the Butterworth documentary."

"One and the same. But I'm afraid a different ploy will be needed with her. Don't believe *fireplaces* will cut it this time. . . ."

It was late afternoon when we walked into Scene of the Crime, Mary Beth Beckman's mystery bookstore, relocated across from the community college in an anonymous strip mall.

Inside, the gray carpeting looked new as did the floor-to-ceiling blond-wood bookcases and other nondescript fixtures. Blown-up covers of mystery best sellers covered any remaining wall space, along with candid photos of the proprietor with visiting authors. (I noticed that none of the ones taken of Brandy and me were among them.)

Scene of the Crime was certainly clean and pleasant in its sterile, modern way. Mary Beth had labored hard to make the shop inviting and cozy and (dare I say) mysterious, including taping a white "dead body outline" to the carpet. Nonetheless, the store carried none of the charm (much less the infamous history) of her former location in the old murder house.

Seated behind a low-slung display case of valuable books and signed first editions, the heavy-set proprietor was hunkered at a computer. Wearing a black wool poncho and a preposterous Victorian black hat with red feathers, she looked like an extra in a Harry Potter movie (way in the background) (the third one was my favorite) (how about you?).

"Well, well, well," she said smugly upon seeing me. "Vivian Borne. If you're here to use your author's discount, I'm afraid I've canceled it."

I gave her my loveliest smile, dripping with sincerity as only a fine actress can drip it. "My dear, Mary Beth, I realize we've had our differences of late, but not long ago we were fellow professionals in the world of mystery. So I am hoping, in the wake of the tragedy in the old Butterworth place, that we might, perhaps—"

"Bury the hatchet?" Her smile was wicked.

Was this a reference to the current murder, or the vintage one? If the former, then the bookseller knew more than she should. If the latter, not a bad joke!

"If we might cast sarcasm aside," I said, "your underlying sentiment has merit. We should make peace or at least declare a truce." I gestured to the cameraman. "You remember Phil Dean?"

She got to her feet behind the counter. "Yes. What do you want, Vivian? What's he doing bringing a TV camera into my store?"

Temper in check, I said, "Now that our reality show is on hold—"

"Don't you mean D.O.A.?" She snorted a laugh, proud of this remarkable display of wit.

I faked a chuckle. "Very droll, dear. No, I'm here because Phil and I, while we're waiting for word on our series, are working on a documentary for Iowa Public Television. It's on the boutique businesses of Serenity, the antiques stores, Pearl City Plaza's shops, and of course, it would not be complete without Serenity's own mystery bookstore . . . that is, unless you are too put out with me to cooperate with an interview and a video tour of your charming shop."

Well, dear reader, Mary Beth Beckman did a flip-flop worthy of the sleaziest politician, scurrying excitedly out from behind the counter. "You mean you want to shoot it now?"

"Well, we are *here*, dear. But, of course, if you're not interested. . . ."

"No, no! I most certainly am interested." She gazed down at herself. "But am I dressed all right? For the camera, I mean."

"You were born to wear black," I said, "and that hat is simply *you*. And I mean that from the heart."

I hoped Mary Beth would read Phil's grin not as derision, but as a reflection of his positive attitude.

"Can Edgar Allan Paw be in it, too?" Mary Beth asked, bubbling with enthusiasm now.

Edgar Allan Paw was her tabby. I believe it's a federal law that all mystery bookstore owners must own a tabby with a cute mystery-oriented name. Here are some Brandy and I've encountered on book tours: Pawrow, Furry Mason, and (sadly) Sam Spayed. Our favorite non-cat mystery bookstore pet names: Nero Wolfhound and Mike Hamster.

"Absolutely Edgar Allan Paw can be in it," I said. "He can sit on your lap, if you like, and be ever so cute." I turned to Phil. "Where do you suggest we set up?"

"Anywhere away from the front windows," he said.

"There are some armchairs in the back," Mary Beth said helpfully, "in the events area . . . Will that do?"

"Perfect," Phil said with a nonderisive smile. "I'll get set up. In the meantime, there's a release you need to sign."

Shortly, Mary Beth and I were seated in matching leather chairs, angled toward each other, the fat tabby, looking quite bored, on her lap. As for any customers, Mary Beth had turned the CLOSED sign outward.

Phil, behind the tripod, checked the viewfinder on the camera, then said, "On three . . . two . . . *one.*"

I looked into the lens. "Hello, fellow Iowans. This is Vivian Borne. Today I'm with Mary Beth Beckman, of Scene of the Crime, and we're going to talk about her new store location." I leaned forward, beaming at her. "Mary Beth, tell us why you decided to move your bookstore to the Park Avenue Strip Mall. The community college across the street must have been a factor, as was perhaps the rent, since yours is one of only three stores of a possible seven."

Mary Beth glared at me. "Now what the hell am I supposed to say?"

"Cut," Phil said.

"Oh, I am sorry," I said, putting hand to bosom. "I'm afraid I'm leading the witness again."

Mary Beth frowned. "What do you mean by that?"

"Merely a figure of speech, my dear. Shall we go again?"

"Rolling," Phil said.

"Hello, my fellow Iowans, this is Vivian Borne. Today I'm with Mary Beth Beckman, of Scene of the Crime, and she's going to tell us all about her new store location."

Blah, blah, blah.

After ten or so not terribly interesting minutes, I called an end to the interview. As before, Phil said he wanted to do some close-ups, but (you're ahead of me, aren't you?) first needed to step outside for a smoke.

After he'd gone, I said to Mary Beth, "Lovely job, dear. Lovely job. Just fascinating."

"Thank you," she said, shifting in her chair. Disturbed, the cat snarled, clawed at her, and ran off to parts unknown. "The little angel."

"By the way, dear, not to touch on an unpleasant subject, but you do have a right to *know*. . . ."

She frowned. "Know what?"

"I'm afraid, dear, that during my interview with the police, I simply had to tell the truth."

"The truth about what?"

"About your little tiff with Bruce Spring the other day."

She sneered at me, examining her hand where her angel tabby had scratched her. "I just *thought* you might. So I went in on my *own*, and explained the whole thing."

"Very shrewd, dear."

"What do you mean, 'shrewd'? I was just being a good citizen." She tossed her head and the floppy hat slid off-kilter. "They didn't seem at all concerned."

I whispered conspiratorially: "No surprise— they like keeping suspects in the dark, you know. Or perhaps you don't read police procedurals."

Her eyes flashed. "I'm no suspect! The very idea that I could harm a fly is outlandish."

That's what Anthony Perkins said about his mother.

"You *were* pretty ticked off, dear. What *did* you tell the police?"

She drew in a breath and lifted her chin grandly, the hat returning to its proper position. "I told them that I'd worked here in the store that night, stocking shelves, until well after midnight."

"This was after hours?"

"Certainly."

"Was anyone with you?"

"No. I only have help on the weekends. Still, I'm sure someone could confirm that the lights in the store were on. One of the other merchants, or the security man. Even someone just driving by."

Which meant nothing.

Now she leaned forward conspiratorially. "I'll tell you who *I* think did it. . . ." She gestured with her head toward the front of the store, the hat tilting off the other side this time. "The very person you're traipsing around with. Your precious cameraman."

"Really? And why do you say that?"

She finally sensed the hat was off-kilter and

straightened it. "My little sister Alice Jean is the bartender at the Holiday Inn, and she told me Phil Dean and Bruce Spring had a heated argument that afternoon. That it nearly came to blows. *And* that Phil came right out and threatened Bruce."

"Threatened him how?"

"Why, to kill him, of course. Alice Jean said that Phil said, 'I could just *strangle* you, you bastard.' *Is* that how Spring got it? *Was* he strangled? The paper doesn't say, and the police wouldn't tell me."

"I'm sworn to confidentiality about the murder method," I said, making a mental note to get to know Alice Jean. She sounded like a heck of a snitch. "Did your sister say what started the argument?"

Mary Beth nodded, the hat flapping in agreement. "She most certainly did," she said, in a Stan Laurel sort of way.

When she didn't continue, I said, "Well?"

Her smile was more a sneer. "Not that easy, Vivian. I want something in return."

"What?"

She sucked at where Edgar Allan Paw had scratched her hand, then said, with eyes as gleaming as the cat's had been: "I want a part in your next play. Now it doesn't have to be the *lead* . . ."

And it wouldn't be. She'd played a supporting role last year in *The Mousetrap,* and if she'd been any hammier, Oscar Meyer might have packaged her.

". . . but it has to be more than a walk-on."

"All right," I agreed. I had just the part in mind: the cow in our upcoming production of Sondheim's *Into the Woods.* Or at least one end of the cow.

"So," I said, "what precipitated the fracas?"

"Spring fired him. Fired your man Phil. So then I guess you've been fraternizing with the enemy, huh, Miss Marple?"

Later, after we'd finished with Mary Beth, and Phil was loading up the car, he asked, "Did we get anything interesting out of her?"

Meaning the secret-camera footage.

"Something," I admitted.

"What?"

"Really want to know?"

"I really want to know."

So I told him.

"Vivian," he said, with a nervous smile, "that was only an expression. Haven't you ever said, 'I could just kill that guy,' or gal, or whatever?"

"Yes. Probably. But I never said I wanted to strangle anyone. That's fairly specific, Phil."

"Is that how Bruce was killed? Come on, Vivian. You owe me that much. Tell me."

"I just can't, dear." And kind of a pity, since Spring had been chopped not choked.

"Are you going to tell the police?"

"About what, dear?"

"About the argument Bruce and I had!"

"I'm sure they already know, or soon will, and won't need my help to find out. Between Mary Beth and her sister Alice Jean and whoever else was in that bar, you're likely to be on Chief Lawson's short list of suspects."

Almost pleadingly, he said, "Look, I didn't kill Bruce. What is it you think I did exactly? Lure him to that house in the dead of night and murder him, in some as yet to be specified way?"

"I didn't say that."

"Vivian, I may have been mad at Bruce for firing me, but hardly *that* mad. In my business, jobs come and go, and there's always another gig waiting for a good cameraman. Hell, I was on the verge of quitting Bruce, anyhow."

"I believe you, dear," I said. "But who *did* lure Bruce to the house in the dead of night, as you say? And kill him in a terribly, horrible, gruesome unspecified way?"

Phil goggled at me—**:-O**. (*Sorry, Brandy! Just that one!*)

"I don't know," he said. "I really don't. I was nowhere near there. By then, we weren't even speaking. I went to my room, and stayed there. Even ordered room service, so I wouldn't run into him in the restaurant."

"Not the most stunning alibi I ever heard."

"Well, that's because I wasn't aware I was going to need one."

We drove out of the strip mall. Rather than return downtown with Phil to take the trolley home, I asked my somewhat dejected cameraman to drop me off.

We sat for a few minutes in front of my house, the conversation turning to what footage was still needed.

"I'll spend tomorrow getting B-roll of the town," he said. "You know, just location footage. Establishing shots."

I nodded. "And I have some investigating to do on my own. If there's more work to be done for Iowa Public Television, I'll let you know."

We exchanged smiles, rather warmly, and I got out of the rental.

And as my chapter winds down, I see that through efficient storytelling, I have curtailed my word count, giving me the opportunity to spend just a little more quality time with you, dear reader.

In our last book, *Antiques Disposal,* I had started to relate my even *funnier* trolley story (funnier than the one about little Billy Buckly, whose grandfather was one of the Munchkins in *The Wizard of Oz*) but, apparently I had exhausted my word limit, and was not allowed to finish the tale. So, here it is now:

There was a spinster in town who bought a chimpanzee to keep her company, and who she called Mr. Muggs (after J. Fred Muggs of the old *Today Show* chimp). One day she wanted to take Mr. Muggs with her on the trolley, but since the driver wouldn't allow pets on board, she dressed the simian up as a little girl, complete with a Goldilocks wig. Well, no one seemed to notice (most were older folks with cataracts) and everything went swimmingly until an elderly fellow seated across from the monkey, reached over, saying, "Isn't she cute," and pinched a furry cheek. And Mr. Muggs promptly bit off his finger. It was quite funny. I mean, not right then, of course, because they couldn't find the finger at first, but later, when you thought about it.

Or perhaps you had to be there.

A Trash 'n' Treasures Tip

Keep a list of your customers' purchases so you can contact them about similar items of interest. E-mail alerts are preferable to phone calls, or at least that has been the case with Mother's customers, many of whom have caller I.D.

Chapter Nine

Chop Lifting

Brandy at the helm again.

Everybody feeling all right? Anyone need a break after Mother's last chapter? Some aspirin maybe? A tiny little swig of cooking sherry? Possibly just stick your head under the faucet and run that water nice and cold for a while? I can wait. No?

Okay, then, onward (if not upward).

The following morning, more autumn crisp than yesterday, I walked Jake out to the Hummer, where Roger was already behind the wheel and loaded up to head back to Chicago. With Jake.

Roger had called Brian and asked for permission, assuring him he'd drive Jake right back for any legal proceedings that might be necessary.

Brian okayed that, and while Jake was not thrilled about leaving, he didn't act out.

Mother, who had already said her good-byes, did not make the walk to the curb with us.

"I'm glad you're not giving your dad a bad time about this," I said.

"I'd really like to stay and help you guys with your"—he lowered his voice; his father was only a few yards away at this point—"investigation."

"We're gonna leave that to the police," I said.

"You lie worse than I do." He shrugged. "But I guess I can't blame Dad for wanting to get me out of here. I mean, I did bump into a chopped-up corpse, and there is an ax murderer running around somewhere in Serenity. So, you know, I guess he has a point."

"Uh, yeah. I guess he does."

"Don't *you* get hurt." He hugged me. "Really, I agree with Dad. I wish you and Grandma would leave this one to the police."

Then he was up in the Hummer, his dad behind the wheel, both father and son looking down at me. Good Lord, the size of that vehicle.

"Brandy, you take care," Roger said.

"I will."

"I mean it." He shook his finger at me in a mildly scolding way, blew me a little kiss, a sweet gesture, really, then went roaring off.

I didn't go back in till they were out of sight.

Soon after, though, I was once again seated on the piano bench in the library/music room.

Mother was saying, "Well, I'm glad *they're* gone."

"What a terrible thing to say."

She was standing at the blackboard, pondering the suspect list, which had been updated. "I am merely glad to have Jake out of harm's way, and not to have your ex hanging around, inhibiting our inquiries. If that Roger had his way, we'd butt out of this one!"

"He's probably right to think that. Jake just reminded me that we are dealing with a very violent culprit here. This isn't fun and games, Mother. Not this time."

"Pish posh," she said. "*I'm* certainly having fun, and any time you pursue a murderer, it's a game of sorts—cat and mouse."

"Well, this time the cat has an ax."

Mother turned and frowned at me. "Not true. That ax is in the evidence lock-up at the police station. And would I like a look at it! Now. Study the blackboard, dear. You'll note I've added a new category."

Rocky and Sushi drifted in to join our little confab. Rocky sat on the floor next to my bench, and appeared to be listening, while Sushi curled up on the Persian rug and promptly began to snore.

Dutifully, I studied what Mother and her piece of chalk had wrought.

MURDER OF BRUCE SPRING

Suspect	Motive	Opportunity	Alibi
Joe Lange	valuable ax	Yes	None
Phil Dean	being fired	Yes	None
Mary Beth Beckman	grudge over documentary	Yes	None
Andrew Butterworth	documentary	Yes	Sarah
Sarah Butterworth	documentary	Yes	Andrew

I said, "You should just go ahead and write 'none' next to both Andrew and Sarah."

Mother nodded, stroking her chin like the Big Bad Wolf contemplating a straw house to blow down. "They could very well be covering for each other. At the very least, they've made no mention of Andrew leaving the house for a late-night stroll."

Earlier Mother had told me about Andrew having been seen walking near the murder house the night of Spring's demise.

"I think," she said, "it's about time we dropped by the Butterworth place, to confront them about their duplicity."

"You mean, accuse them of lying? I'm up for that."

We gathered our coats and, as we went out the door, Rocky did his best to go with us.

"We'll be back soon," I promised him, "and then I'll take you and Soosh for a walk."

That last word I whispered, to keep Sushi, dozing in the other room, from hearing. But Rocky was clambering at the door, up on his hind legs, batting at the wood with his paws, barking as we left.

So much for Sushi's nap.

"Poor dear," Mother said over the dog wails, which included Sushi's yapping now. "He just hates to be left out of the fun."

And games.

In just over ten minutes, we were on the porch of the Butterworth mansion, Mother again cranking the handle of the ancient doorbell.

After three or four more tries, and still no answer, I said, "They must be out."

"No way, Jose," Mother replied. "I saw a curtain drawn back. They just don't want to face the music!"

Raising her voice, she called out in her patented singsong fashion, "I'm not *leeeeav*-ing!"

Persistence was one of Mother's best traits. Also one of her worst. Yin and Yang kind of thing.

After some more spirited ringing of the non-electric doorbell, the front door opened, the space all but filled by the tall, mannishly attractive Sarah Butterworth, exhibiting colors perfect for this late fall day—green wool slacks, orange cardigan over gold blouse, over which blazed a scarlet face.

"I can't *believe*," Sarah said, biting off the words, "that you have the *audacity* to come back here."

"My dear, you simply *must* calm yourself," Mother responded, the soul of concern. "All that blood rushing to your face just *can't* be good for your rosacea."

"I don't have rosacea!"

"You *don't?* Oh, well, I do. It's the Scandinavian curse, you know. Red patchy spots on both cheeks—most annoying—and I've *tried* cutting out spicy foods, to no avail I'm afraid."

"What do you *want,* Vivian?"

Mother pointed toward the inside of the house, past Sarah, whispering, "I think this topic of discussion might be better handled inside. The neighbors, you know. The last thing I would ever want is to embarrass you."

Sarah's eyes and nostrils flared, and she folded her arms across her chest, ever more the sentry. "And what topic of discussion is that?"

"Why, dear," Mother said, still sotto voce, "I have learned that the alibi you and Andy provided me was a big old fib. And I wanted to give you the chance to correct the record."

Sarah's face, the red having softened to pink, now paled. She drew in a deep breath, then let it out. Then, with some reluctance, she took a step back and another to one side, allowing us to enter.

In the foyer, Mother said, "I think it would be best if Andy were a part of this conversation, too, my dear."

"He's not in."

Mother raised an eyebrow.

Sarah closed her eyes in a moment of frustration, then said, "We do go out from time to time, Vivian. And Andrew isn't here right now. And he did *not* say when he'd be back."

I touched Mother's arm and gave her a glance that said, *Maybe that's just as well.* Maybe we could get more out of the sister without the brother around.

Mother nodded to me, then turned to our reluctant host, saying, "Could we go somewhere and sit down? I do so hate to impose, but my darn bunions are just killing me."

Sarah sighed and nodded, and led the way.

She took us only a few paces into her domain—no veranda with wicker chairs and fabulous river view this trip—gesturing for Mother and me to sit on a mission-style couch, while our put-upon hostess took a matching chair.

"I won't beat about the bush," Mother said, settling back. "I have it on good authority that Andy was seen walking out of the old Butterworth homestead, the very night Bruce Spring was killed."

She was taking some liberty with her statement—Andrew had been seen walking near the murder house, not exiting it. Whether this was theatrics or entrapment on Mother's part, I couldn't say.

Either way, it certainly got results.

Sarah buried her face in her hands and a wail came out that echoed through the big room like a banshee. I jumped in my chair a little, but Mother only sat forward, eyes glittering.

Then, with little choking sounds, Sarah moaned, "It's . . . it's going to start all *over* again, isn't it?"

She meant that Andrew would be accused of another murder. Another ax murder, at that.

I dug in my purse, found a tissue, and leaned forward to hand it to Sarah. She snatched it from my fingers as if the thing had always belonged to her. She dabbed her eyes, but said nothing.

Mother made the terrible silence go away by asking, "Had Andy arranged to meet Bruce Spring that night, for some reason? Perhaps something to do with that scurrilous documentary?"

"Yes," Sarah sniffled, looking down at the wadded tissue in her hands. "My brother discovered from that horrible Beckman woman that it was Spring who produced that awful program. So Andy went down there to meet with him, and tell him in no uncertain terms that he was withdrawing the use of the house for your series."

Mother frowned, and I was afraid she was going to say something inappropriate, so I took the lead, asking, "The meeting did take place?"

"Yes."

"Had it been arranged in advance?"

Sarah nodded. "Andy called Spring at the Holiday Inn, and insisted on a meeting at the old house, that evening. That man could hardly turn him down."

"How did Spring react, learning that use of the location was now denied him?"

Sarah shrugged, fingering the tissue. "Well, obviously, he wasn't pleased, but what could he say? What could he do? Anyway, for a gentle, genteel human being, Andy can be quite forceful and even stubborn."

She looked up sharply, realizing her last words might condemn him.

"But my brother *swears* Spring was alive when he left that house! He never laid a hand on him."

Mother had been strangely silent as I'd taken over the questioning. I think for a while she was sidetracked by the news that the murder house wasn't going to be available for our series—like *that* would still happen!

But Sarah, sitting there crying, was an old friend of hers, and while Mother can have a cold, calculating streak where her sleuthing is concerned, the sight of her old chum wracked with dismay did seem to move her. She got to her feet and stood next to the seated woman and slipped an arm around her.

"I'm telling the truth!" Sarah blurted.

"Of course, dear," Mother said soothingly, patting a shoulder in *there, there* fashion. "I believe you. I do believe you. . . ."

I wasn't sure I did. Couldn't the sister be covering up for her brother again? Just as she must have done, all those years ago, for a disturbingly similar murder?

Leaving Sarah with her thoughts, we returned to the Buick to discuss ours, and were about to climb in, when a squad car rolled up behind us, and Officer Munson got out.

As he approached, he said, "The chief wants to see the both of you—toot sweet."

The officer's hound-dog face was hard to read. But this didn't feel like a social visit.

Mother, on the other hand, seemed pleased to be summoned by the town's top cop.

"No problem, Officer," she said cheerily. "We'll be along shortly. I think we're *all* due about now for a debriefing."

I wondered if that would be the kind of "debriefing" where they took your clothes and underthings and gave you a shower and a cell.

"No," Munson said firmly, "you're going to the station *right now*."

"Very well, Officer," Mother replied politely. "Never let it be said that Vivian Borne does not pay local law enforcement the respect it deserves."

Just don't ask her how much respect that is.

On the short drive to the station, Munson was so close behind us, he must have figured we might make a break for it.

"Doesn't that imbecile," Mother said, in a typical display of her respect for local law enforcement, "know that tailgating is illegal? In the sense of following a car too closely, I mean. It's quite legal to have baked beans and beer out of the back of your vehicle in a parking lot before a football game."

"Good to know, Mother. But what is this about, do you think?"

Mother shrugged rather grandly. "The chief likely wants to know what we've learned about the murder. Those poor boobs probably haven't gotten past first base." A less grand shrug. "Well, I suppose we can throw him a bone."

I'd leave the bone-throwing up to her.

In the station lot, I took a visitor's spot while Munson moved past us to park with the other police cars. We waited dutifully for him to join us and, shortly, he was escorting us into the station via the side door, where perps were hauled in.

An omen perhaps?

But once inside, it was just a few short steps to the chief's office, where Munson deposited us in visitors' chairs, then disappeared.

Brian, sitting behind his big metal desk, did not rise to greet us. His face—unlike hound-dog Munson's—was about as hard to read as Dick and Jane.

"I told you two to stay *out* of this case," he said, voice dripping with rancor.

I was flying low, hoping to keep under the radar, letting Mother take the blame and the lead, expecting her to rush to our defense. But she appeared uncharacteristically tongue-tied, as if she'd stepped out on stage having learned the script for one play only to find herself in the midst of another, already going on.

As Brian ranted, his perhaps unintentionally patriotic-themed attire (white shirt, red tie, navy slacks) somehow added weight to his righteous indignation. At least it went well with the American flag behind his desk, anyway.

"It has come to my embarrassed attention that you have been sticking your noses into the Spring investigation, interfering with police business! You are treading very close to obstruction of justice charges."

Mother finally found some words, if not very

original. "There is freedom of the press in this country, young man. Or have you forgotten that?"

"You aren't reporters."

"We are the authors of a number of nonfiction true crime works, I'll have you know."

And she stuck her tongue out at him.

I slumped in my chair and covered my eyes, but I didn't have to see Brian to know that Mother had only turned him whiter with rage.

Still, he worked to contain himself. "Vivian. Brandy. Do you have any idea what this case means to me, personally?" He swallowed thickly. "The D.C.I. is watching my every step."

That was Iowa's Division of Criminal Investigation.

"Hell," he continued, "once this finally hits the media, the whole *nation* will be watching! I'll be lucky to find a job as a mall cop. Brandy, I expect this kind of self-absorption from your mother. But I thought I deserved better from you, at least."

So this was about him. Talk about self-absorption. . . .

I raised a hand like a kid in class. "Brian, we're not interfering. We're caught up in the middle of this, through no fault of our own. So we're merely conducting a few inquiries."

"There's no 'merely' about it!" He glared at Mother but spoke to me. "*This* Looney Tunes has been questioning our suspects! *And* taping those interviews."

How could he know that? And how could I get that darn "The Merry-Go-Round Broke

Down" song from playing in my brain, after his Looney Tunes crack?

Mother laughed unconvincingly. "Why, you're the loon, young man. All I've been doing is working on a documentary for Iowa Public Television. It's all about the fireplaces of—"

"Horse hockey!" he yelled.

Only he didn't say "hockey."

Mother drew herself up indignantly. "I would respectfully request that you, as a servant of the people, refrain from using such foul language in front of my impressionable daughter."

From infancy, I'd heard much worse from her, especially when she hit her thumb with a hammer.

"Besides," Mother went on, "what proof do you have? I can show you the signed releases that indicate what the program is going to be about. Uh, and I'm also doing a documentary on our town's boutique businesses, and—"

"Spare me the bull crap," Brian said, although (yup) he didn't say "crap." He opened a desk drawer. "I have what we call in the business a smoking gun."

What he held up was not, of course, a smoking gun, rather a little piece of black plastic hardly bigger than a credit card, reading Panasonic P2.

"Where did you get that?" Mother blurted.

"From Phil Dean. He thought it would be in his best interests to cooperate with actual law enforcement, as opposed to the Serenity branch of the Nancy Drew fan club." Then, in response to my puzzled expression, Brian said, "It's a disc,

Brandy—the stored footage of the interviews your mother conducted. Under false pretenses, by the way."

I frowned. "Did you have a warrant to get that?"

"Didn't need one. As I said, Mr. Dean has been quite cooperative, particularly after I informed him that we knew of his conviction for third-degree manslaughter in a bar fight some years ago."

Mother said huffily, "Chief Lawson, you are an underhanded, conniving so-and-so."

"And you, Mrs. Borne, are a meddling busybody."

Nobody, and I mean *nobody,* calls Mother a meddling busybody but me! (Looney Tunes was harder to take issue with.)

"You should be *grateful* to her, Brian Lawson," I shot back. "She has saved this department's bacon half a dozen times. Name an officer on your stupid department who has solved more crimes than Mother! You can't, can you?" I should have stopped there, because what I said next was childish. "Know what? You aren't my boyfriend anymore."

That stopped him. As if I'd slapped him.

Finally he said, softly, "Was I ever?"

Which hurt. Truth does, sometimes.

Brian said, his tone almost conciliatory, "Look, I got you girls in here to give you fair warning—if I get any more reports of your interference, I won't have any choice."

"Any choice?" I asked.

"I'll have to throw the book at you . . . both!"

Well, like Mother's remark, that wasn't very original, either. So why did it scare me?

Mother straightened regally. "May we leave? Or do I need to call our legal representation?"

That scared me, too—the thought of Wayne Ekhardt riding to our rescue in his Lincoln, sideswiping everyone in sight.

"Yes," Brian sighed. "You can go."

We did.

I halfway expected Brian to ask me to stay behind for a private moment. So that maybe we could make up (or at least pretend to).

No such luck.

In the hall, an attractive female dispatcher with chin-length reddish-brown hair and red glasses flagged us down.

"Are these your scissors, ma'am?" she asked, addressing Mother. "I found 'em by the plant in the outer room."

Mother looked down at the small scissors the woman held in one hand. "Oh, my, yes. I'd been trimming the dead leaves. Thank you, dear."

In the parking lot, back in the Buick, I waited before starting up the engine to get Mother's tirade out of the way. She would surely rail on and on about how we had just been so ill-treated by *Interim* Chief Lawson. But what emerged from her mouth surprised me.

Her eyes gleamed behind the magnifying lenses. "We're going to meet her in half an hour."

"Who?"

"Heather?"

"Who's Heather?"

"My new mole! The woman in red glasses who passed me this note along with my cuticle scissors, which by the way I was missing last night, after my evening bath."

"When did you have time to recruit a new police mole?"

But Mother ignored that and handed me a scrap of paper, which I took and read out loud: " 'Library parking garage. South stairwell. Noon.' " I looked up from the note. "What does she want?"

"*That* is the question!" Mother said, quoting Shakespeare in a completely nonsequitur fashion. She settled back in her seat. "To the library, dear! That is, if you still want to continue assisting in my sleuthing, despite Chief Lawson."

"Heck, yes." Only I did not say "heck." I also said, "And that's *our* sleuthing, if you don't mind, not *your* sleuthing. We established a long time ago that neither one of us is Watson."

"We're both Holmes sweet Holmes!" She patted my knee. "*There* she is . . . my little defiant Brandy. For a while there I'd thought I'd lost her."

"Not on your frickin' life!" I said. And actually I *did* say "frickin'." Sorry to disappoint. "We're going to find out who killed Bruce Spring, cost us our reality show, put Joe in the slammer, and endangered my son and your grandson!"

"That's my girl!"

We drove off with considerably less drama than the dialogue that led up to it. The Buick needed a tune-up and the shocks were out, so we just jostled along.

It was a chilly, brief wait in the unheated garage stairwell. We'd gone straight there, with not enough time to do anything else before our meeting with Heather.

I was praying that the dispatcher would arrive soon, as Mother's hyperjabber was starting to drive me bonkers.

"Isn't this *exciting?*" my cohort in crime was saying. We were seated on the dirty cement steps, she one above me. "*Very* 'Deep Throat'."

That was us—the Woodward and Bernstein of Serenity, Iowa.

She continued. "Such a odd code name for an informant—'Deep Throat.' What's the significance?"

I looked up at her. "You're kidding, right?"

She looked down at me. "No, dear." She lowered her tone to a gravelly mannish timbre. "Did the informant have a deep voice?"

The stairwell door opened, a businessman with briefcase entered, and we had to scoot over to allow him to pass.

Mother went on. "Perhaps Deep Throat was a snitch under *deep* cover, who passed on information verbally—thus *throat.*"

"Mother, let it go. Or we *really* won't ever get our books into Walmart. . . ."

The door opened again—please, Lord, let it be Heather—and my prayer was answered. First one in a while.

We stood, Mother moving down a step to slip past me and greet the woman.

"My dear," Mother cooed, "this is such a surprise! And a pleasant one."

"I don't have much time," Heather whispered. She had a deep, throaty timbre herself. "So just listen."

She handed Mother a manila envelope.

"This is a copy of the coroner's report on Bruce Spring. Also, there are photos of the ax."

"Any possibility of viewing the weapon in person?" Mother whispered back.

The dispatcher shook her head. "It's been sent on to Des Moines for analysis."

Mother gushed, "Well, my dear, we can't thank you enough—just let us know your terms."

Heather frowned. "Terms?"

"Yes," I said. "What you want for your trouble. But keep in mind we're not rich."

"Yes, dear," Mother said. "We need a more quid pro quo kind of arrangement. A part in one of my plays, perhaps, or possibly an autographed photo of George Clooney, even prescription drugs, if you don't abuse the privilege—you name it!"

The dispatcher's frown deepened. "I don't want anything from you. Only that you catch the killer. Oh, the department *might* eventually get him . . . but you two? You can do it quicker. I mean, how many killers have *they* caught in the last year or two? Now, I *must* go."

Heather opened the stairwell door, then looked back at us—were there tears in her eyes?

Had one of the murders we'd solved involved some friend or family member of hers? Was that the debt she seemed to think she owed us?

But her parting words said otherwise.

"I just don't know *what* I'm going to watch on TV now that Bruce Spring is gone! He was the best reality show host around!"

I don't know whose mouth was hanging open wider—Mother's or mine.

Well, probably Mother's.

Like everybody says, she does have a big mouth.

A Trash 'n' Treasures Tip

To attract more customers, offer a variety of price ranges on merchandise—high, middle, and low. But best avoid Mother's innovative tactic (since rejected) of putting all the higher-priced items on the top shelves, the middle-priced on the middle shelves, and the low-priced on the low shelves. All that does is cause backaches for bargain hunters.

Chapter Ten

Chop Class

After our secret parking-ramp meeting with our new dispatcher snitch (whom Mother was now referring to as "Sore Throat" because of Heather's husky alto), we headed home, arriving about one o'clock.

Knowing Mother would want to pore over the coroner's report and evidence photos herself, I figured I'd wait for the Cliffs Notes. Sushi and Rocky had been promised a walk, and they danced around my ankles until I delivered, taking multi-tasking to new limits (two dogs, two leashes, one pooper scooper).

That took twenty minutes, but when I got back Mother was still going over the files, having taken over the dining room table. I made us lunch, finally getting around to those egg salad sandwiches.

Half an hour later, I brought the sandwiches, iced tea, and a bowl of chips in on a tray, set it down, and sat myself down, too. I positioned the tray and yours truly down a ways at the Duncan Phyfe, not wanting to put scrumptious sandwiches in too close a proximity to grisly evidence photos. I'd intended for Mother to come down and join me, but she was busy peering at photos under a large magnifying glass (the photos were under the glass, not Mother).

She glanced up at me, momentarily bringing the round glass to her face, magnifying an already enlarged eye behind its round frame, a terrifying effect perfect for an old B-movie horror flick. *The Fly*, maybe. Or *Dr. Cyclops*.

"Anything?" I prodded, nibbling the sandwich. Say what you will about Wonder Bread; it knows just what to do with egg salad, even if it doesn't really build strong bodies twelve ways.

"I'll need to study these further," she said, tapping a photo with a finger. Even from my end of the table, I could see the pic was of the murder ax.

As for me, I was eating a potato chip, and not about to seek a closer look at a blood-caked weapon.

But I did ask, "Can they tell at this late date— the lab in Des Moines, I mean—if *that* ax was also the one used to kill Archibald Butterworth? Would there still be fingerprints after so many years?"

Mother frowned. "I doubt it, dear. But a DNA match from old blood should certainly be possible. At least, according to Gil Grissom and Catherine Willows."

"I don't think *CSI* reruns are admissible in court as forensics evidence, Mother."

She ignored that and reached for a document headed CORONER'S REPORT—CONFIDENTIAL. "But now, this is particularly interesting. In fact, it changes everything. It's a breakthrough, all right."

"And you're going to make me ask, of course."

She nodded with a smile no more demented than Daffy Duck's dodging the little man from the draft board.

So I asked, "What's particularly interesting, Mother? How does it change everything? What makes it a breakthrough?"

"When you're sarcastic, dear, I notice that you reflexively smirk, and that digs lines in the epidermis. Not a good idea for a young woman heading past thirty."

"Yeah, yeah, yeah. What is it, already?"

"Oh, nothing much," she said. "Just that our late producer Bruce Spring was *not* hacked to death by an ax-wielding maniac."

"*What?*" A bit of chopped egg salad stuck in my throat, and I pushed the rest of the sandwich aside.

"He was strangled, dear," she said as I was choking on egg salad. "Seems he was very much dead when he was, uh . . . disassembled. Pass me a sandwich, would you, dear? There's a good girl."

I pulled my chair around closer to hers. "If he was already dead," I said, "why would the killer chop up the body?"

"Isn't it obvious?" Mother replied, munching. "To create the impression that this crime was a repeat of the Archibald Butterworth murder."

"You mean, cast suspicion on Andrew? The prime suspect in the *earlier* ax murder?"

"Yes . . . or his sister, Sarah. She *is* a large woman, sturdy as a stevedore, easily several inches taller than Bruce. Many of the articles about the crime, over the years, have posited her as Archibald's slayer. It even came up in the Bruce Spring documentary."

"You think Sarah would be capable of killing her own father?"

Mother frowned in thought. "I couldn't hazard a guess, dear, but you know, I have always felt there was something rather on the calculating side about her, a certain cold-blooded quality." She leaned closer, conspiratorial. "She never married, you know."

As if being single makes a killer of a woman. Being married seems a more likely cause.

"Maybe she is another Lizzie Borden," I said, going along with Mother. "Didn't you say the father was overly strict—almost cruel?"

"Yes. But by today's standards, Ward Cleaver would seem such. Applying a belt to a bare bottom was a standard punishment then. And many fathers in those days believed in the old edict that children should be seen and not heard. That last, I must admit, has its appeal. . . ."

"What if," I said, ignoring her last remark,

"Archibald gave Sarah too *much* fatherly attention? The unwanted kind. That kind of abuse rarely came to light back then."

Mother frowned. "A religious man like Archibald?"

"Hello! All those articles and that documentary, too, speculated that the oh so pious Archibald was having an affair at the time of the murder. Perhaps he was some kind of sicko behind his pious, proper public image."

"Dear, we're not trying to find Archibald Butterworth's killer. We're looking for *Bruce Spring's* killer."

"Unless that's the *same* killer."

She slapped the table with both hands and her pilfered files jumped. "It *couldn't* be! Not unless either Andrew or Sarah or both of them are involved, and in that instance, why chop up the corpse afterward to overtly connect it with the other unsolved crime? If you had committed that crime yourself."

I had no answer for that.

Mother continued: "No, the murderer was trying to implicate one or both Butterworth siblings, and your poor friend Joe just stumbled into the thick of things, confusing matters."

"Then the original murder is irrelevant, except for providing a way to implicate the Butterworths."

"Yes."

"So solving the *old* murder is not a goal?"

"No. I mean, yes. I mean . . ."

"Mother!"

"What is it? What's wrong, dear?"

"It just occurred to me—this is terrible news for Joe."

"What is?"

"Death by strangulation." My hand went to my forehead as if checking to see if I had a temperature. "And it explains why Joe is still being held."

"Not following you, dear. Do try to stay on point."

"Here is the point: when this was an *ax* murder, the blood on Joe's clothing wasn't enough to suggest the kind of mess that violent crime would make."

Mother clapped once and it rang in the room. "You're right! A dead body, with no blood flow, would not create the likely arterial spray of an ax murder. . . . Are you going to finish that sandwich, dear? I'm working up an appetite."

"Forget eating! I thought Joe was more or less in the clear, but he's still in big trouble. And what about that cameraman friend of yours, who threatened to strangle your late producer? We *have* to solve this thing!"

Mother flew to her feet, pushed her chair away from the table, and began to pace along its length.

I let her pace and think, going over to have a look at the photos and even using the magnifying glass myself. What I saw made me risk interrupting her mulling process: "Mother . . . didn't you see this? Didn't you notice it?"

She was still pacing, barely paying any attention to me. "Dear, I'm trying to think. Please don't bother me."

"Hey! *You!* Listen for once!"

That froze her. She looked like a deer in the headlights, if a deer in the headlights had on glasses that magnified its crazy eyes.

"Take a look at this," I said, gesturing with the magnifying glass.

She came over and peered down through. Then she reared back, as if alarmed. "Oh dear. I missed it. That's it. That's the key. The clue!"

"You're welcome," I said. "So. What now?"

She extended her arms, palms up, as if balancing something on them. "Obviously. A return visit to Andrew and Sarah Butterworth."

"You have *got* to be kidding me," I groaned. "We were practically thrown out of there this morning. Couldn't we just call Brian and hand this over to him?"

Mother gave me a hard look. "After the way he treated us?"

She had a point.

This time it was Andrew who answered Mother's unrelenting doorbell-twisting.

Looking positively murderous, he growled, "I came home to find my sister in *tears!* Vivian Borne, you aren't just a busybody, but a cruel and unfeeling *monster*. If you don't stop bothering us, I'm calling the police. There are laws against such harassment!"

"That strikes me as rather an overreaction," Mother said, pleasant, businesslike, and utterly unfazed.

He thrust his finger past us, pointing to the rest of the world. "*Go! Both* of you!"

But Mother didn't go and, for that matter, neither did I. I was watching Mother reach into her copious bag. It was like seeing Harpo Marx reach in his pocket—you never knew what was going to come out.

"Andy, my old dear . . . before you cast me into the storm like a fallen daughter with a babe in arms, you might want to feast your eyes upon *this.*"

"What is it? What's that, a photo?"

"Might we come inside?"

"No, you can't come inside! My God, woman."

"Very well, we'll conduct this charade out here." She thrust the photo toward him. "This is a picture of the ax associated with the murder of Bruce Spring—the very one *also* was used in the killing of your father."

Andrew recoiled, refusing to take the picture.

"Actually, it's a close-up of the handle," Mother explained further, "with the initials AGB burnt into the butt."

Archibald (middle initial G) Butterworth.

Why hadn't the police noticed that? They really were helpless without us.

Now, finally, he took the photo, studied it for a moment, then said, "My father's middle name was *Louis*. It's a matter of public record."

Mother arched an eyebrow. "And yours?"

"Louis, also. My grandfather's name." He thrust the photo back at Mother. "This ax was *not* ours. I already talked on the phone to that

Lawson fellow, the chief of police, about this. Now, if that's all, would you please, once and for all, *leave?*"

He turned on his heel, and slammed the door.

Back at home, Mother was pacing next to the Duncan Phyfe again.

"Brandy, Brandy, Brandy," she muttered. She threw her hands up. "This case is driving me absolutely out of my mind!"

No comment.

She halted so suddenly I jumped a little. Then she thrust an Uncle-Sam-Wants-You finger in my face. "Bring down the box of tangled Christmas lights from the attic," she commanded.

"What? Why?"

"I must do something mundane to clear the little pink cells," she announced, tapping her head with a finger.

"You mean little gray cells."

"Actually, that's a misnomer on Hercule Poirot's part. Really they're pink. Or *pinkish-*gray, anyway. Get the box, dear! Get the box."

I made a face. "Don't tell me you're going to start decorating for Christmas already!"

"And what if I am?"

"That's disrespecting Thanksgiving. Thanksgiving is not a step you can skip. It's a special holiday, too."

"What's so special about it?" Mother huffed, her eyes large and wild. "A woman spends a whole morning cooking, the meal is eaten in half an hour, then she's left to an afternoon of clean-up while everyone else watches football. And—just as she sinks exhausted into a chair—the family wants to know what's for dinner."

"Well, leftovers, of course. Turkey. Duh."

Her eyes flared. "I forbid you to say 'duh' ever again! It is childish and beneath the dignity of a woman who is no longer a child."

This coming from the woman who had earlier this afternoon stuck her tongue out at the chief of police.

I said, "Well, your tale of Thanksgiving travails is very moving, but I'd be moved more if it had anything to do with you. When was the last time you cooked Thanksgiving dinner? We always go out."

"Get the Christmas tree lights!"

And so I headed up to the attic to retrieve the heavy box of hopelessly ensnared lights, which Mother dumped out on the Persian rug in the library/music room in front of the flat-screen TV that had been the only worthwhile item from our last win at a storage-unit auction. Then she put on a DVD of *A Christmas Story* ("for mood").

I found a chair and watched the movie, which had been a favorite of mine long before the world caught up with it. Such a funny, unsentimental story of childhood. Maybe after this we could watch *Miracle on 34th Street* (the original black-and-white version), then Alastair Sim in *Scrooge.* Who needed Thanksgiving, anyway?

And who needed solving murders? It was Christmas in November!

The dogs joined us, curling up together on the rug for a nap, while Mother worked at taming the tree light snakes. Right now one of my favorite *Christmas Story* scenes was unfolding, and probably yours too, the one where a boy gets his warm tongue stuck to the freezing flagpole.

But a few minutes into the scene, Mother suddenly sat up straight, eyes riveted to the screen.

"That's *it!*" she exclaimed.

"*What's* it?"

"The key to the murder of Bruce Spring!" Still seated on the floor, she shook a fist at the screen, where the boy's classmates were rushing to the window to see their fellow student stuck to that pole. "And perhaps even to the murder of Archibald Butterworth!"

Her level of excitement either meant she was really on to something, or had been off her meds for maybe a week without my knowing.

So, calmly as possible, I said, "Mother, perhaps you could explain what a little boy getting his tongue stuck to a frozen flagpole has to do with the price of tea in China."

"It has nothing to do with China, dear, and anyway, there just isn't time to explain. We need to see Tilda *right now*, before it's too late. Shake a tail feather!"

Matilda Tompkins—Tilda to her friends— was Serenity's resident New Age guru and part-time hypnotherapist.

"Too late for what?" I asked, helping Mother to her feet.

"Why for the leetle peenk cells!" she said, lapsing into her idea of a French accent (actually Belgian), little brain cells, pink or gray, being the province of Agatha Christie's prissy detective, whose adventures she'd been reading lately in her Red-Hatted League mystery book club.

But as she moved into the living room, the accent disappeared by the time she ordered, "Now get our coats, dear. It's getting chilly out there."

Tilda lived and toiled across from Serenity's main cemetery in an old, white two-story clapboard house of the sort that people nowadays call shabby-chic. Originally more shabby than chic, the house had seen enough repairs and remodeling to put the emphasis on chic. This was thanks to an uptick in Tilda's business—she taught various New Age classes out of the bungalow.

Three o'clock was approaching when Tilda answered Mother's insistent knock, and—though we hadn't called ahead (just not Mother's way)—the guru seemed not a bit surprised to see us. Maybe she'd had a psychic vision.

Pushing fifty, Tilda could have passed for far younger, thanks to her slender figure and long golden-red hair, translucent skin, and freckles. Her attire was strictly latter-day hippie—patchwork peasant skirt, funky necklace (her own creation), white gypsy blouse, and Birkenstock sandals (brown suede for fall).

"Ladies, come in," she said in her husky, sensual voice. "Your timing is impeccable. My Tantric Sex Class isn't for another hour."

Tilda has assisted us on several investigations in the past, using hypnosis to reveal information locked in a subject's mind. Early on, we'd been greeted about as warmly as a bill collector, but now she welcomed us as loyal students in her classroom of greater enlightenment. And like all classrooms, there was inevitably a registration fee.

Mother and I followed Tilda into her small living room, a mystic shrine of soothing candles, healing crystals, and swirling mobiles of planets and stars—much of it for sale. Incense hung heavy as a curtain in the air, and from somewhere drifted the tinkling, mystical sound of New Age music. This was an odd combination living space, waiting room, and gift shop.

At the moment, we were the only students/customers present, but we weren't alone. There were also Eugene Lyle Wilkenson, Constance Ruth Penfield, and Franklin "Frankie" Carlyle, who took up the floral couch.

They were Tilda's cats—and not just any old cats, but reincarnates (reincatnips?) (sorry) of people whose spirits had (she assured one and all) floated across the street to take up residence in her rescued felines. With all of the great unknown to explore, why these spirits had made such a short trip to their next life remained unexplained.

"Who's that?" I asked, pointing to a new addition, a small black kitten, sunning itself on a windowsill.

"That's Cheryl Jean Stewart," the woman said, beaming. "She showed up on my doorstep a few weeks ago."

That was around the time the real Cheryl Jean Stewart, a young fifty-five, had died of a heart attack. I had known Cheryl, who worked at a local bank. We weren't close, but I gave the cat a nod and smile, just in case.

At the same time I made a mental note to make sure my will stipulated that under no circumstances was I to be buried in the cemetery across from Tilda. Just not that wild about incense. . . .

Tilda was trying unsuccessfully to shoo the reincarnates off the couch to make room for us, but Mother said, "There's no time for further pleasantries, my dear—we simply must get to it."

Our hostess half bowed. "I am not surprised. I had a premonition all day that you may need my help."

"You must put me under immediately so that I may recall certain details about our current case, before they are lost forever."

Like Mother had ever forgotten anything, except maybe that she wasn't supposed to drive without a license.

"Very well, Vivian," Tilda said, with another little nod/bow. "We'll go into the hypnosis chamber."

As we followed Tilda, she moved with ethereal, dreamy grace, leading us back to the kitchen, off of which was a small, dark, claustrophobic room, its single window shuttered. The only source of light came from a table lamp, the revolving shade with its cut-out stars sending its own galaxy swirling on the ceiling.

Mother stretched out on a red-velvet Victorian fainting couch (as they are called) while Tilda took an ornate straight-back chair next to her. I stood behind Tilda, with my hand-held tape recorder ready to capture Mother's every utterance.

Tilda took Mother's handwritten instructions on what to ask, and then began the session by reaching to the lamp table for a long, gold-chained necklace with a round shiny disc. Dangling the jewelry before Mother's face, Tilda started to swing it, pendulum-like.

"Watch the medallion, Vivian," Tilda said softly.

As if at a tennis match, Mother's eyes moved back and forth.

"You feel relaxed . . . so very relaxed. You're getting sleepy . . . so very sleepy." This she repeated, progressively slower, ever more soothing.

Mother's eyelids fluttered.

"Your eyelids are heavy . . . very heavy . . . so heavy . . . so heavy you can't keep them open. . . ."

Mother's eyelids closed.

"I'm going to count backward, from ten to one. When I say 'one,' Vivian, you will be asleep, completely, deeply asleep. Ten . . . nine . . . eight. . . ."

At "five," Mother's body went limp, but Tilda finished the count.

"Now, Vivian, I want you to go back in time."

But before Tilda could provide the exact *point* in time, Mother began to speak in a somber yet fluid manner. "My name is Iras. I was first handmaiden to Cleopatra, and in charge of her asps—the care and feeding thereof, that is. Cleo thought Mark Anthony had the hots for her, but it was me he used to meet secretly beneath a fig tree in the garden, after Miss Egypt 44 B.C. had gone to sleep. The way that woman snored, wow, what a racket! You could hear her all the way from Alexandria to Rome. And she had quite the big honker on her, too, I have to say. Greatest beauty of the ancient world, my asp—"

"No, no, dear," Tilda said gently, "not back *that* far. . . ."

But once again, before Tilda could be more specific, Mother began. "My name is Matoaka, younger sister of Pocahontas. It 'twas I—not that Poca face sis of mine—who saved the life of the captured Captain John Smith. Pocahontas didn't throw herself upon him, at all! As if! She tripped and fell—clumsy oaf! My sister was always taking credit for—"

Again Tilda interrupted Mother. "No, no, Vivian. I only want you to go back in time a few days—to the night of the murder."

"Oh." She grunted. "You might have said so."

I was smiling. This tape would make excellent blackmail material. But right now I was doubting that *A Christmas Story*, Cleopatra's handmaiden, and Pocahontas's younger sister could provide much traction for our murder inquiry.

Tilda consulted the paper Mother had given her. "It's the night of Bruce Spring's murder. You are at the scene. The police cars have just arrived. You are waiting outside the old Butterworth house . . . neighbors are beginning to gather, because of the commotion. Who are they?"

Mother's eyeballs began moving back and forth beneath their lids. "Ken and Joanne Fisher . . . Jerry and Marilyn Truitt . . . Jeff Lee . . . John and Carolyn Deason."

Did I mention that Mother knew everyone in town?

"Anyone else?" Tilda asked.

Mother frowned in deep thought. Then: "No."

"In the neighborhood, lights go on in houses up and down the street. Are there any exceptions?"

"Yes. One house, across the way."

"Directly across?"

"No. Up one house. No lights on. Just darkness."

"All right," Tilda said. "Now it's a little later, and you and Jake are in the police car, waiting for Brandy. Has anyone else joined the crowd?"

Mother rattled off the names of a few more people I didn't know, and included the nameless detective in the red Toyota (Froggy to me). Finally, when Tilda had wrung every bit of information out about the murder night from Mother's "little pink cells," she brought her subject out of the trance.

"Well," Mother said, looking first at Tilda, then me. "How did I do?"

"Just great," I said. "We got the inside dope on two boyfriends of yours I never knew about."

She goggled at me. "What? Who?"

"Mark Anthony and Captain John Smith."

She began to nod. "I was in high school with them. No, wait, there was one boy named Mark, another named Anthony, and John Smith. Captain of the basketball squad! But what does that have to do with the Bruce Spring murder?"

"I wouldn't know," I said. "But we do have a laundry list of everybody who lives up and down West Hill."

Mother's smile was mysterious. "Everybody?"

I didn't bother answering that. We bid Tilda and her reincarnate cats good-bye, getting out of there before we had to deal with whoever was signed up for her Tantric Sex class.

In the car Mother had me play back the tape, fast-forwarding through the Cleopatra and Pocahontas stuff, and at the conclusion of what I felt was a fairly boring account of the murder evening, she said, "*Bon.*"

That was Hercule Poirot for "Good," the equivalent of "Satisfactory" from Nero Wolfe, and the extent of what Vivian Borne had to say on the subject.

Starting the engine, I said to my uncharacteristically silent (and characteristically smug) passenger, "You know, Hastings wouldn't be such an imbecile if Poirot would clue him in, once in a while."

"All in good time, Hastings," she said.

"That's *Brandy.*" At least the French accent was gone. Belgian. "What is going on, Mother?"

"All will be revealed."

Soon we were in the library/music room; me on the piano bench, Mother at the blackboard, a teacher ready to enlighten her pupil.

She picked up the eraser from the ledge, then with great sweeping motions wiped the board clean.

"What are you doing?" I asked.

"Disposing of red herrings." She turned around to face me so quickly, I about jumped out of my skin. "None of these suspects is the killer."

"And you know this how?"

"Because of the movie we watched, my dear, and of course, my session with Tilda."

I clapped my hands, once, hard, loud, and this time *she* jumped.

"Okay, lady," I said, "that does it. No more cutesy stuff. No more diva dopeyness. You are going to cut the subterfuge and tell me what that kid getting his tongue stuck on a cold flagpole has to do with the price of beans."

"Flick."

"Say what?"

"The unfortunate boy in *A Christmas Story.* His name was Flick. Everyone remembers that scene. Do you know how they pulled off that effect? It's really quite interesting. They rigged a suction device up the pole and—"

"Could we stay on point? What does Flick, the pole, and his tongue have to do with the murder!"

"You don't have to be rude," Mother said, folding her hands in front of her like a stern schoolmarm; if she'd had a ruler, I'd have gotten my knuckles rapped. "And it has nothing to do with anything—not Flick, the pole, or his tongue."

"Kill me now," I said to the universe. "Kill me now."

"It wasn't what was happening *outside* in the schoolyard that provided the key clue," Mother explained, finally. "Rather, what was taking place *inside* the classroom."

I frowned, recalling the scene from the movie. "Everyone was at the window, looking out at the kid ... at Flick ... with his tongue stuck to the pole."

"Everyone?"

"Well, everyone except for a couple of boys."

"Ralphie and Schwartz."

"Yeah."

She got a crinkly smile going. "And why, pray tell, did they not rush to the window?"

"Because they were trying to be inconspicuous about it, which wound up being actually more suspicious. They're the ones who put Flick up to it. Anyway, what was there to see? They already knew what had happened."

Mother's smile was really quite lovely. "Precisely, dear. Just as when *all* the neighbors came out the night Bruce was killed, to see what was going on. All but one, that is."

I squinted at her. "You mean, the murderer."

"Yes, dear. Trying to be inconspicuous and ultimately tipping his guilt. A man who already knew exactly what was being discovered across the street."

Mother turned back to the board, picked up the chalk, and wrote a name.

I simply sat there and stared, agape. It had all sounded so good until she had written that name, writ large where all the other suspects previously had been.

I was shaking my head. "Did your little pink cells go to sleep, Mother? You *can't* be saying that Samuel Wright is the killer. The deacon of Amazing Grace Church?"

"Ah, but that wasn't the name of the church back in 1950, when Samuel's father was its head."

And my little pink cells started to work.

"Amazing Grace Baptist," I said.

AGB.

Until a few years ago, Baptist had been part of the church's name, dropped when Amazing Grace ended its affiliation with the denomination.

"The ax belonged to the church," I said numbly. "Where Samuel's father, Gabriel, was pastor. . . ."

"Yes, dear."

My head was spinning. "And the chopper wound up in the old Butterworth house because . . ."

". . . because," Mother picked up, "that's where it was hidden all those years ago."

I squinted at her again, hoping this would all come into focus. "Are you saying that Samuel Wright—then a teenager—killed Archibald Butterworth, and fifty-some years later, used the same ax to murder Bruce Spring?" I blinked. "But that's wrong, isn't it?"

"It's wrong," Mother agreed. "We know from Heather's files that the ax wasn't used to kill Bruce Spring. That the modern-day murderer strangled his victim, and used the ax for misdirection."

"And the modern-day murderer is Sam Wright?"

"Right." Or maybe she said "Wright." Same difference.

"So," I asked, "who killed Archibald Butterworth?"

Mother was gloating now. "Very likely it was Samuel's father, Gabriel, who did it."

I snapped my fingers. "Because Archibald was having an affair with Gabriel's wife!"

She nodded. "I have come to believe the tryst was more than just idle gossip. Jealousy would explain Archibald's viciousness in committing the murder."

I could only shake my head. "A man of the cloth."

"But not a gentle one, dear. A fire-and-brimstone believer, whose rage and repression resulted in a brutal crime. Did you know that Gabriel's wife, Elsie, disappeared in 1950? Apparently leaving Gabriel to care for fourteen-year-old Samuel?"

"No."

"Well, it's in the articles. And the documentary. Or *did* Elsie leave town? Perhaps Gabriel killed *her,* too."

My head was spinning. "And Sam *knew* his father had murdered Butterworth?"

"Yes. How, we can't be sure. Perhaps he assisted his father in cleaning up the murder scene. Maybe his father came home covered in blood, traumatized, and the boy stepped up and helped out. Sam may have been the person who hid the ax in the house. Certainly he helped in one key way—he testified in a manner that threw strong suspicion on his good friend, Andy Butterworth."

"Okay, okay," I said, holding up two hands before she got too carried away. "But explain this to me. Why would Samuel kill Bruce Spring?"

She answered my question with one of her own. "Why do you think the ax remained hidden, undisturbed, until only a few days ago?"

"Well . . . maybe because we started repairs on the house, that made it possible, even likely, the ax would turn up."

Mother nodded. "It must have given Sam quite a start, seeing that old carpet hauled out to the curb in the sunshine, along with some broken floorboards, knowing the ax might be discovered. So he waited until the cover of night to retrieve it, and tragedy ensued."

"How do you suppose it went down?"

"Dear, a number of scenarios occur to me."

Not one involving a little boy sticking his wet tongue on a cold flagpole, I hoped.

"But perhaps the most likely one would go as follows," Mother said. "From his window, Sam notices Andy going into the old house, then quickly coming out, having had his brief meeting with Bruce Spring."

"Why brief?"

"Because, first, there would be little to it, just Andy indignantly telling Bruce off and withdrawing his permission for the house to be used as a location. Second, with no electricity, the house was dark, which would not encourage a lengthy discourse."

"Okay. I'll buy that."

Mother gestured with a gently lecturing finger. "The key to this scenario is Sam not knowing that Bruce was in the house—all Sam knew was that Andy went in and went out, rather quickly. But for whatever reason, Bruce lingered, and when Sam crossed the street, probably with flashlight and tools, the producer was still inside. Sam was probably prepared to break in, possibly in back, but came upon an open front door—perhaps even an ajar one—and took advantage of the invitation. Likely Sam didn't see Bruce at first—Bruce may have stayed behind for a quick look at the progress of the renovation."

"In the dark?"

"With a flashlight. Possibly Bruce was upstairs doing as much and Sam, unaware of the producer's presence, quickly went to work on retrieving the ax he'd hidden so long ago. This tableau is what Bruce came upon—you can picture it, can't you? Bruce shining a flashlight beam on a kneeling Sam, floorboards to one side, revealing the long-sequestered murder weapon . . . a weapon that Bruce would immediately recognize, as the producer of the documentary on the crime!"

I was nodding, right with her. "And a confrontation followed, a physical one. But not involving the ax."

"No. Two men struggling until one got the upper hand—or, in this case 'hands.' Strangulation, you know. The cover-up followed—Sam's *second* cover-up in that murder house."

I nodded. "Samuel throwing suspicion on Andrew, by making Bruce's murder similar to Archibald's."

Mother said, in disgust, "And just yesterday, he even tried to use *me* as the tool to implicate Andy, saying he saw Andrew Butterworth on the night of the murder near the house."

"But he actually did see Andy."

"Yes, and it's possible other neighbors could corroborate that."

We fell silent for a moment.

Then I said, "Okay. So. What proof do we have?"

"Not much, dear. We need more than speculation, and some initials on an ax."

"Is there any way we could get more?"

"Yes."

"And?"

"And you won't like it."

She told me.

I didn't.

A Trash 'n' Treasures Tip

If you've had merchandise sitting around for a while—and lowering the price hasn't helped—send it to an auction house. But don't attend that auction. There's always the possibility some sentimental attachment will rear its head, and you'll bid on your own item. That's how Mother wound up with the brass commode she keeps under her bed.

Chapter Eleven

Window Chopping

"Can you help me with this, dear?" Mother asked.

We were standing near the front door, both dressed in commando black—slacks, tennies, hoodies, and gloves. Outside, dusk was smudging the sky a darkening gray.

Mother handed me the black mini-recording HD video camera with audio feature, about the size of a pack of gum. She had ordered the gizmo from a spy-oriented Internet site, thinking it might be helpful in our investigations. At the time, I had made fun of her. Now I was grateful.

"Where do you want it?" I asked.

"Clip it to the side of my spectacles, dear— like a third eye! Very *Blair Witch*, don't you think?"

She had been much impressed with that "found footage" horror flick and the various imitations thereof. Come to think of it, she did look like a witch, in her black ensemble. Which I guess made me a witchette.

"How much recording time does this thing have?" I asked, securing it to the eyeglass temple piece next to one ear. "About three minutes?"

"More like three hours, oh ye of little faith. So we can activate it now."

But before I did so, I said, "You *do* realize, don't you, that along the way, this thingie of yours? It'll be capturing not just any evidence we might uncover, but incriminating evidence against thee and me."

Mother shrugged. "We can always erase the recording later, if need be. Anyway, we've crossed legal lines before and generally gotten away with it—hard to arrest the parties who nab the bad guy, wot?"

"Mother, no British accent tonight, or I'm jolly well out. Got it?"

"Got it," she said, taking no offense. "Do we have everything else, dear?"

"Flashlight," I said.

"Check."

"Rope."

"Check."

"Cell phone."

"Check."

Please.

I said, "I think that fills your list. But what do we need the rope for?"

"Who knows? Scaling a wall, perhaps. Tying up a miscreant, possibly."

"No one's supposed to be home! Let's leave the rope behind."

"No, it might come in handy. 'Be prepared,' we Girl Scouts say."

Boy Scouts, actually, but why quibble on a night where breaking and entering was on the docket?

"Of course, I may have missed something," Mother said. "Anything else you can think of that we might need?"

I shook my head, but was thinking a flask of whiskey would be nice.

My cell I slipped into one hoodie pocket, the small megalight in the other. The rope I concealed beneath the jacket, winding it around my waist like a makeshift belt in an old hillbilly movie. Mother carried her own cell and flashlight.

Meanwhile, Sushi was whining at my feet, doing a sad little samba.

I stooped to pet her. "No, honey, not this time. We'll be back soon."

I hoped.

To Rocky, I said, "Take care of my little girl, okay, boy?"

Last time Rocky had been the one impatient to tag along, practically knocking the closed door down behind us. But this time he took the news well, and my instructions, too. Nice to know I had such a good touch with dogs— Rocky seemed to understand exactly what I'd said, and was obedience personified, or anyway doggified.

Only when I opened the door, he dashed out like he'd spied a squirrel. I followed quickly, seeing him disappear around the side of the house, but when I got back there he was gone, swallowed by darkness.

"Damn!" I blurted. I called for him and called for him, but nothing. Then I whirled, upset. "What are we going to do?"

"Let him go, dear," Mother said. "He's a big boy and he'll find his way home. Anyway, we don't have time to go looking for him now. Maybe it's just a beauty call!"

I did not correct Mother's malapropism, but she had a point—on our walks, Rocky had shown definite interest in a neighborhood terrier, much to Sushi's jealous dismay.

"You're *positive* Samuel Wright won't be home?" I asked as we headed out to the car.

"Pos-i-*tute*-ly. We will have a good two hours. Sam always attends choir practices on Thursday nights, from seven to nine. As the deacon, he never misses a rehearsal because that would set a bad example."

"So does covering up and committing murders," I said.

"Apples and oranges, dear."

As we headed for the Buick in the driveway, Mother raised a warning finger. "Still, that doesn't mean we can afford to dawdle."

"Right. I was planning to sit in the man's den and knock back a beer and maybe smoke a cigar."

"Well, don't."

Which was just her way of saying, *Not funny.*

I was behind the wheel when I asked, "What's the game plan?"

Mother's brow furrowed, as if my question had been in a foreign tongue. "Game plan? Why, none in particular, dear. We'll improvise."

The keys were in my hand, not yet in the ignition. "That's not what I want to hear. I want to know you have a plan, a goal."

"My goal is to wing it. Start 'er up and let's roll!"

Here is an example of Mother "winging it": burning down the hundred-year-old grandstand at the Serenity County Fairground. Granted, it did attract the attention of the police and enabled the capture of a killer; yet for some reason, to this day, a number of people in town remain upset about a local landmark going up in smoke.

As we rode through an unsuspecting Serenity, Mother said, "We are looking for evidence— that much of a game plan I can give you."

"Any evidence in particular?"

"Bloody clothes. While there would be no spray with a d.b., a dismemberment would still certainly be an untidy task. 'D.b.' is dead body, dear."

We were going to break into the home of a murderer who had been capable of a grotesque and gruesome cover-up. *How had I let Mother talk me into this?* But she had, and more easily than I like to admit. I was caught up in it, just like her.

But most of all, my friend Joe was sitting in a

jail cell right now, looking like a much better suspect today than he had yesterday. We simply had to clear him.

I parked the Buick on the street near the mouth of the alley that ran behind Samuel Wright's house. We got out, Mother taking the lead as we walked briskly up the single-lane asphalt incline, coming to a stop behind the easily recognizable back of Wright's Gothic Revival home, silhouetted like a massive crouching beast against the ever-darkening night sky. The moon, peeking over a tall gable, seemed to give us a wink, a sly one like on the old sheet music covers—it apparently knew what we were planning and maybe even approved.

Why was I not reassured?

A stand-alone garage with steeply pitched roof and iron cresting—the original carriage house?—sat just off the alley. Mother tiptoed over (yes, tiptoed) to a narrow arched window, and peered inside.

"Good," she whispered. "His car is gone."

"You said you were absolutely positive he wouldn't be here," I whispered back.

"I did. And I was right. Now, you just get with the program, missy! I won't have you tying tin cans to my little red wagon."

Was that an old saying, or just her being a nut?

I was standing beside a plastic garbage can with WRIGHT printed on the side, when she came over, grabbed the can's lid, and yanked it off.

"Good," she said, the third eye of the clamped-on microcamera next to her magnified God-given eyes making her look like something out of an *Alien* movie. "Here's our first break!"

"Oh?"

"The trash hasn't been picked up yet this week. Dump it out, dear."

"Why?" I didn't want to go through my own garbage, let alone somebody else's.

Mother stared at me as if a box of candy was missing and I had chocolate smeared all over my mug. "The bloody clothes could be in there."

"Come on, if finding bloody clothes is your best shot, we should go back to the car right now, while we still have the chance."

She glared at me with all three eyes. "Go through that garbage, Brandy. *Right now.*"

"Don't you think they would have been disposed of already? Like thrown off the high bridge?"

Mother shook her head. "Sam couldn't risk being seen doing anything out of the ordinary, and tossing something into the river certainly is."

I gaped at her. "But putting blood-soaked clothes in the garbage *isn't* out of the ordinary?"

"Dear, you could have done it by now."

I sighed, took hold of the can, then tipped it upside down, causing a cacophony of clanking glass bottles and rattling tin cans and other refuse, that echoed in the alley.

"Be quiet!" Mother yelled.

I shushed her with a finger to my lips, then whispered, "You *told* me to dump it out."

Turning on her flashlight, she slowly scanned the mess with its beam, a searchlight looking for an escaped prisoner.

"Good Lord!" Mother said. "Do you see what I see?"

"What?"

Had she been right about the bloody clothes?

"The man doesn't *recycle!*"

"Criminal," I said, the word dripping with sarcasm.

"Well, it *should* be," Mother huffed. "We have to protect Planet Earth, you know. Global warming is no joke."

"Neither is us getting caught," I reminded her, pointing to my wristwatch. "What now?"

"Put the garbage back in the can, of course."

I laughed, once. "Like I'm *touching* that junk! Not even with gloves on."

"Very well." She shrugged. "Sam will blame a racoon for it."

"Or a skunk," I said.

"Is that a dig, dear?"

"No comment."

A six-foot wood fence separated the house from the alley and garage, and we walked over to it.

Locked.

"Afraid you'll have to scale it, dear," Mother said. "And open it from the other side."

I gave her a hard stare.

She gave me one back. "Surely you don't expect *moi* to climb this Everest? With my artificial hips?"

"Oh, *fine*."

I grabbed the top of the fence door, and pulled myself up, then with some difficulty (you try it) straddled it, and was about to lower myself over, when Mother said, "Oh. What do you know? There's a little latch to pull!"

And before I could say, "Don't do it," she did it.

The door flew open with my weight, flinging me windmilling to the ground, where I lay sprawled on my back, stunned, like I was making a snow angel, only sans snow.

"Well, I didn't expect *that* to happen," Mother said, her face looming over mine, eyes wide. "Are you all right, dear? That was quite a fall."

I reached out and up with both hands as if to strangle her—well, *maybe* "as if"—and she grabbed one of my hands, pulling me to my feet.

Dusting myself off, I said, "So far, I am *not* having a good time."

"We're not here to have a good time, dear. We're here to find vital evidence that will convict a killer."

"Could we try to do it without breaking my neck?"

"We can certainly give it a go," she said, chipper. "Now come along, we're losing valuable time."

Leaving the gate ajar ("for easy egress"), she led me up a cracked sidewalk to a small open porch under a flat roof supported by two stone columns topped by openmouthed gargoyles, neither of whom seemed to be saying, "Welcome." Mother had picked for us, for our first major breaking-and-entering caper, probably the creepiest house in town.

Mother tried the door onto the porch and reported, "Locked," then sighed.

"If that's an unexpected setback, maybe we better abort."

Ignoring that, Mother muttered, "There must be a key around here somewhere."

But hunt as we might, a spare key couldn't be found, not above the door, or under the mat, nor hidden in a nearby flowerpot. I even stood on a porch chair and looked in the gargoyles' mouths, managing to avoid the temptation to add, "Say 'ah.' "

Finally, Mother said, "I'm afraid a window may simply have to be broken."

Meaning *I* would have to break a window.

As uninviting as that prospect might be, I was eager to expedite things and get back home.

"Stand back," I told her.

I looked in the nearest window, flashed a light in, saw a mudroom and nothing blocking our path. With the butt of my flashlight on the bottom pane of a window, I gave the glass a quick, hard *WHAP!*

Which was followed by a sharp crack and then the brittle rain of tinkling glass as it fell to the floor within.

A few shards clung stubbornly to the window frame, and these I carefully extracted, like little sharp teeth, with a gloved hand. I tossed the chunks inside, as if keeping the porch tidy and safe for little gargoyles was a priority.

I was about to turn to Mother for her approval, when the back door opened.

My heart leapt in my chest. *Caught already!*

Mother leaned out, like a friendly neighbor woman offering milk and cookies. "Discovered an unlocked window on the side of the house," she beamed, pleased as punch with herself. "So you needn't have broken that window."

My fingers curled into fists. "A little late *now,* isn't it? Besides, you told me to do it!"

"I did not."

"Did, too."

"Did not. I believe my exact words were '. . . a window *may* simply have to be broken.' "

For the sake of propriety and Walmart, I will not report *my* exact words in response.

Closing the door behind us, we sent our flashlight beams around the mudroom, taking in the scarred wood floor, long wooden bench, narrow pine wall paneling, and multiple coat hooks.

A door leading to the kitchen was unlocked, and we stepped into the large room, flashlight beams flitting like oversize fireflies, illuminating a stone floor, pine cabinets, and ceiling fixtures, all appearing to be original—or early last century, anyway. But the appliances—fridge, stove, dishwasher—were modern enough.

In the room's midst was a dark-wood rectangular table, a bowl of red apples in the center, and six high-backed, ornate, churchlike chairs. To the left, a walk-in pantry door yawned open, revealing more cabinets, drawers, and well-stocked shelves.

I whispered, "What are my instructions, again?"

Mother whispered back: "Look anywhere and everywhere the damning clothes could be hidden."

"Like in here?" I asked, and opened a narrow, floor-to-ceiling door.

And an old ironing board fell down, hitting me on the top of my head.

"Probably not there," Mother said.

"Remind me to kill you later," I said, rubbing my sore skull.

"I should never have allowed you to watch the Three Stooges after school," Mother said disappointedly. Then: "We can cover more ground if we split up."

"That's when all the trouble starts in the horror movies," I said. "We should stick together."

"This is not a horror movie," Mother said, and of course, she was right—it was *The Three Stooges Meet Laurel and Hardy*, and I was the brunt of all the gags.

"We have limited time," she said. "Remember—choir practice!" She had sung the last two words, off-key.

Was I in a dream? A delirious dream?

She went on: "I'll search the first floor and you take the second. Don't turn on any light that isn't already on, and stay away from the windows."

"Right."

She consulted her watch. "Let's meet back here at eight. We'll search the basement together."

That was good, because I wasn't going down there by myself. Even if we weren't in a horror movie, we were certainly in a horror-movie house.

"And stay alert," she said. "You might run across something else significant besides bloody clothing."

"Like what?"

"How about the missing Butterworth ax?"

"Well, the police have the ax."

"They have the *Amazing Grace* ax, dear, the murder weapon. But the *Butterworth* family ax, assumed to be the murder weapon at the time, is *also* missing. Doesn't that stand to reason? Perhaps Sam Wright carried it away as part of the original cover-up."

What a bunch of twaddle.

"Right," I said. "It'll probably be displayed someplace upstairs. Maybe in a glass case, or on a nightstand."

"Sarcasm does not become a young woman," Mother reminded me.

Leaving the kitchen, we entered the dining room, our flashlights revealing another table—this one larger than the one in the kitchen, with chairs that were even more ornate, a thronelike one at the table's head—as well as a buffet with carved-leaf theme, the back cupboard topped with spindly spires. Heavy brocade drapes covered the room's three long, narrow windows.

Despite the castlelike grandeur of the home's exterior, the interior rooms (but for the kitchen) were proving to be rather small, exacerbated, of course, by the massive gothic furniture, creating a claustrophobic feeling that even the high ceilings couldn't relieve.

We moved down a dark hallway to the living room, which was illuminated by a lamp in the front window—a boon for Mother, as it would both assist her search and prevent anyone on the outside from seeing in.

The living room, too, was oppressively overstuffed with gothic furniture, but among the antiquities was a comfy brown leather couch and matching recliner, as if Samuel Wright had declared, "Enough is enough."

We had paused at the archway of the living room, next to a curved, thick-banistered staircase that led up into darkness.

"Mother," I said, "be sure to put everything back *exactly* the way you found it."

She shot me an acerbic glance. "Dear, if anyone knows how to snoop properly it's Vivian Borne."

On the wall behind her, just over one shoulder, a framed Sunday school–type print of Jesus seemed equally put out by my lack of faith.

We parted company, she going into the living room, me heading up the stairs, my flashlight carving a path through the darkness. All I could think of was that scene in *Psycho* where the detective goes up the stairs and . . . *Come on, Brandy, that was only a movie, only a movie. . . .*

The second floor had five rooms (and no mommy mummies), four bedrooms, and a bath sharing a wide central hall. The first room I entered had more modern furniture, the bed carefully made, a set of towels on the dresser-top, and a little wooden suitcase rack, telling me this room was used by guests. So I didn't spend much time there.

The second room I tried, also furnished in a more up-to-date fashion, was Samuel Wright's bedroom, as indicated by the unmade bed and confirmed by numerous prescription bottles on a nightstand. Further proof came by way of a closet of men's clothes—none of which were bloody.

The third room, the bathroom, I checked, looking under the sink and in the bathtub (in case bloody clothes were being washed there). Nada. Nothing bloodily incriminating in a closet hamper, either.

The fourth room, a bedless bedroom used for storage, offered some possibilities for hidden evidence, and I poked around opening boxes for a while, finding nothing of apparent import. Box after box contained business-related church documents, with cartons of Amazing Grace memorabilia and photographs, heavy on the father's era.

The fifth room immediately piqued my interest; much larger than Wright's own, this apparently had originally been the master bedroom, graced with the most impressive gothic furnishings yet: massive four-poster bed with exquisitely carved headboard depicting cherubs and roses; a huge armoire (with similar motif); two marble-topped bedside tables; and several dressers (one, a lady's, with large mirror).

Since the windows were shuttered, not curtained, I risked turning on a ceiling light.

And immediately something became apparent, something that gave me a chill: this had been the elder Wright's bedroom, where nothing appeared to have been disturbed since his death, rarely if ever cleaned in the decades since. A layer of dust covered everything.

It would be hard not to leave indications of disturbing things here.

I crossed to the grand armoire. Inside hung an array of men's suits—a larger size than the ones I'd seen in Samuel's closet—as were the shoes neatly arranged on a bottom shelf. Narrow ties on a rack dated these clothes to the 1980s, about the time Gabriel Wright departed this world for another.

But there was more in the closet: women's clothing. Fashions from the fifties, but not the dowdy matronly dresses Mamie Eisenhower wore. No. These were colorful, gay in the former sense of the word—an array of flirtatious, formfitting frocks.

How odd. *Why would Gabriel Wright keep the clothes of a wife who had been faithless?* These seemed to date to about the time Mrs. Wright had run off and abandoned her pastor husband. Funny that she left them behind . . . and that he had kept them.

Or was it Samuel who couldn't bear to get rid of his mother's things?

This was starting to feel like *Psycho* again. . . .

I took a lingering look at the room, at the wedding photo of Gabriel and Elsie Wright on the nightstand, the cupidlike cherubs looming above the bed, the pearl-handled hairbrush set carefully arranged on the dressing table, along with an assortment of perfume bottles.

This space was one big valentine to Elsie Wright, who had been a very attractive woman, based on the wedding photo anyway.

But who had sent her this valentine? Gabriel or Samuel?

I checked my watch. *Yikes!* Eight-fifteen.

Turning off the light, I scurried out of there.

Mother was at the bottom of the staircase, where I joined her.

"Look what I found in the family Bible," she said excitedly, waving a piece of notepaper, its edges yellow with age. "Tucked away in a writing desk—listen to this. . . ."

She began to read: " 'Samuel, I haven't always been the best of fathers, but I want you to know how much I have loved you, even if I have rarely said so. I am depending on you, son, to carry on and protect the many years of good works I've accomplished with the Church. Keep faith. Leviticus 20:10. Dad.' "

I shrugged. "What's so special about that?"

"Dear, if you had paid attention in Sunday school, you'd know. This is a virtual murder confession."

"Well, we can talk theology later." I tapped my watch. "We have *got* to wrap this up and get out of here before choir practice is over."

"Quite right, dear." She stuffed the letter in a pocket. "To the basement!"

"Lead the way."

She did so, back through the dining room to

the kitchen, then into the pantry to an open door, steep stone steps going downward.

We were back in horror-movie country—you just don't go in the basement in those kind of movies, not unless you want to run into an evil leprechaun or a guy in a hockey mask or something. Dark and dank down there, like a dungeon. I wouldn't have been surprised to find shackles waiting on the wall or even a torture rack. As we descended, flashlights showing the way, the floor revealed itself to be cement, at least.

Mother pulled the string on a ceiling light— the bare bulb helped greatly, exposing a washer and dryer, a card table with detergent and a plastic laundry basket, a furnace, some old buckets, mops, wooden boxes, ceramic pots, paint cans, and an old workbench with a variety of tools, some on adjacent pegboard.

While Mother poked around the workbench, I tackled the furnace, opening the front, checking inside. Nothing.

"What's this thing?" I asked Mother.

She joined me, and I pointed to a metal panel in the stone wall behind the furnace.

"That's where they used to store the coal," Mother explained. "That would be an *excellent* place to hide an ax."

I pulled down a metal handle, opened the door, and something flew out, going like a bat out of hell!

And there was a reason for that.

"Just a bat, dear," Mother said lightly. "Not to worry."

"Not to worry!" I said in a reflexive crouch. "May I remind you they carry rabies?"

"Not all of them."

"How do you know that one doesn't?"

"Dear, dear, please. We can discuss bats all you like, later, perhaps over mugs of cocoa with marshmallows. Doesn't *that* sound delightful! In the meantime, tick tick tick!"

I noticed something else. "What's that contraption?"

I was referring to a rust-pocked metal unit the size of a tall kitchen garbage can next to the furnace.

"That, my dear, is an incinerator. In the good old days there was no such thing as garbage pickup." She examined it closer. "Hmmm . . . looks like it's still hooked up to the gas line."

"Which means it's still being used."

We looked at each other.

Then I shook my head. "If the clothes were burned in there, they'd be ashes."

Mother smiled. "Forensics can tell quite a bit from ashes—even extract DNA . . . Find a plastic sack, dear."

I hunted around, then came back. "Will paper do?"

"Nicely," she said, taking the bag that had formerly been filled with nails (I'd dumped out on the workbench).

Knees popping, Mother bent, then pulled out a bottom drawer of the incinerator, which was used to collect the ashes.

I leaned over and held the paper sack open, as she emptied the contents inside, ash dust billowing up, tickling my nose, nearly making me sneeze. Charred DNA will do that.

Winding the bag shut, I held its neck tightly with one hand, using my other to help Mother to her feet.

"Now, dear, I have another interesting discovery to share. And I will do my best not to say, I told you so."

"Okay. Show me."

She walked me over to the workbench, from under which she had pulled out a big wooden crate—some long-ago machinery had probably been shipped in it. With a glance, I could see it was filled with old tools, hammers, several saws, screwdrivers, what have you.

"People never throw away their old tools, dear," Mother said. "Take a closer look."

There, propped alongside one edge of the box, was a very old ax.

"It's not necessarily the Butterworth ax," I said. But I could only be impressed with her sleuthing.

"Oh, I beg to differ. Take a look at the butt of the handle."

As with the murder ax, this one had initials wood-burned in. Oddly, they were the *same* initials: AGB.

"This is just another Baptist church ax," I said.

"Take a closer look, dear. What do you notice about that wood-burned 'G'?"

"Hey . . . you're right. It's squared-off, and the 'A' and 'B' *aren't*. And part of the 'G' has thicker lettering, like it's from another tool. As if someone doctored it."

"Someone did," Mother said. "That 'G' started out life as an 'L.' "

My wide eyes met hers, all three of them. "*Louis,*" I said. "Archibald's middle name. And Andrew's. This *is* the Butterworth family ax . . . Should we take it?"

"No. I hate to say so, but it's time to go find that boyfriend of yours and report our suspicions and tell him what we've seen. We have to act fast, because it's just possible we'll have left a few signs of our break-in for Samuel to pick up on."

Like the window busted out in the mudroom, maybe?

"You're right," I said. "Let's get the H out."

We had paused in the middle of the basement, Mother about to pull the string on the ceiling light, when we saw the man's feet poised on a step near the top.

Too late to hide, we froze, as the legs that belonged to the well-shined shoes revealed themselves.

"Well, well," Samuel Wright said coldly, coming into full view.

He was one of those skinny older men with a little pot belly, with thinning hair and stooped shoulders, in a preacherlike dark suit and tie.

"I *thought* I heard rats rustling around down here," he said. "I tend to take rather extreme measures with vermin."

Just a skinny old man . . . with a gun. A revolver in a fist that had more than its share of age spots, but wasn't old-man shaky at all.

Mother blurted accusingly, "*You're* not supposed to be back yet!" As if she thought he should explain his presence in his own home.

So he did: "Choir practice got out early, Vivian. I'm so glad it did. Now I can entertain my guests."

He was almost at the bottom, him and his gun.

In a rush of words, I said, "We don't have any right to be here, but I have a friend in jail, so we got a little desperate and came looking for evidence. But we didn't find a thing. I wouldn't blame you for turning us in to the police."

"Skip it," he said, at the foot of the steps now. "I didn't just get home. I've been listening from up there." He jerked his head toward the door above. "Now, empty your pockets—everything on the floor. Carefully."

We set down both our cell phones and flashlights; the paper bag I held onto, at my side.

Wright was studying Mother. "What's that by your ear?"

"What, dear? You'll have to speak up . . . I have a new hearing aid, and it doesn't seem to be working so well." She tapped the camera with a finger and continued conversationally, as if his gun were a party favor he was about to hand her. "Darn thing is expensive, too."

His eyes narrowed. "You weren't wearing it the other day. Didn't seem to need any damn hearing aid."

"You would be surprised how well I've learned to read lips, dear."

This bit of nonsense apparently passed muster,

because Wright—if I was reading him correctly—seemed to have moved on from harboring any suspicions to the next pertinent topic: deciding what to do with us.

And—if I *was* reading him correctly—he had come to a decision that wouldn't be mutually beneficial.

Mother was saying, "Sam, if you killed Bruce Spring, it had to have been self-defense. He attacked you and you defended yourself, simple as that." Then she added with a shrug, "I grant you it's difficult to strangle someone in self-defense, and of course, it doesn't account for why you chopped him up."

Mother just never knew when to quit.

Wright said dispassionately, "I'm glad you brought up that brutal murder, Vivian. It's gotten people awfully skittish in this neighborhood." He moved forward to kick our cells and flashlights off to one side.

"I came home tonight," he went on clinically, his gun trained on Mother, then me, "only to find the gate open, a broken window in back, and two intruders in the basement, dressed in black. Who could blame me for defending my hearth and home?"

Mother stepped in front of me.

Then I stepped in front of her.

Which brought me closer to Wright. Close enough, I thought, to throw the sack of ashes in his face . . . a waste of good evidence, maybe, but a necessary sacrifice. . . .

Before I had the chance, a blur of white hit Wright from the behind, knocking him down.

Then Rocky's powerful jaws clamped down on the man's forearm, a savage snarling echoing off the cement, Wright howling in pain as the gun tumbled from his hand.

"Good *boy*, Rocky!" I said, retrieving the weapon.

Rocky *hadn't* run off—he'd hidden, then followed us! The devil. The angel.

"Steak for you tonight!" Mother said, retrieving the gun. "Eat your heart out, Rin Tin Tin!"

I let the snarling Rocky enjoy a taste of Wright for a while—well, he *was* going to shoot us!—but with the frightened, hurting deacon hollering again and again, "Get him off," I finally ordered the dog to stop.

Then I used the rope around my waist to tie the man up.

Mother had been right—it did come in handy.

I called the police and they quickly came. Brian himself was in the lead, backed up by Munson and that new cop, Horton. Mother had already told Wright that we had everything on HD ("Captures video even in low light!"), so our reluctant host didn't bother trying to explain why a couple of burglars had tied him up and called the cops on themselves.

We turned over the ashes to Brian, and showed him the ax, and he said to us, "You girls are pretty proud of yourselves, aren't you?"

"Oh, yes!" Mother said, but there was something about the way he said it that I didn't like.

Rocky was behind the furnace, pawing at the floor, barking, making a real racket.

Brian went back there and I followed him. While we did this, Wright was trading in his ropes for a pair of handcuffs courtesy of Munson.

Rocky looked up at us, whining terribly.

"What's his problem?" Brian asked.

I remembered the women's clothing upstairs, dating to about the time Sam Wright's mother disappeared.

Brian was kneeling. "Some of this cement seems newer than the rest. I don't think this section is original to the house."

From where he stood, getting his hands cuffed behind him by Munson, Samuel Wright seemed suddenly interested.

"I think," I said, "Rocky may have just found Mrs. Gabriel Wright."

"*No!*" Wright said. "No! He wouldn't do that! He didn't do that! She left town! Papa said she left town! Papa said . . ."

Brian said to me, "What's that about?"

But it was Mother who answered him: "I think Sam just figured out his father killed his mother. Has to come as a shock."

And Wright had dropped to his knees, head hung, weeping, in a prayerful posture, only I didn't think he was praying.

Mother said, "Elsie Wright had been having an affair with Archibald Butterworth, and they both had to die for it—according to the Bible, anyway."

Brian said, "What are you *talking* about, Vivian?"

"Leviticus twenty-ten," she said. " 'The adulterer and the adulteress shall *both* be put to death.' "

The sobbing deacon had obviously not fully understood the significance of that passage himself, until just now.

A Trash 'n' Treasures Tip

If you rent out space to other dealers, they should understand that what they display (and how their booth looks) reflects on you—don't let junk or mess define your store. Where did I get this advice? From anyone who has ever rented space to Mother and me.

Chapter Twelve

Chopping Block

I'm having to finish this last chapter in long-hand, on my cot, because the "screws" (as Mother calls the guards—more UK speak) won't allow me to have a laptop in jail.

Mother's cell is next to mine. That's one small blessing, that we aren't sharing space—surely any court in the land would consider putting me in with Mother cruel and unusual punishment. (Just the same, a simple foot of concrete is not enough to protect me from her snoring.)

Brian, true to his word, carried out his threat of "throwing the book at us," and, backed by Judge Jones (whose patience had been exhausted by Mother over the course of several arraignments) charged us with breaking and entering, for which we were remanded to the county jail for thirty days.

Mr. Ekhardt, representing us as usual, argued that we should be given a medal, not jail time, for solving three murders: Archibald Butterworth slain by a jealous Gabriel Wright for having an affair with his wife, Elsie; Elsie Wright slain by Gabriel over her unfaithfulness; and Bruce Spring by Samuel Wright, to protect the legacy of Samuel's father's church, not to mention that church's moneymaking capacities.

Samuel claims not to know that his mother was buried in the basement (the body had been recovered, with much difficulty) and, having seen his reaction to Rocky's discovery, I tend to believe him. Still, if he did know, that might help explain why Samuel Wright refused to leave the ancestral home, even at the cost of his marriage.

A few other details have come to light. According to Mother's new snitch, Heather, the DCI in Des Moines was able to extract from the incinerator ashes evidence of the bloody clothes; and while it would take several weeks for a DNA match on Spring to come through, the outcome seemed a foregone conclusion. The recovery of the missing

Butterworth ax, stored beneath the workbench, would go a long way toward clearing up that first, long-ago murder and the suspicions whose shadow had for decades been cast upon Andrew.

As for Andrew, he and Sarah have consented to allow us to use the old murder house for an antiques shop, whether the _Antiques Sleuths_ show ever happens or not. Sarah, who has decided to move back to Serenity and live with her brother, expressed her gratitude for restoring the Butterworth name by looking after our house while we are "in stir," as Mother likes to put it. Me, I prefer "in the slam."

Tina, my BFF, and her husband, Kevin, have taken Sushi and Rocky into their home, even though they have their hands full with baby Brandy. Sushi adores Tina, who has an especially good touch at administering the doggie's insulin shots. Meanwhile, Kevin and Rocky are caught up in a major bromance.

And you know what? It's not so bad in here, not anything like the British series _Bad Girls_ (a guilty pleasure for both Mother and me). The cells are new and clean, and I'm getting plenty of rest; but the food is fattening and bland, and the orange outfits we wear are as scratchy as they are baggy.

Other than that I can't complain.

On our first day in, Mother was welcomed back with open arms by the female inmates, many of whom she knew from a recent solo stay (Antiques Knock-off).

You longtime readers may recall Mother's jailhouse repertory company that performed for other prisons. Well, the two women who escaped during a production at the Ft. Dodge pen are back, and once again there is talk (spearheaded by Mother, natch) of reviving the theater program, though Sheriff Rudder so far isn't terribly supportive.

Mother is working on a letter to Mel Brooks with an idea for building an all-jailbird musical around his song "Prisoners of Love" from his great movie, The Producers. She has taught the catchy ditty to her "posse" and their surprisingly in-tune harmonies echo off the walls during evening free time.

When lock-up is over, I head out into the common room to hang with "the girls." Mother originally introduced them to me by their court charges: "This is Aggravated Assault, dear, and this is my sista from anotha mutha, Embezzlement, and shake hands with Grand Larceny...."

And so forth. She was afraid that her own

charge of Breaking and Entering (quite a come-down from her previous stay as Felony Murder) would diminish her big-house stature. But she was instantly embraced by her old pack and appointed Top Dog of the block, once again. (I'm happy to be Bottom Dog, and have no aspirations to climb the jail hierarchy.)

In the outer room, Mother often holds court at one of the plastic, bolted-down picnic-style tables with some of the others: Sarah, midtwenties, tall, shapely, with shoulder-length red hair and green eyes; Angela, thirties, dark-complected, short curly black hair; Carol, early forties, husky, crew-cut; and Jennifer, young, rail-thin, blond. (Carol and Jennifer, an item, were the aforementioned escapees.)

Mother was saying, "After Sam's trial, the footage that I shot will be returned, and my shooter Phil Dean and I are going to use it for the _Antiques Sleuths_ pilot . . . No, Angela, not _that_ kind of shooter. . . ."

La Diva Borne still holds out great hopes for our TV show, but I figure her footage is probably more likely to turn up on _America's Funniest Home Videos_.

Jennifer said, "Girlfriend, if that pilot sells, I'll have somethin to brag about! We _all_ will—we'll have served time with a couple of real-life reality TV stars!"

I wasn't so sure that was all *that* special, since a lot of reality TV show stars have done jail time; but I didn't burst anybody's bubble. Bottom Dog keeps a low profile.

I was just sitting watching Mother hold court when guard Patty approached. Patty's on the up-hill slope of forty, with dull, short, blond hair and an apparent hatred for her job.

"You have a phone call," she sighed, the inconvenience of carrying this message such a terrible burden for her.

We are allowed three such calls per week. I had already heard from Jake and Roger—the former thought my incarceration "very funny and kinda cool," while the latter displayed a different "kinda cool" that indicated any thoughts he might have had about getting back together had, well, cooled. As for Tina, she always came in person (bringing Sushi), so I couldn't imagine who the call could be from.

I walked over to the alcove and picked up the receiver on the wall phone, then waited while Patty returned to her station to patch me through.

"Hello?"

"Brandy?"

"Yes."

"It's . . . it's Tony."

<u>Tony Cassato!</u> Ex-boyfriend, ex-Serenity police chief, current Witness Protection Program enrollee. I nearly dropped the receiver. How had I not recognized his voice?

"Tony, thank God," I blurted. "Where are you?"

A pause. Then: "You know I can't tell you that."

"Oh . . . yeah. Well, of course. Duh. But how did you know I was here?"

"Can't tell you that either."

Probably from someone in WITSEC, or maybe Brian.

"You always did know how to sweet-talk a girl."

I loved his laugh.

I asked, "What <u>can</u> you tell me?"

"Just that I'm grateful to you for taking care of Rocky. I hope he's getting along with Sushi."

"He is. Did you know that his police training saved my life? Mother's, too."

"I heard. How is Vivian? I almost miss her."

"Never better. Lording it up 'in stir' as 'top dog'. . ."

That earned me some more musical, baritone laughter.

Then silence.

"Tony?"

"Yes, Brandy?"

"How are you doing? Really?"

"All right, considering."

"I miss you." It just came out.

"I miss you, too."

"I mean . . . well, you _know_ what I mean."

"Me too, you." Then: "Brandy? Do me a favor?"

"Name it."

"Try not to be a repeat offender, okay?"

"See what I can do."

"Really. Stay out of trouble."

"I'll try."

He said good-bye and I said good-bye and that was all. But I was floating. You know that expression, short but sweet? That was that phone call. That was exactly that phone call.

I returned to the common area, taking a seat next to Mother, who interrupted her performance to ask me why I looked like the cat that ate the canary.

"Oh, I just heard from an old friend."

"That's nice, dear," she said, absently, then

she went on regaling her jailhouse audience with the details of our recent case, building to the exciting part where she took the old ax from under the workbench and charged the revolver-wielding killer.

I stopped listening, but I kept on smiling.

A Trash 'n' Treasures Tip

It's important that your store offer discounts, not just to other dealers, but to customers who spend a certain amount. Everyone likes a bargain. Mother once bought one hundred antique potato mashers for a dollar a piece. She sold two at fifty dollars each and recouped her investment. Uh . . . anybody interested in picking up ninety-eight antique potato mashers?

Ready for more murder and mayhem?
Turn the page to enjoy a preview of the next
Trash 'n' Treasures mystery, *Antiques Con* . . .
Coming from Kensington in May 2014.

Chapter Two

Con Fusion

No, your eyes are not deceiving you, nor has the publisher made a printing error by beginning this book with chapter two. Rather, chapter one has been omitted, having been deemed by our esteemed editor as inconsequential to the murder mystery about to unfold.

But Mother and I beg to differ!

Mother being Vivian Borne, seventies, bipolar, widowed, Danish stock, local thespian, and amateur sleuth; and me, Brandy Borne, thirty-two, Prozac popping, divorced, and frequent reluctant accomplice in Mother's escapades since coming home to live with her in the small Mississippi River town of Serenity, Iowa, bringing along only a few clothes and my little blind shih tzu, Sushi.

The following is our defense for writing chapter one, however bereft of mystery content it might be.

Several loyal readers have written to inquire as to whether we have as yet found poor Aunt Olive. Olive—actually my great-aunt—wasn't "missing" in the face-on-a-milk-carton manner, since she was, after all, deceased, her ashes encased in a glass paperweight and entrusted to Mother for safekeeping. Unfortunately, during a well-meaning flurry of downsizing our antiques-cluttered home, Olive had gotten herself mixed in with a collection of paperweights and erroneously sold at a garage sale to Fanny Watterson, a third-grade teacher visiting Serenity from Akron, Ohio.

But, as Mother would say, I digress.

Thanks to the prodding of our readers, we— that is, Mother, Sushi, and I—set out by car on an eastern trek to the Buckeye State to retrieve her/it. But, in Akron, we discovered that the third-grade teacher who had purchased Auntie had done so with a paperweight-collecting friend in mind, to whom Olive had been mailed as a birthday present, in Scranton, Pennsylvania. Then, upon our arrival in Scranton, we were told by said friend (a fourth-grade teacher) that she had found the paperweight rather unattractive and possessed of "an odd vibe," so she'd regifted it to a sister (presumably not her favorite one) in Hackensack, New Jersey.

Now, just how Aunt Olive ended up in a torpedo hole of the USS *Ling* at the New Jersey Naval Museum in Hackensack is a fascinating, amusing, and remarkable set of circumstances, but—and here we must reluctantly bow to editorial wisdom—wholly inconsequential to the mystery at hand. (Chapter one *will* be available for your reading pleasure on our website, www.BarbaraAllan.com.)

Just the same, Mother and I would like to point out that if it hadn't been for the quest to recover Aunt Olive, she (Mother) and I would never have considered incorporating into our plans a trip to New York City, where we became innocently involved in yet another murder, giving us material for this, our eighth book.

So forget Akron and Scranton and Hackensack and, for that matter, Aunt Olive (meaning no offense to those cities nor our beloved late relative). Our story proper begins in Manhattan, in late March, where we were on our way to attend a comic book convention, to sell a rare Superman drawing by creators Siegel and Shuster that we had found in a storage locker won in auction last October. (We refer you to *Antiques Disposal*, available from your favorite bookseller.)

Still with us?

Specifically, we were traveling south by car on the Henry Hudson Parkway, having just crossed the George Washington Bridge, when the old burgundy Buick that had done amazingly well for us on our travels thus far began to shudder violently.

Luckily, I was able to ease the car over to an emergency lane before it shuddered its last shudder, dying with a long, mechanical death rattle, punctuated by a final *conk!* and one last steam-heat sigh.

After using my cell to summon help, I was informed by a dispassionate dispatcher (did my lack of a local accent brand me as an outsider?) that our situation was not worthy of a 9-1-1 call in the city, and not to bother her again.

No, Toto (that is, Sushi), we were not in Serenity anymore. Quiet Serenity, where a police car would have been dispatched to assist us toot-sweet. Sweet Serenity, where Mrs. Clyde Martin—monitoring a scanner in her kitchen— would begin preparing an apple pie to present us on our doorstep, in a few hours, as a consolation for our travails.

But no such assistance (and certainly no pie, apple or otherwise) had been dispatched to aid us here on the HHP, where cars cruelly whizzed by two helpless women and a blind dog next to an obviously broken-down car in the late afternoon March wind.

Mother was still quite attractive at her undisclosed age—porcelain complexion, straight nose, wide mouth, large eyes admittedly magnified by her glasses, wavy silver hair pulled loosely back. And I was no slouch—button nose, blue eyes, and shoulder-length blond hair. Plus, Sushi was cute as all heck. Yet our collective predicament failed to soften the hard-hearted New Yorkers, who continued to stir the wind as they passed, ignoring us as if that were a requirement of Big Apple citizenship.

Now might be a good time to mention that Mother was handcuffed. To a black briefcase, that is, which held our valuable Superman drawing. My insistence that the artwork would be safe in a suitcase did nothing to sway her; once Mother got an idea in her head, that was that, even after I pointed out that she would be attracting undue attention to herself (as if that would dissuade Serenity's most notorious diva).

Still, I had smirked. "Why don't you carry a big sign that says, 'Hey world! Here's something so valuable that I'm willing to lose an arm over it'?"

Her frown was almost a scowl. "Dear, I hope you're not going to be a Debbie Downer."

And I had replied, "I hope *you're* not going to be a Nutty Nancy."

Then she said something, to which I responded in kind, none of which can be reported here, if we are ever to have any hope of Walmart stocking our books.

Let's just say it had been a long cross-country trip.

One more thing about the handcuff-briefcase: Mother didn't want to spend the bucks ordering one from her spy catalogue, so she had borrowed a beat-up case from a neighbor, then stole (or as she puts it, "borrowed") cuffs from the police department, where she had recently dropped by ostensibly to give a neighborhood watch report.

Anyway, as soon as we'd crossed the George Washington Bridge, she'd hooked herself up to the briefcase.

And now she and I and the briefcase and our

blind dog stood next to our dead car in an emergency lane, where I began to suspect we would spend the rest of our lives.

Mother, pulling her coat collar up around her neck with her spare, uncuffed hand to combat the icy river wind, sighed, "I'm afraid getting someone to stop won't be easy, dear. If you weren't wearing sweatpants, I'd suggest you lift your skirt in time-honored Claudette Colbert fashion."

"What?"

"*It Happened One Night,* dear!"

"You don't want to know what'll happen to us if we are still *here* at night."

Then I had an idea. It could happen.

I positioned Sushi on the car's hood.

"Dance!" I commanded the cute little fur ball.

At first she just looked at me, in the way you're just looking at this page right now.

But then I began singing "Shake Your Booty," and the dear got up on her hind legs and hopped around, wagging her furry ears, flopping her front paws rhythmically, and twitching her doggie booty.

I hadn't gotten to the song's bridge by the time a tan Subaru suddenly veered off the highway, pulling in front of us, then backed up to the Buick.

I gave Mother a self-satisfied smirk. "Who needs Claudette Colbert?"

Grabbing Sushi, I rushed over to the driver's side of the vehicle, just as the woman behind the wheel powered down her window.

"Oh, thank you so much for stopping," I said.

"Car trouble?" the lady asked.

She was middle-aged but nicely preserved, with chin-length honey-blond hair and striking, light brown eyes. She was wearing a red wool coat and black leather gloves. Next to her in the passenger seat was a large gray gym bag.

"Our car *is* the trouble," I said. "I'm afraid we need a junk dealer, not a tow truck."

She gave me a winning smile. "Been there, done that. But with an old Mustang." Then, "Where are you headed?"

"The Hotel Pennsylvania on Seventh Avenue."

She nodded. "Not too far from where I'm going. Hop in."

I thanked our Good Samaritan, then went back to the Buick to collect Mother and our luggage, giving its battered hood a final pat. We'd arrange at the hotel for a proper burial for our old friend.

We filled our savior's trunk with our belongings and settled into the Subaru—Mother in front, gym bag on her lap, the blond Samaritan giving the handcuffed briefcase a curious look; me in back holding Sushi. Then we were once again traveling south on the Hudson Parkway.

Mother introduced herself and me, ending with, "And the little dancing dog that caught your attention is Sushi."

"You should put that mutt on YouTube," the woman said, eyes on the traffic. "But it was your license plate that caught my eye."

Mother's head swivelled toward her. "Oh?

Are you another native of the great state of Iowa?"

"Des Moines, originally." She took her right gloved hand off the wheel, thrusting it toward Mother. "I'm sorry, I haven't introduced myself."

She said her first name.

Which prompted Mother to ask, "Do you use a *c* or a *k* in the middle?"

"Two *k*s, actually."

"And end with a *y* or an *i*?"

"An *i*."

I could see our new friend *Vikki*'s face in the visor mirror; she had a sideways smile going, in response to Mother's insistence on detail.

But the woman wouldn't be smiling if she knew Mother's purpose. Before ride's end, she would wheedle from Vikki her last name as well as her address, and the unsuspecting lady Lancelot who'd ridden to our rescue would find herself on Mother's ever-growing Christmas-letter list, receiving—year after year—a long and laborious Yuletide report ("Merry Christmas, my darlings!"), from which the only known escape was death, either the recipient's or Mother's—and Mother felt just fine.

Moved with no forwarding address? No problem. Mother will find you. Returned to sender? Out goes the letter again. Addressee deceased? Next time, it goes to "Family of," so maybe even the Grim Reaper couldn't get you off Mother's Christmas-letter list.

This would very likely be the last time Vikki with two *k*s and an *i* helped anyone ever again on the Henry Hudson Parkway (especially with Iowa license plates).

Mother was asking her, "What's your trade, dear?"

"I work backstage on *Wicked.* I'm a costume dresser."

I interjected, "Oh! That's the show we're hoping to see while we're in town. What theater is it playing in, again?"

Vikki looked at me in the mirror. "The Gershwin on West Fifty-first. That's where I'm going after I drop you off."

With trying-too-hard sincerity, Mother said, "My dear, your job sounds *simply* marvelous." Then, instead of inquiring how long Vikki had been with the play, or how many witches she had seen come and go during its long run, or even if she'd been a dresser on other Broadway shows, Mother shifted the subject to herself.

Just like a wicked witch would.

"Ah, how well I remember waiting for reviews at Sardi's," she expounded.

"Oh?" Vikki replied politely. "You've appeared on Broadway?"

"Oh, my, yes," Mother warbled, as if the woman should have known. "My stage name was my maiden name—Vivian Jensen. But you are so young, and that was so many years ago."

"What were you in?" Vikki asked, interested.

Mother waved a dismissive hand. "I'm sure you've never heard of it, dear. Way before your time."

She had dug herself in a hole.

"Try me," Vikki said.

Confronted with an actual Broadway professional, Mother hesitated, then finally said, "Well, it was just a little production, dear . . . not so much Broadway as off-Broadway."

"Where off-Broadway?"

"Off-*off* Broadway."

I'd never heard this story before, but my guess? If the play had been any farther off Broadway, it would have been performed in Hoboken.

Mother was saying, "This was in the late sixties, you see, when I was single and had come to Gotham to make my mark."

Maybe in answer to the Bat signal.

"And did you?" I asked, lending her a hand digging that hole. "Make your mark, I mean."

"*I* like to think so," Mother said regally. "As a matter of fact, *I* was the first actress to bare her breasts on a theatrical stage!"

"Oh," Vikki said. "Were you in *Hair?*"

"No, dear, this predated that production by some time."

"Ah. *Old Calcutta*, then?"

"No, this was before *Oh! Calcutta*, as well. Of course, nowadays I suppose they might call my landmark performance a 'wardrobe malfunction.' You see, the strapless bra I was wearing in a boudoir scene suddenly came unhooked and shot into the audience like a huge rubber band. But this unintentional piece of improvisational business went over so well, the director decided to incorporate it into the production." Mother sighed. "A week later, the police closed us

down." Then she added, chipper, "But nothing
was held against me!"

Vikki gave me a look of astonished amuse-
ment in the rearview mirror, and I smiled back,
raising my eyebrows in quick succession. *Welcome to my world.*

Mother was saying, "These days I'm the director of our community theater playhouse . . .
along with playing leads."

"She also founded a theater group in our
county jail," I offered mischievously.

"That is commendable," Vikki said, seeming
impressed. "You go to the jail and hold classes?"

"No, dear," Mother replied. "I was *in* jail—for
murder."

The car veered onto the shoulder, then Vikki
regained control.

"But the charges were dropped," I said.

The Hudson Parkway had changed to Joe
DiMaggio Highway, and then Twelfth Avenue.
Soon we were turning onto West Thirty-fourth
Street, the crosstown traffic—much to our blond
chauffeur's relief, I'm sure—relatively light, and
in another few minutes we veered onto Seventh
Avenue, where the stately Hotel Pennsylvania
loomed on the corner of Thirty-third Street.

Quicker than one can say "Good riddance to
bad rubbish," Vikki whipped her car into the
hotel's unloading zone and hopped out. Mother
and I disembarked, too, to speed things along,
and together we got the luggage to the curb.

Holding Sushi tightly, I said to the woman,
"Thank you again for helping us."

Mother took her by the hand and said, "My dear, after we take in your show, we would just *love* to visit you backstage."

Vikki smiled nervously and withdrew her hand. "Ah, well, I *am* rather busy back there. Can't promise anything."

I could see the backstage notice board now: *Vivian and Brandy Borne Not Admitted!*

Mother pressed forward, all big eyes and bigger teeth. "Perhaps we could call you and arrange for tickets to be held at the box office. Let me get my cell phone out and add your number. . . ."

But our rescuer was already leaving. "It's been very interesting," she said. "I don't imagine we'll be running into each other again, so I'll just say so long. . . ."

"Don't be so sure," I said with a smile. "It's a *wicked* old world, you know. Always another witch waiting in the wings."

She looked a little startled, then hurried back to her Subaru, relieved to unburden herself of her charges. In another moment, she pulled skillfully out into busy traffic, courtesy of Penn Station and Madison Square Garden across the street.

Pedestrian traffic was no lighter. As we stood beneath the hotel's golden overhang—above which four American flags fluttered between massive Grecian columns—Mother and I made speed bumps in everyone's path.

Sushi gave out a little whimper, bothered by all the big city hubbub, and I held her tighter.

"Welcome to the Hotel Pennsylvania," someone said.

A doorman had materialized, smartly attired
in a black uniform with red stripes around his
coat cuffs and down his pant legs. Middle-aged,
with reddish hair, a ruddy complexion, and
friendly smile, he cut an impressive figure.

But the most impressive thing about him? He
gave but a brief glance at Mother's handcuff-
briefcase, no doubt having seen much stranger
things in his line of work.

"Thanks for the welcome," I said.

Mother beamed at him, just a little less crazily
than Norman Bates's mama at the end of *Psycho*.
"It's a pleasure to be here at . . ." And shaking a
forefinger in the air, yowza style, she sang,
"Pennsylvania six five thousand!"

Then Mother, in response to my horrified expression, waiting a beat for the Andrew Sisters
to turn over in their graves, said defensively,
"It's a Glenn Miller tune, dear. Very popular,
back in the day. After the hotel's phone number?"

The doorman smiled gamely. "We do get that
from time to time. But you're the first one to
mention it *today*, ma'am."

"Do I win a prize?" Mother chirped. "A discount coupon perhaps, or a hotel beanie?"

The game smile turned a trifle strained. "I'm
afraid not."

Sushi yapped her impatience.

And I yapped mine: "Mother, could we *please*
get checked in? Soosh needs to be fed and to
get her insulin shot, and I'm hungry, too."

Mother thought about whether to frown or to smile, decided on the latter, and said, "Very well, dear, we could *all* do with some vittles."

If you like, you can just put this book down and wait for the movie: *The Serenity Hillbillies Take Manhattan*.

"Just go on in, ladies," the doorman said. "I'll bring your luggage to the counter."

"Splendid, my good man," Mother said, lapsing into the British accent that was her default setting to impress strangers, and handed him a dollar bill. Apparently she didn't have a quid on her.

I'll give the doorman this much: he didn't flinch. And after Mother turned away, I slipped him a fiver. I mean, five spot.

We made our way into the vast rectangular lobby with its tan-and-gold marbled walls, mirrored columns, and shining floor with motif of large diamonds and circles.

In case you were wondering why I sauntered into a hotel brazenly brandishing a dog, the Pennsylvania was (and as far as I know still is) pet friendly, playing host every year to the Westminster Kennel Club dog show.

The check-in counter ran the distance of the cavernous room, above which rows of flat-screens projected a variety of cable shows—from business to politics to sports to reality programs. But, despite the possibility of ten check-in stations, only two were open. And to my dismay (and my stomach's), a long line of patrons snaked around, corralled by black nylon ropes, as if they were trying to get tickets to the latest blockbuster flick.

"Well," an unhappy customer said, passing us, having finally checked in, "at least I got to see a complete episode of *Storage Wars.*"

"Mother?" I whined. My stomach seconded that question with a growl.

"Courage, dear," she responded. "I just spotted another Good Samaritan." Waving her free hand wildly, she called out, her voice echoing across the lobby, "Oh, *yoo*-woo! Mr. Bufford! It's *Vivian!*"

A heavyset, unmade bed of a man, with a convention bag dangling from a shoulder, gave us a momentarily bewildered look that turned into recognition and a wave back at us before hurrying our way.

Mother whispered, "Mr. Bufford is the convention organizer, dear."

"Yes, I know," I whispered back. She'd had many conversations with him on the phone, and on Skype, arranging for us to come, and I'd spoken to him once or twice myself.

Our host—who I guessed to be about forty— wore wrinkled khaki shorts, a plaid short-sleeved shirt open over the convention's logo T-shirt, and white socks with sandals. His black-rimmed glasses, which rode his night-light bulb of a nose, were adhesive taped at one temple. The comb-over of his thinning sandy-colored hair seemed to have exploded, and he bore the wild-eyed look of a dude rancher who had just been tossed off a bull.

And the convention didn't even officially start till tomorrow.

Mr. Bufford stuck out a chubby hand to Mother. His smile was as big and sincere as it was yellow. "Vivian, so nice to finally meet you in person!"

Mother had taken the hand. "And you, likewise, young man."

"And this must be Brandy." He had stepped my way. "This is a real thrill. You know, first and foremost, I'm a fan."

"Pleasure is mine, Mr. Bufford, " I replied, my smile straining a little. Frankly, our host could have used a stronger deodorant. But then, after our long day, I probably didn't smell dew-drop fresh myself.

"Please, call me Tommy," he said. "All my friends call me Tommy." He scratched Sushi's head. "Cute dog. Just like in your books!"

Soosh sniffed at him, and (unlike me) seemed to relish his bouquet as she licked his thick hand.

Then his eyes flew to Mother's handcuffed briefcase like magnets seeking metal.

"Is *that* the Superman drawing?" he whispered, eyes wide.

"Yes, indeedy." Mother nodded, patting the case.

"You know, Vivian," Tommy said, an eyebrow arching above a slightly tilted black eyeglass frame, "that might be better kept in the hotel's safe."

"Oh, no," Mother replied, tightening her grip. "This super-duper drawing doesn't leave my sight. It will go to bed with me. It will go to the bathroom with me. Of course, I *will* entrust it to Brandy when I shower, but—"

"Mother," I said, "too much information."

Tommy was looking at me for support, but I shook my head. "I've already tried. She saw a spy movie and got the briefcase idea."

Mother's grin went well with her magnified eyes. "The character with the briefcase got killed! They had to cut his hand off to get it."

Why Mother found this reassuring is anybody's guess.

"Very well," Tommy sighed. "But it would be a disaster if anything should happen to it—it's the showpiece of the auction, you know."

And the reason we were all-expenses-paid guests.

"Tommy," I asked, "is there any way we can avoid the check-in line?"

"Certainly," he said, grinning big again. "I have all convention guest keycards right here."

From his convention bag, he produced several small hotel folders holding keycards, then, fanning them out like a deck of playing cards, handed one to Mother.

He dug in the bag again. "And here are your badges—which will get you into all the events."

Those, I took.

"I'll get you a schedule later," he said. "You're on a mystery-writing panel Sunday morning."

A striking-looking woman rushed up. She was about my age, tall—at least six foot—curvy but muscular, with raven-black hair worn in a shoulder-length pageboy, à la Bettie Page. Her makeup was

heavy—darkened brows, black-rimmed violet
eyes—but the pink painted mouth gave her
goth look a feminine touch. As did her dress, a
fitted black and white polka-dotted number, its
low neckline revealing a spray of flowers tat-
tooed across her chest. Red heels with bows on
the toes completed her mixed-signals ensemble
of hard and soft.

"Sorry to interrupt . . . ," she said, addressing
Tommy.

He gestured to us. "Violet, this is Vivian and
Brandy Borne. They write the Antiques mysteries." Then he added in a whisper to her, "The
Superman drawing," and then to us, "Violet is
my assistant."

Which surprised me; I thought her to be a
fan or guest professional.

"Hello," the woman replied quickly, with
barely a glance our way. Neither Superman nor
the Antiques books impressed her much, at
least not in the throes of the big job she was
caught up in. "Tommy, we've got a problem with
the Buff Awards."

"Not *too* serious, I hope," he said, frowning.

"We're missing one."

"Ah . . ." Tommy looked at Mother and me.
"Will you excuse me?"

Mother replied, "But of course."

And before I could say, "Nice to meet you
both," they were gone.

Mother and I stood for a moment, then I
took hold of the brass cart with our luggage, not
waiting for a bellhop (I had a limited number of
fivers), and pushed it to the elevators, Mother

following, holding Sushi in her arms like an unlikely baby.

Our room was on the fourteenth floor, and I
had to admit I was surprised by how small it
was—my bedroom at home was larger.

"We were promised a suite," I said.

Mother was kicking off her shoes. "Dear,
don't be ungrateful. Free is free. Now, where
did I put the key to these darn handcuffs?"

"I'm not being ungrateful," I said ungrate-
fully. "But there's only *one* bed."

Which didn't bother Soosh, already snuggled
between two plump pillows.

"Yes, that is a problem," Mother admitted.
"You *do* snore so. *You* must have the handcuff
key."

"*I* snore? You could blow out these windows,
on an off night. And I *don't* have the key."

Mother stood with hands on hips and a single
eyebrow arched, like Mr. Spock regarding Dr.
McCoy. "Dear, I *know* you're tired, but let's not
be a Grumpy Gus. If I happen to snore a wee little bit, you can *always* sleep in the tub. We can
request extra pillows for that purpose, if need
be. You're *sure* you don't have the key?"

"No," I snapped. "Look in your purse."

"Besides," she went on, digging in her bag
with her free hand, "this is a *lovely* room—perhaps a trifle cramped, I'll grant you—but this is
New York, the City that Never Sleeps. . . ."

"I thought Las Vegas was the city that never
sleeps, and with you snoring, I'll be the one that
never sleeps."

". . . and simply *no one* comes to the Big Apple

to spend much time in a hotel room. Ah, *here's*
that naughty key—I had it after all." She unlocked the cuff, which fell to the floor with a
thunk, then she rubbed her wrist. Her eyes
gleamed with possibilities behind the thick
lenses. "Do you realize that the Empire State
Building *and* Macy's flagship store are a mere
block away?"

I had stopped paying attention, having spotted a gift basket of fruit and goodies, compli-
ments of the convention, sitting on a side table.

With my mouth salivating and stomach growling, I moved eagerly toward it.

But Mother blocked my path. "*Oh, no* you
don't, missy!" she said. "We're going to send
that over to the Gershwin Theater to reward that
nice woman for picking us up."

Mother made regifting an art.

"Over my dead body," I snarled.

And she grabbed the basket, and I grabbed
the basket, and she tugged, and I tugged, and
we both tugged, and suddenly the contents
were airborne. Then the room was raining fruit
and snacks.

A packet of gourmet salmon landed on the
pillow next to Sushi and in a blink of a blind eye
she had torn it open with her sharp little teeth.

"*Now* look what you've done," Mother said
crossly.

"You did it, not me!"

"You need an attitude adjustment!"

A knock at the door interrupted our squabble.

I let Mother answer it.

"Is everything all right?" Tommy asked, probably having heard bickering through the door.

"Fine, fine," Mother said. Then, "But, Tommy dear, there is a *slight* snafu. . . ."

"Yes, I know," he said, and he looked stricken. "This isn't a suite—my mistake. I know I promised you that, as a perk, for being our honored guests."

"Think nothing of it," Mother said, and I—having joined her—discreetly kicked her in the calf. Not hard. She barely ouched.

"But I *do* have a solution," Tommy said. "You ladies take *my* suite—it's 1537, just up one floor. I haven't moved in yet. Until tonight, it's been easier for me to work out of the convention's office a few blocks from here."

I was feeling a little bad about my behavior, and heard myself saying, "You're sure? Because that would really be wonderful."

"Yes, it would," Mother chimed in. "Not having to share a bed with Brandy is a lifesaver. The girl kicks like a mule."

Maybe so, but not when I'm sleeping. . . .

After exchanging keycards with Tommy, we thanked him again, and he left.

"You forgot to mention I snore," I said.

"Dear, we needn't air *all* our dirty laundry."

"Just mine." I sighed, but my mood was improving. "Help me pick up the fruit."

Our new digs were a corner suite with two rooms elegantly decorated in gold and blue, the bedroom separate from an outer area that had a fold-out couch, coffee table, desk, and mini-kitchen with sink and small fridge.

While Mother disappeared into the bathroom to wash off the dust from our trip, I put her suitcase on the king-size bed, leaving my things in the outer room by the couch, where I would sleep. Fold-out beds were never wonderful, but compared to sleeping with a world-class snorer, this one would be a magic carpet to slumberland.

After giving Sushi her insulin, followed by a dog biscuit reward for taking the shot, I helped familiarize the blind little darling with the layout of the suite so she could move around and about without bumping into anything.

I also set up a little pee station for her, having brought along a plastic tray with pads designed for emergency situations.

Finally, Sushi and I played the "maid game" I had taught her on other trips (including at those accommodations where dogs were not welcome): I would rap on the door and call, "Housekeeping, housekeeping," and she would scurry into the cracked-open closet, out of the way, until the maid had gone.

Mother, now dressed in her favorite emerald green velour top and slacks, held out a hand to me.

"What's this?" I asked, taking the silver object she offered.

"A rape whistle, dear."

"Oh-kay . . . I'm not wearing that."

"Then keep it in your pocket." She had hers around her neck on a silver chain.

"No, I don't think so."

Mother shrugged. "Suit yourself. But we're in the *Naked City* now, where there are eight million stories, few with happy endings."

She had conveniently forgotten that I'd lived in Chicago for ten years before my divorce.

But to placate her, I said, "I'll think about it," and set the whistle on the coffee table.

Mother stared at me with a frown. "Dear, meaning no offense and not intending in any way to redraw battle lines, but . . . you do look a fright. I hope you're going to freshen up before we go out to the reception."

There was a preconvention get-together in one of the ballrooms for the guests and professionals—artists and writers—along with staff members. Most of the pros were involved in the comics industry, but others—like Mother and me—were from related fields, like movies and books.

This was also preview night—when preregistered attendees got a three hour "sneak" look at the vendors, before opening tomorrow to the general public. But we were skipping that.

"This is as fresh as I'm gonna get," I said grumpily.

Mother took my hand and led me to the couch, pulling me down to sit with her.

"Brandy," she began gently, "I know what's troubling you."

"You do?"

"Yes. You miss *him*."

By "*him,*" I knew she meant Tony Cassato, former Serenity chief of police, with whom I had begun a romantic relationship before circumstance and fate intervened. Tony had been forced to flee into witness protection after New Jersey mobsters dispatched a contract killer to retaliate for his testimony against them.

Mother was saying, "Taking your frustration out on me won't help, dear. You've been a grouch all day. You are better than that."

She was right. About the me being a grouch part, anyway.

"I'm sorry," I said, nodding, sighing. "I'll try to be better."

Mother patted my knee. "There's my sweet, good girl."

So I washed my face, combed my hair, reapplied makeup, and put on a Max and Cleo geometric-print dress, little Juicy Couture cardigan, and short tan Frye boots.

Mother had once again locked herself to the briefcase and, after we'd pinned on our convention badges for the reception, we headed out.

The reception, held in one of the smaller ballrooms—PennTop North on the eighteenth floor, with a spectacular view of the city—was in full swing as we arrived, the guest professionals and staff talking and laughing, competing with a disc jockey in one corner who was playing loud dance music. That disco beat never seemed to go out of style in NYC.

I was both disappointed and kind of relieved that there was nary a costumed superhero in sight—they were lined up in the lower lobby, outside the huge Globetrotter Ballroom where the booths were set up, waiting to get in. And their presence would increase on the day of the costume ball and contest.

While Mother stood in the doorway—whether expecting to be noticed, planning her next move, or choosing a new victim to befriend—I made a beeline for the buffet, where I filled up my small plate to overflowing.

How to be a one-trip salad bar cheat—a.k.a. salad bar hacking: First, fill a bowl with food, then lay carrot sticks on top as a second "floor." Next, build a circular wall of cucumbers, tomato slices, and/or oranges. Finally, fill the tower in with other salad bar goodies. (Be careful your tower isn't the leaning Pisa kind, because more than one of mine has toppled all over a restaurant floor.)

Balancing my plate, utensils, napkin, and bottled water, I surveyed the tables, looking for an empty chair, but found none. Then I remembered passing by a little alcove outside the ballroom, with end tables and two overstuffed chairs, and decided to go there.

Mother was across the room, flitting from person to person, inserting herself into one conversation or another, showing off her briefcase bracelet. I wanted to get her attention, to motion I would be out in the hall, but had no free hand to do it.

Which didn't matter; I wouldn't be missed.

Finding the alcove empty, I settled into one of the comfy chairs. The food on my plate looked yummy, but admittedly at this stage of my long day, I would have found cardboard a feast. I was in the process of removing juicy bits of meat and vegetable from a skewer when an altercation between two men outside the alcove interrupted.

One of the pair I immediately recognized: our host, Tommy Bufford. The other was tall, slender, with wavy dark hair and an angular face; he wore a yellow polo shirt and tan slacks, a preppie alternative to train-wreck Tommy.

"You signed an *exclusivity* clause, remember?" the wavy-haired guy said angrily, poking Tommy in the chest with a hard forefinger. "You weren't supposed to operate a competing convention for five *years,* and I'm gonna sue your stinky ass."

"So sue me," Tommy said, and shrugged. "But you'll be wasting your time and money, Gino. I'm just a hired hand here."

The wavy-haired guy snorted. "That won't wash. You're *running* things—your name is being used."

Another shrug. "Just because we co-founded the Manhattan comic convention doesn't mean you have any claim to *my* name. Or do I need to sue *you* over *that?*"

Now Tommy poked the other man's chest.

"And that goes double for the Buff Awards," he added. "Buff is short for Bufford, you know. If you wanted to keep presenting those at the *old* con, then you should've included *that* in the contract."

As Tommy walked away, the guy yelled, "Sometimes I could just *kill* you, you *bleeper.*" Fill in the bleep yourself.

Then he was gone, too.

* * *

I had meant to tell Mother about the scrap, but when we returned to our suite—Mother having made countless new friends, me having gone through three plates at the salad bar—I was so full and so tired, I just flopped on the couch, not bothering to unfold the bed, still in my dress and cardi.

I don't know how long I'd been asleep, when something woke me. The room was dark, as was Mother's bedroom, though I could hear her snoring behind the closed door, like a sea storm roaring behind a shut porthole. That was probably the noise I'd heard, I thought, and rolled over.

I felt around for Sushi, but she wasn't with me, having deemed a soft bed with Mother more appealing than a cramped couch with her mistress.

As I lay curled up with my head on one of the small davenport pillows, my eyes accustomed to the dark, it seemed to me as if something or someone was coming through the wall directly across the room!

I froze as a figure moved stealthily toward the bedroom.

The intruder had not seen me, apparently not expecting anyone to be camped out on the couch . . . which gave me an advantage.

I grabbed my rape whistle off the coffee table, stuck it in my mouth, and blew.

The shrill, eardrum splitting sound startled our uninvited guest, who stumbled into the dinette set, toppling a chair.

Suddenly the door to the bedroom flew open and Mother, in red flannel pj's, came rushing out, crying, "*Rape! Rape!*" at the top of her voice. And Sushi was not far behind, yapping for all she was worth.

The intruder fled back through the wall, which I realized held a connecting door to the next room. And there was a little "click" as it was being locked from the other side.

How had our side gotten unlocked?

"Quick, dear," she said. "We can catch him."

I shook my head. "No! I'm in no mood for a struggle. Anyway, he's gone by now. And I think you'll find that the room next door is empty."

"You're no fun," she said poutily. "But surely those whistles, our yelling, will result in help arriving unbidden!"

"You're in Manhattan," I reminded her, and a siren underscored my point. "Anyway, this is what you *get* by letting everyone under the sun know we've got that Superman drawing in our room. The first thing tomorrow, we're putting that thing in the hotel's safe!"

"I suppose you're right," Mother replied sheepishly. "But we should call security."

"In the morning. Go back to sleep. He won't be back. If it makes you feel better, I'll leave the lights on out here."

"Very well," Mother said disappointedly. "But I still think, with a little effort, we might well have caught him."

"Good *night*, Mother," I said with finality.

She shuffled into the bedroom, making a decidedly untheatrical exit. For her.

And I went back to the couch—after making doubly sure our side of the door was locked and had a chair propped under the knob.

But I didn't sleep. Couldn't.

Because there was something I hadn't told Mother about our intruder—and the reason I didn't want us running after him.

When she had opened the door coming to my rescue, the light from the bathroom caught the glint of metal in his hand.

In the shape of what seemed to be a knife.

A Trash 'n' Treasures Tip

Comics conventions are not just about selling or buying funny books. You'll find at these fun functions a wide array of pop-culture memorabilia and collectibles: cartoon figurines, autographed photos, original comic artwork, and even clothing. I'm looking for a set of Shmoo salt and pepper shakers, because I think they're so darn cute! The Shmoo was a famous critter in the *Li'l Abner* comic strip. But Mother finds them repellent, insisting they are "phallic symbols with eyes, dear."